THE BEAST HUNTERS
BLOOD OATH

THE BEAST HUNTERS
BLOOD OATH

Christer Lende

C. A. Lende Publishing

DEDICATION

This book is dedicated to Emma Kristine Skjæveland. You've been there for me since high school, and I love our little family. Thanks for reacting the way you did on that train ride when I told you for the first time that I had started writing a book.

ALSO BY

CHRISTER LENDE

THE BEAST HUNTER OF ASHBOURN SERIES:
The Beast Hunters
The Beast Hunters Dark Sovereign
The Beast Hunters Blood Oath

The Dollmaker of Kalastra
Bleeding Ink

SIGN UP FOR MY AUTHOR NEWSLETTER

Be the first to find out all the super-duper exciting news about Christer Lende's new releases and life, and get some free short stories while you're at it: https://www.authorcal-ende.com/newsletter-signup

ACKNOWLEDGEMENT

First, I must thank Emma Kristine Skjæveland for standing by my side. Thank you. Are you happy now? I put you first.

Now that that's out of the way, here we go:

The only part my mom has read of this trilogy is the dedication of the second book thanking her, but still, thank you Anette Lende, for giving birth to me.

My friend Brage Ariel Lindell Eidsvik came up with the most sinister way of solving the problem the beast hunters now face. It was sickening, you vile man. Thank you for reading.

Nichole Schramm was the first to read this book too, so she was the first one to know how it all goes. Thank you for your enthusiasm, I loved talking to you about it. For a while, we were the only two people to know the ending.

Tom Haugen printed this book out too, and read it on his way to the ferry. We later discussed it in the gym. It was incredibly inefficient workouts, but they were the most fun ones too.

Sin-Jace Blix-Torres has got to be among the fastest readers out there. This book lasted half a day, and it was more fun to talk with you about it than vacationing in Rotterdam.

Ole-Marius Skulbru is the kind of guy you need to force to read the first sentences, and then he just won't stop until he's through. He said this book left him emotionally exhausted, and there was nothing to do but lay in bed, and wait it out. Your praise and love for my work have kept me going, thank you.

Thank you Are Bråthen for reading this book and letting me know you liked this one the best. I do agree with you. And thank you for your continued interest in my work.

Tom Christian Klingsheim, you're a crazy dude hiding behind a guise of calmness, but you sure let your insanity out to express how you felt about this book. We've had such fun conversations and laughs about this trilogy, and I'm glad you're as devoted to my newer work as well. I miss you, bro.

I want to thank Luke Schulz too, for being a fantastic author friend. Thank you for giving my books a chance and talking about them. We authors are so lucky to have a soul such as you in our community. Thank you for all your help and great conversations. You and your lovely dog are awesome.

Esmay Rosalyne, you are fantastic. Thank you for your love and appreciation for my books. I love seeing you talk about them and I love your reviews. Thanks a lot for welcoming me into the community.

Davie Docherty, I'll never forget your post on Twitter about how I could end the second book the way I did, and I have to thank you for your engagement. It truly means so much to me, and you're an awfully funny guy. Thanks a lot, man.

Willow's Pass
Paradrax
The Lake Fields
Norda
Nordwind
Ponteria
Kavadash
Carnagar
Peligon
Varost
The Sangerian Grasslands
Avania
Mandranar
Westlin Pass
The Moutainlands of Harrendale
Harrendale
Kolridge
Borders, The Mud Lands
Varanos
Eastern Veridim
Sak Lake
Dimbar Forest

THE ASHENBORN

31 Years Ago

A bead of sweat ran down Adenar's brown hair and hit his face as the sun beat down hard on his skin. The heat from the furnace didn't exactly help either, sparks taking on a life of their own before succumbing to the outside temperature. Adenar wiped his forehead with a wet handkerchief that never got to properly dry up before each use.

He had to finish forging the spear today. His father, Tennindar, could return from the hunt at any moment, and Adenar wanted to have his gift ready and surprise him. It should almost be ready for sharpening and cooling. He'd kept his blacksmithing skill hidden, only working while his father was away on hunts.

Soon eighteen years of age, he would have to choose a profession, and having a head start like this would be good. He had learned a lot from the months it had taken forging this spear, and the occasional help from the town's old blacksmith, Erill, had been invaluable. Erill had been a good friend to Adenar's mother for as long as Adenar had lived, and seemed to relish helping him.

Adenar pulled it out of the fire and thrust it into the cold water. Steam rose; excitement grew in his fingers and bones. It shone marvellously, the light of the sun bouncing off its sharp edge.

"That spear looks good," Erill's cranky voice sounded from the second forge. "Your dad will kill many razorboars with it, I'm sure."

"I hope so," Adenar said and started sharpening it. With Erill's guidance, it turned out a fierce weapon. Adenar's eyes ignited with it in hand, feeling mighty, and he rushed out of the smithy to show his mother.

Adenar ran quickly through the small village of Morrowdar, reaching his parent's house with haste. Only about a hundred and fifty people lived there, and their greatest export was supplying Ashbourn with grain. But growing crops never interested Adenar, nor any in his family. His father had the heart of a hunter, and his mother knitted clothes and ate the spoils of the hunts.

His mother, Ilia, sat in a rocking chair outside knitting on some piece of clothing, enjoying the sun. She wore her yellow dress, indicating her good mood.

"Mother!" Adenar called out. She shielded her eyes from the sun and smiled as he approached. "It's done!" He handed it to her.

"Wow!" she gasped in what seemed like genuine awe. "It's magnificent! I honestly can't believe how great it turned out." Rising from her chair, she gave the weapon a spin. "Adenar, I'm truly impressed."

"Do you think father will be too?"

"You won't have to worry. What will you call it, young Master Blacksmith?" She asked in a respectful, but mocking tone.

Adenar smiled. "Heartfire."

"That is a great name. He will love it."

"When is he coming?"

"Anytime now," she said, looking to the horizon, but saw no sign of him and turned back to the spear. Heartfire's long wooden shaft rested comfortably in her hand, while the spearhead glimmered so strongly in the sun that it looked like a smaller sun itself. The tip had the shape of an arrowhead, so it could rip off razorboar scales, making it possible to actually kill the beasts.

"Why don't you wait for him like you used to?" his mother suggested. Adenar nodded and went to his small scouting hill at the edge of the village. From there, the Sangerian Grassland laid itself bare in front of his eyes and he would spot his father from a long distance away.

Hours went by with no sight of his father or his fellow hunters. Just as Adenar's worry set in, he spotted something small appear far away on the horizon. It turned into small dots, and finally the hunters Adenar expected, his father riding in the middle as usual. They rode slowly to keep the horses from going exhausted while carrying the dead razorboars. Adenar counted five people, meaning everything had gone well.

A nervous feeling grew in his gut as his fingers danced over Heartfire's spearhead. It laid in the grass next to him, as ready as it would ever be. *Will he like it? What if he doesn't like its balance?* Erill had approved every aspect of the spear, but suppressing the worry proved hard.

The hunting party approached and Adenar waved back to his father while making sure the spear stayed hidden from sight. He rose proudly, pushing his shoulders back. "Posture makes the man."

Something glimmered in the air far above the hunting party, like an ember from the forge, but it seemed to move downward. Hidden behind the strong rays of the sun, Adenar couldn't spot it properly, but it grew larger with haste. What seemed like an ember grew into a plummeting inferno, approaching with great speed.

"Father!" Adenar yelled and pointed at the incoming danger. They turned and shot their horses into motion, screaming wildly. Adenar's father pulled out his knife and cut the razorboar off his horse and kicked it into a gallop.

Bright fire dove down from the sky before large wings expanded to flatten out its descent as it soared across the endless fields. A large eagle-like head stayed locked on the riders ahead, its speed many times faster than that of the horses.

Adenar froze in fear as the giant flaming bird crashed towards his father. Fire cascaded off it like rain, leaving a burning trail in its wake.

"Ride!" Adenar yelled at them, but the monster would catch up. His father fired an arrow at it, but the fire consumed it.

"NO!" Adenar roared as the bird flew through the hunting party with devastating speed. Horses capitulated and riders flew into the air before a blistering hot inferno swallowed them in a violent explosion. The bird continued, taking to the sky, leaving behind a scorched landscape, but no sign of Adenar's father or the other riders. The village erupted in panicked screams at the commotion, but Adenar remained silent, his eyes searching for the winged monstrosity in the sky—he found it, and it soared straight towards the village with lightning speed.

Adenar threw himself to the ground as it shot over the hill. The heat made him scream in agony before the shockwave ripped him from the ground and into the air. He crashed and rolled on the hot ground, holding on to Heartfire for dear life. Flames rained down around him, but he came to a stop before rolling into fire. The gigantic beast blasted right through a house. It exploded, shooting debris to all sides. People ran around wildly, trying to avoid the rain of fire. Adenar shot to his feet before a horde of villages trampled him on their way out of Morrowdar. He had to find his mother. He tried spotting the beast, but thick smoke rose from all around, obscuring his view.

"Mother!" he shouted, his eyes searching for her, but his words drowned out in the screams and commotion.

Blazing infernos spread from house to house, and he had to hurry. He ran, shoving others aside and passed the burning houses before it became too late—the bird shot through the smoke inches above his head, its speed tearing the village apart. He threw his hands up to protect his face from the blistering heat before the shockwave threw him off his feet again. He rolled along the ground, hearing people screaming their lungs out behind him. Breathing felt almost impossible in the heavy smoke, but he got back on his feet. He suppressed the anger alive in his heart and focused on saving his mother. He turned to spot if the bird returned, but his gaze fell to the ground. Endless of his fellow villagers laid dead or wounded behind him, either burnt to a crisp or mortally wounded, screaming in agony. *You can't save them*, he told himself. *Go find mother.*

He ran towards his house, feeling the heat of the bird as it flew through the village again, obliterating several houses, including the large noble house in the centre close to the bell tower. His forehead and underarms burned with pain, but he ignored it, nearing his house, which had caught on fire. He kicked the door open and stormed inside, not finding Ilia anywhere.

Coughing, he went back outside as the beast came down upon Morrowdar again. Debris from buildings crashed into the ground near him, together with charred body parts. Thick smoke blackened his surroundings, making it hard to orient himself.

Where is she?

Someone on fire ran towards him, throwing themselves at him screaming for help, but he shoved the man aside with his spear. Burning corpses laid amidst the ruins of the village, and anyone could be her mother. His fingers trembled with fear and anger, feeling completely helpless. A burst of screams echoed through the smoke as the beast descended upon them again, but he couldn't see anything through the smoke.

It felt like a stone dropped in his stomach as his eyes noticed something yellow in front of him. He ran to it, jumping over planks and bodies, finding the remains of a woman wearing a yellow dress. His guts churned as he felt the fabric with his thumb, knowing for certain she had been burned alive. He couldn't even recognize her, all features gone. He couldn't speak. He couldn't think. *Both of them are d-dead.*

The monster tore the village apart once more, the terrifying sounds breaking Adenar out of his trance. His hand gripped Heartfire. *I will kill you.* The heat of the bird struck him as it flew overhead. He rose amid the burning chaos, seeing people he'd known his whole life die in front of him. *Why? Why is it doing this?* The village he'd grown up in smouldered around him—where all his greatest memories had been created.

He ran through the burning village, heading for the still-standing tower beside the destroyed noble house. It burned, but it was his best shot. He struggled breathing, but he didn't care; he wouldn't survive this anyway. He only cared about bringing down this terrible beast.

He stormed past people who just wandered around without purpose, while others had their senses to flee or try to save their loved ones. Adenar kept his eye on the tower, reaching its door. He felt and heard the bird fly through Morrowdar yet again, the sound of wood breaking filling the air, but he stayed focused and grabbed onto the first ladder.

He climbed to the top of the tower, where he laid his eyes upon the total obliteration of his birthplace.

Flames, ash, ruins, bodies, everywhere.

And through the smoke, he spotted it circling back for another assault.

Breathing hard and trying to fend off the heat, Adenar tightened his grip on Heartfire. The bird flew straight towards him, crashing through the village, killing too many. It neared the bell tower and Adenar jumped, thrusting his spear into the air and releasing a roar of anger.

The bird crashed into his weapon, and it sank deep into its flesh, shooting fire from the wound. It screeched wildly, erupting into molten fire that enveloped Adenar. He screamed, his flesh burning away as he melded with the beast. They crashed towards the ground; Adenar barely conscious. In his final moments, he knew he'd killed it, avenging his family and his village. They hit the ground together, moulding into each other in the intense heat. Then . . . darkness.

* * *

"*Well done, little human,*" something said. "*You ended me.*"

Adenar sat up sharply and sucked in air as if his lungs expanded for the first time. He coughed harshly as white ash cascaded down from his hair, obscuring his already blurred vision. He rubbed his face, but the ash clad his hands as well. His breathing finally calmed down. *What's happening?* he wondered.

The smell of charred wood filled his nostrils as his vision slowly cleared. The sun cast its crimson light on . . . on the remains of Morrowdar. Adenar's eyes widened in horror at the destruction—it all came back to him; the winged beast and what it had done to Morrowdar, to his father and mother.

He screamed with a raspy voice, immense sorrow striking deep in his heart. Ash around his eyes absorbed his tears. His mind didn't know how to comprehend his loss, but his body crumbled into the crystal-white ash surrounding him. He wept until his body would yield no more water. *Why am I alive? How am I alive?* Adenar frantically ran his fingers over his skin, searching for burns, but found none. In fact, his skin felt healthy and in perfect condition. He rose out of the ash around his body, which stood out from the black soot that remained of Morrowdar, being otherworldly white and clear.

He tore his eyes away from the peculiarity and gazed upon the village. *How am I alive? Is this a dream?*

"Mother?" he shouted into the wind. "Father?" No answers came. Nobody had been left alive, but him. His knees buckled. He hammered the ground with his hand.

"The privilege to walk among the living," a soothing, calm voice spoke in his mind, interrupting his pounding. *"Comes with the great toll of loss."*

He looked around, ready for someone or something to appear. "What?" he whispered. "Who said that?"

"It was I," the voice said again, seeming to come from everywhere and nowhere simultaneously. *"I am the one you slew. The great, winged fire in the sky. Your kind calls me pharlanax."*

"The great, winged fire? The bird? You are the bird of fire?"

"Correct. My name is ancient and I have lived for longer than your kind has existed."

"Where are you? Why can I hear you?" Adenar yelled into the air, anger seeping into his words. "Come out so I can kill you again!"

"You already won, little one. Slaying one of my kind is a feat sought by kings and heroes of all races aeons ago. You're brought back from my ashes, and once you perish, I shall emerge forth from your ashes yet again."

"Why did you kill them?" Adenar demanded. "They were my family."

"It is my nature."

"Your nature? That's a coward's excuse. Why punish innocent people like this? Why destroy so many lives?"

"I am not so different from you or yours. You do the same to each other for reasons of land, vengeance, love, grief, and even lust. I do what I do because I am what I am."

"That makes no sense," he said.

"Then I am sorry I cannot make you understand."

"Why am I alive?"

"You are granted life anew and have been reborn from my remains. The kings of old would call you Athaena or . . . Ashenborn."

Reborn? he thought, his mind struggling to understand. He ran his fingers over his naked body again, feeling bulging muscles and veins, with not a single scar. The sun shone directly into his eyes, but he didn't have to shield them, seeing clearly, despite the strong light.

"Fire is no longer your enemy. You are not the same boy that felled me. Pieces of you remain, but pieces of everyone who has slain me reside within you too. Their strength, valour, and courage. I am made from those who have slain me and they are made of me. Small pieces of them transcend through time through you, preserved within me. You now belong to a long line of kings and heroes who sought a fraction of my power. Some used them for good, others for evil. And once you die, I will carry a piece of you with me."

"This cannot be," Adenar said. "I mean . . . this is impossible."

"I understand. Let time heal your mind and you will see clearly. My name is Mattronia, and you and I are one. I see what you see, and feel what you feel."

Adenar didn't know how he felt about that. Having someone in his head at all times seemed like a good reason to end himself right here and now. "Can you hear my thoughts?"

"Your mind is your own," Mattronia answered. *"Your thoughts are shielded from my intrusion, and you cannot hear my thoughts."*

"So you're speaking?"

"In a way. It is difficult to explain, but I have thoughts not shared with you."

Great, he thought, but understood he could not kill himself and unleash this monster back into the world. *It's better she's with me than 'following her nature.'* "I will call you Matt. It's easier."

"You may."

"Matt, I hate you, and I will for all of our time together."

"Then that is what you will do."

He sighed, not liking the pharlanax's willingness to accept his resentment. He wanted Matt to show some emotion—or, at least, regret for what she had done. But she wouldn't. It was her nature. Razorboars killed people sometimes too; it was their nature.

Adenar walked through the ruins of Morrowdar. *What will I do now? Where will I go?* A window, almost completely hidden by ash, reflected his face and he saw his blonde hair, which used to be brown.

"You have gone through changes," Matt said. Adenar went over to the windowpane, seeing that his face had stayed the same. *"There are other changes too."*

"Like what?"

"You have the fighting instinct and reflexes of the pharlanax. Few can best you in battle if you learn to handle yourself. Skills will come to you faster—skills like riding, marksmanship, fighting, knitting, black-smithing—even playing an instrument. Your memory is enhanced too. You can access my raw power, fuelled by fire."

Strangely, Adenar understood what she meant, feeling something surging in his veins; a fire wanting to be released. "You said 'fire is no longer my enemy?'"

"In time, I shall teach you. And we have enough time. Go back to my ashes, they should not be wasted."

Adenar did so and looked upon the white ashes of her remains.

"You must forge my ashes into a sword. It will never fail, never break, nor yield to any foe. It will be a sword made from the remains of a divinity."

A horn rang through the air in the far distance, and Adenar leapt upon a rock effortlessly with uncanny balance. Riders approached from Ashbourn, their flags clear to his eyes despite the distance. "They must have seen the smoke," Adenar said. "There's no time to forge a blade."

"Then gather the ash," Matt said with a hint of urgency. *"People trade kingdoms for such a treasure."*

Adenar surveyed the area. After running through two houses, he found a suitable, unburned pouch and a pair of linen pants. He scooped almost all of the ash into the pouch and put it over his shoulder.

The riders neared, waving at him. Adenar walked towards them, leaving the village of his birth, death, and rebirth behind.

"Who will you be?" Matt asked. *"You have capabilities others can only dream of. You can perform feats unmatched by your kind, so spectacular you will be immortalized in history. So, I ask you, who will this new man be? What is your name?"*

The soldiers caught up, all except one riding into the village to search for survivors. The captain had a broad build with a strong face and beard. He looked at him with great wonder, eyes wide.

"H-how? Are you the only survivor?" he asked.

Adenar nodded. *It's true what Matt says,* he thought to himself, turning his eyes to Morrowdar for a final time. *I am no longer the same person that fell into her fire. I am someone else. And I will be someone great.*

"What is your name, son?" the captain asked, extending a hand.

He met the captain's eyes, grabbed his hand with a strong grip, and said, "Koradin. I am Koradin Banner."

CHAPTER 1

A Grand Betrayal

Darkness spreads across the world. The night becomes eternal. In darkness he shall come, with the strength of the voreen. The world will be his, and through him, ours. Kill in his name, murder by his wish, and relish in his glory. Give his blood to those unbending or remove them from this world. Few shall stand in his way, and those few will become his greatest warriors and help him bring the end.

A prayer of war from "The Dark Traitor", chapter two.

Night had fallen over Ashbourn earlier than usual and the wind howled with might. Eranna Carner walked from her large office in the Warborn Headquarters and to the new throne room that Chronor had demanded built. One day since the coronation and her plan had worked perfectly. She'd never admit it, but her eyes had grown tired and her heart had trembled during this important phase of her plan, but she pulled it off. The people of Ashbourn chose an ancient voreen god as their king, and the city, the kingdom, and herself would rise to their true potential. First, conquer the city, then the world. With Chronor's help, the kingdom would bend to her will. She knew he was the god—she just a human—but she would become the most powerful woman to ever exist, especially with almost no more voreen left to oppose them.

Walking through the hallway, she passed window by window, spotting Ashbourn in glimpses. The city bled, and she had inflicted the wound, all she had to do was to keep it open. It had come at a high cost and a lot of luck. That bullet would have killed Chronor in his previous phase, but did nothing to wound him after the announcement. Had it come moments before, it could all have been over before it started. After his elevation, the assassination attempt had actually helped. She'd used it as an excuse for him to stay away from the public eye so they could progress their plan faster.

Eranna stopped next to a window showing the Meritocrat Headquarters in the distance. *Smart move, Koradin,* she thought. *Grabbing the beast hunter that fast.* Thinking about the beast hunter made her tighten her fist so hard her knuckles whitened. They had been so close to losing it all because of him and his gang. Losing Ronoch that close to the coronation would have ended with her head on a pike.

And still, those beast hunters remained a problem—an irritating thorn in her side. *But what can they do now?* The whole city of Ashbourn would soon be in Eranna's hands. Brattora would fall next, and his legions would grow unstoppable.

On her way, she passed several guards with dark eyes and orange irises. They looked terrifying, their minds replaced with Chronor's will. When Chronor laid out the plan of lacing the soldiers's food with his blood, Eranna had her doubts it would work, but as soon as he reached his new phase, they turned into mindless minions. It couldn't have happened any later, as maintaining control over an army of soldiers with the blood of a voreen god running through their veins, proved almost impossible. Unwarranted fights had to be broken off between previously friendly soldiers before they killed each other. With most of the Warborn army under Chronor's direct command, any still free souls had been forced to take in his blood or die.

She pushed open the large doors into the throne room. A few torches dimly lit the dank hall. On the large throne sat her lord in his fullest form, a head taller than the tallest men she'd seen, and broad as the throne itself. From his menacing armour protruded several dark spikes, hiding his grey body from sight. The black metal seemed unnatural as if it had a mind of its own, slowly churning around his body with a dark haze. Large pauldrons rested on his shoulders, bristling with metal spikes and thick smoke. He was gorgeous, glimmering in the light of the moon, with black flames sparking to life infrequently on the different armour pieces without producing any heat. The green firelight coming from his eyes still unnerved Eranna, but she tried not to let it show. It made his gaze all the more oppressive, as he sat alone in the chamber.

"It did not work." His deep godly voice vibrated in her chest. "I am not as strong as you promised."

Eranna frowned at his remark. "What do you mean, my Lord?" she asked, kneeling in front of him.

"It seems not all of my new citizens have devoted themselves to me. I cannot perform the oath of blood yet."

"That cannot be," she answered, and rose to look out a window. "The people of Ashbourn always rally behind their new king."

Chronor rose from his throne and joined her in front of the window, his footsteps shaking the floor. "Had they all been devoted to their new king"—he put a large, dark hand on her shoulder—"then I would have reached my final phase." He turned his head toward the city. "There is still resistance out there. We must make them bend."

Eranna ground her teeth together, taking the failure personally. "The boy," she said. "He was from the Meritocrat District and had leads on us. It's most likely your book is in the hands of someone there. Assuming they've found out who Ronoch truly is, naturally, they won't follow you." Talking about the book brought her great discomfort. She'd been the one to lose it and it was Chronor's most prized possession. He hated that book, but it could not be destroyed. So he wished to keep it close, as close as he could, but then she lost it to some boy. Chronor's hand tightened around her shoulder and she held back a flinch.

"Yes," his voice rumbled. "My book. The truth can be spread like wildfire if given to the right people, like Koradin Banner."

"I believe," she said through gritted teeth. "Any resistance must come from him and his army."

He finally let go of her and went back to his throne, his armour clinking as he sat down.

"But as long as the people stay hungry," she added, "it won't matter. They may believe what they wish, but only we can sate their hunger."

"What you say is true. And once it is sated, they shall *all* be mine."

Eranna cast one glance over at the Meritocrat Headquarters, fearing what Koradin could conjure. She knew of his intellect and capabilities, and if he *was* against them, he'd put up a fight.

"I will get my army," Chronor said. "And with it, force them into submission. Then, Koradin will be mine."

Eranna walked over to his throne, where Chronor injected a large needle into his vein to drain his powerful blood into a large barrel. One of his slaves entered the room and gathered the other barrel full of blood, moving it down to the stored food.

"Will they turn immediately?" she asked him.

"Once my blood enters their body, their weak minds will have no choice but to give in to my might. With my soldiers, I have blocked every exit out of the city." The barrel started filling with his dark blood. "I will use my new slaves to force the food down the throats of those who refuse to eat. Once they are all mine, we will crush Koradin Banner and the Meritocrats."

"*If* I am right, my Lord," she said. "I could be wrong about your opposition, but it seems most likely."

Chronor turned his head towards the Meritocrat District. "I can feel a vacuum of my power looming over that part of the city. It is him that we face. I have to spread the food through the other districts with haste before the knowledge of the book spreads."

"It won't matter," Eranna said, trying to believe her own word. "What could they do? Knowing how to kill you doesn't mean they have the means to kill you."

"The girl," Chronor said.

Eranna's heart filled with anger, her hands tightening. *You should have killed her when you had the chance,* she thought, but dared not say it. The girl had been right there, tied to the chair.

"Calm your anger. The girl is a threat. A small one, but a threat nonetheless."

"That threat must be minuscule," Eranna said, trying to recover from her emotions. "Even less of a threat than the voreen outside of the city."

Chronor's eyes lingered on the Meritocrat District. "She is still out there. I can feel her and she can feel me."

"Will she try to attack?" Eranna asked.

"She would have done so long ago. Confusion clouds her mind, unsure as to why I am surrounded by humans. If she meant to kill me, she would have done so when she first felt my presence, before I could rise to power." His head turned to Eranna. "The girl is a larger threat—if she is clever. I would end her personally, but this important work weakens me."

She couldn't stop him if she wanted to, so she was glad he wanted to stay safe by his own volition. To distribute the food they had hidden was vital to turn the people to

Chronor's control before their lives became even worse, and they turned to someone else to guide them.

But she knew no one else could provide the food they could. The minions Chronor had created had worked perfectly to take out the surrounding villages, stopping the caravans of food coming into Ashbourn. "I can send assassins," Eranna offered.

"Perhaps," Chronor said. "But she will be protected by the healer."

"If he still roams free, my Lord," Eranna said.

"Koradin was clever to stab him. He tricked the public into thinking he killed my assailant, showing his 'support' for me, making himself immune to future claims of defiance. How he knew the healer had regenerative abilities, I do not know. Koradin will be trouble. His people believe in him strongly. Breaking them will be hard. But if I break him, the rest will follow."

"I can discredit him," Eranna offered.

Chronor looked at her with questioning eyes.

"If I could find proof he keeps the healer alive and safe within his walls."

"Perhaps," Chronor said, which meant he didn't approve. He pulled out the syringe as the barrel reached its capacity. "But I know how to deal with the healer." The boy from before came and rolled away the newly filled barrel, returning quickly with an empty one, but Chronor didn't plug the needle into his arm. "You have been of great use, Eranna Carner. You have helped me rise to power. With my army, I will crush anyone who opposes me. Those who have read the dark book will die by my hands and I will lock it away so no one can read it ever again. That is how I will become forever immortal. Doing so will leave only you with the knowledge of how to destroy me."

Eranna narrowed her eyes.

Chronor fixed his gaze on her. "*You* will be my only weakness."

Eranna's eyes widened; she turned to run. His large hand grabbed her by the neck, dragging her back. "Chronor!" she roared, fury welling in her eyes. "I am your most trusted follower!"

His hand dug into her neck, shooting pain through her body. "I do not doubt your loyalty for a second." He turned her head to look into his green fiery eyes. "I have too many times felt the knife of vengeance in my back from a trusted follower who couldn't take the destruction I bring."

"I . . . swear . . ." Eranna gasped for breath.

"You are of the darkest breed, I will give you that. Strong, resourceful and you do whatever it takes. I am not afraid of *your* betrayal. Rather, it is that you are *human*. And humans can be broken by torture, unlike my voreen. I cannot always protect you."

Something snapped in her neck—the pain excruciating and her voice didn't work.

"You see," he said, "you cannot live, as I won't take any chances." She felt his tentacles push through her skin, into her body, and he drained her blood. Numbness took hold. The pain stopped, and only anger and a feeling of unfairness remained.

I gave you everything, she thought in her dying moments. *I gave you life. How can you do this to me?* She had been nothing but loyal. Chronor's face vanished, her vision blackening.

In the end, her anger disappeared. Everything disappeared. Blackness consumed her.

CHAPTER 2

Connections of the Past

Shadestones are dark rubies that grow in ancient caves, and are a central part of voreen culture, being the origin of our magic and violence. The shadestones emerge from the cavern walls with some predictability, and we sense their strong presence and are drawn to them.

This marks the start of Wrot'zu, a terrible blood feud, as we all crave the rubies with insane determination. We slaughter and kill each other mercilessly, and use the voreen blood for the 'ritual of the blade.' When the victors emerge from the cave with rubies, they use the stones to craft our deadly blades, but they can also be used for other things.

In forging the blade, two things are essential: shadestones and a lot of voreen blood. Many duels are settled during this time, causing even more slaughter, and the blood of the loser is added to the mixture.

To craft my blade, Sa'thun, I needed the blood of twelve voreen and two shadestones.

The blood must be boiled over a fire, lit with the dust from a kindler, to reach the needed temperature. At this temperature, the rubies smelt and mix with the blood, and with the incantation of Ther'ah, the sword is moulded into shape.

From 'The Dark Traitor,' chapter eleven.

Khendric's dry mouth and rumbling stomach reminded him that a night had passed in the cell, after his assassination attempt on Chronor. The cell didn't have a window, but he had a vague sense of time. He wanted to find out his location, but he was all alone. Nobody occupied any of the other countless cells, reminding him of the dungeons below the Warborn Headquarters. *If that's where I am, then I'm dead.*

Pondering why Koradin Banner had been the one to assail him always made him crease his brows. Perhaps he saw it as his duty, or perhaps Koradin worked with Chronor?

His fingers ran over the bandage someone had wrapped him in after being stabbed, but the wound had healed quickly. *They must have noticed my abilities,* he thought. *Why else throw a man you stabbed in prison?*

Khendric drew long, concentrated breaths and hoped someone would come for him soon. Because, behind a thin wall in his mind, his past loomed, eager to fester and torture him. Occasional whispers plagued his mind, but he'd been able to keep them under control. The most annoying aspect of this had been his itching arm, exactly where that beast of Chronor stung him. How could regular people live with itching? He felt it aided in dragging the past forth too, tearing at his mental strength.

He had no idea if Darlaene lived, and if he let that dam of worry open fully he'd be paralyzed. Had she gotten out of the Warborn Headquarters after their infiltration? Hopefully, Topper could answer if Khendric got out of this mess. He couldn't let thoughts about her spiral out of control, so he fought hard to keep to his plan about asking Topper.

He leaned against the bars of the cell, contemplating his foolishness. He'd been led by anger and had left Ara and Adenar to themselves. Did they know what had happened? If not, they wouldn't know his whereabouts and the hope that Ara stormed to his rescue, bending the bars to release him, didn't exist.

The sound of footsteps echoed through the dungeons. *One person, alone.* Despite the danger he might be in, he relished the respite a conversation offered from the thoughts in his own mind. A door opened, but from his angle, he couldn't see anything, until the footsteps came closer and Koradin Banner emerged with his light hair and proud posture. *Could have been way worse,* Khendric thought, stepping away from the bars and meeting his eyes dead on.

"I'm sorry for stabbing you," Koradin said.

Khendric lifted his eyebrows in surprise. "Nobody has ever apologized for driving a dagger through me before."

"It wasn't meant to kill, just incapacitate. My physicians could easily patch you back up, though I quickly discovered there was no need for that." Koradin stepped closer. "I see you're not *just* a man."

Khendric showed his palms and lifted his shoulders, but said nothing.

"You must be thirsty," Koradin said and produced a waterskin from below his cloak, and put it down on the floor outside of the bars. "It's not poisoned. Why poison you when I already have you locked up? I'm not even sure poison would affect you."

Khendric pulled the waterskin through the bars and poured water down his throat, feeling better and refreshed instantly.

Koradin clasped his hands behind his back and started pacing back and forth. "The public believes you are dead. This conversation will determine if they're right or not. I'm here to figure out whether or not you are crazy."

"So you believe there can be a side to this where I'm not crazy? Why would you even consider that?"

"Hmm," Koradin rubbed his chin. "I have an incessant need to explore any alternative."

"Alternative? Does this mean that after you saw me shoot Ronoch in the chest, you kept me alive to find out if I'm crazy or . . . perhaps, on to something?"

The two locked eyes with intense stares, before a yielding smile spread across Koradin's face. "Well, you're not a fool at least."

"That's a good start for me."

"So why storm up and shoot him in broad daylight? You knew you wouldn't get away. I need to know why and who you are."

Khendric narrowed his eyes, clearly seeing that Koradin knew something was happening to Ashbourn, but perhaps he had no idea what—or maybe he just wanted his throne back. But if Khendric had to choose between Koradin and Chronor, he'd choose the former king over an ancient, malevolent voreen god.

"He survived, didn't he?" Khendric asked.

"He did."

"I shot him in the chest. Nobody would survive that without plate armour."

Koradin said nothing, his eyes lingering on Khendric.

Guess I'll spill the beans. "I'm a beast hunter. My name is Khendric."

"Your abilities must come in handy in your profession," Koradin said.

"A while ago, a young assistant at these very Headquarters hired me to investigate Ronoch Steelbane. At first, I thought it only a ploy to discredit an opponent, but the young man was persistent and earnest. I investigated and found some disturbing evidence, which led me to infiltrate the Warborn Headquarters in search of a book. It was hard, but I retrieved it."

Koradin leaned closer, captivated by Khendric's words.

"Reading the book, I found out that Ronoch Steelbane is *not* who he claims to be. And all the evidence lined up with what the book claimed."

"Will you just tell me?"

"Ronoch is an ancient, voreen god, named Chronor."

"Voreen?" Koradin asked, not as astonished as Khendric would have thought. The former king seemed to mull over his words. "Can you prove this?"

"Not right now. But I can get the book."

"No," Koradin said, fishing out a small map of the city. "In case you're lying, I can't let such a dangerous individual as you back on the streets." He held the map up to the prison bars and offered Khendric an inked quill. "Can I send one of my trusted men to a location to gather the book?"

Khendric didn't reach for the map. "I need some assurances: my freedom and all items I had on my person upon being stabbed."

"I can't do anything more than give you my word."

Khendric sighed heavily. "This book can save your city. In the wrong hands, Ashbourn is doomed. Perhaps even the whole kingdom."

Koradin's stare intensified, and his jaw tightened.

"Say you're working with Chronor and I give you the book," Khendric continued. "Then Ashbourn is lost."

"And you think that a possibility? After I've been their good king for twelve years, now I've decided I want them damned to live under the oppressive hand of a voreen god."

"You did stab me," Khendric said.

"To save your life. Even though that sounds morbid, it's true. If I hadn't had my men carry you away, then Ronoch would have you now. I didn't hit any vital organs and I put my best doctor on you immediately after I carried you away. Had I done nothing, I'd lose face in front of everyone. Upon stopping you, *after* you fired the pistol, I gained credibility as a just king *and* could detain you for questioning."

"*After* I fired the pistol?" Khendric asked, a shrewd smile on his face.

Koradin lowered the small map and rolled his eyes. "Well, I did believe there to be something wrong and maybe even malevolent about Ronoch. I might have waited longer than I ordinarily would have. I wouldn't be blamed for acting too late, as I am, after all, only human."

Khendric chuckled at the honesty. "Your logic is sound."

"I can't give you physical reassurance for your safety and freedom, but if I had sided with Ronoch, I'd surely just kill you—"

"And lose your only lead to the book," Khendric answered, growing wary again. "I don't think so."

Koradin shrugged. "Well, I guess that's true. As said, I can't give you any true reassurance, but I can let you in on my plan and hopefully, you'll take a chance on me."

"You've got my ear."

"Good. In losing my kingly title, it's been tough to go from King to Councillor, being equal with those on the Meritocrat Council. I came back to the council, assuming control like I was used to, and told them we needed to look into Ronoch Steelbane. They quickly reminded me of my new station and accused me of 'dealing poorly with losing my title.' I lost all credibility and the council went back to its usual business; the food and crime problems." He paced calmly back and forth with hands clasped behind his back. "I'll admit that a part of me wished to seize control of the party with force, but I suppressed the tyrannical urge. Since then, I came to rely more on my other possible lead: you. To discover you are a beast hunter—and hear of your discoveries about Ronoch Steelbane—both pleases and worries me. Naturally, I wished to be wrong. To simply be beaten by a stronger opponent. But now at least I have a chance to find some proof of my beliefs. So, I plan to get the book and have you come before the council to talk about it. Hopefully, they'll see reason and we can actually do something about this situation."

The former king stopped pacing, and turned to Khendric, who kept his tongue.

"And before you also accuse me of not doing anything to stop Ronoch's war talk: Eranna and Ronoch kept me far too busy investigating their non-existent war claims, rather than addressing my people. The city was still under my protection and talk of war will always rank high on my priorities."

"I didn't say anything." Khendric lifted his hands.

Koradin walked up to the bars and put the map against them. He looked deep into Khendric's eyes. "I know you still have to only take my word for it, but I care deeply about my city. Will you aid me in defending and saving it, Master Beast hunter?"

Khendric searched his eyes for a sign of deception, but found nothing. *Please don't let me be wrong.* He grabbed the map and quill through the bars and drew a circle around the hideout, feeling a knot form in his stomach. He looked up at Koradin once more, who still looked sincere and trustworthy. *You better not play me,* he thought and handed him the map.

"Thank you, Khendric. If what you say is found to be true, I apologize for the imprisonment and you'll be compensated for your temporary loss of freedom. For now, my most trusted commander—Commander Relen—the doctor, a cook, and I are the only people who know of your existence. You must be hungry. I'll get the cook to prepare you a meal. In my experience, people are more talkative when hungry. Sorry about that." The king walked away.

Khendric didn't want him to leave him alone again. But of course, he had to leave. Khendric just begged he hadn't placed a bet on the wrong horse.

Just before he walked completely out of Khendric's vision, Koradin turned and asked, "Am I right to assume that you work with Darlaene and Ara?"

Khendric's mouth fell open, unpleasantly surprised he knew about them, thinking hard about how this would play out. *He knows about them, but he'd most likely find them in the hideout anyway, so does it matter?* If Khendric had made the wrong choice, he could have doomed them all.

"From your look, I take it I'm right," Koradin said. "Don't worry. I just need to know if I should safely bring them back if I find them. It would be better to have the whole team of beast hunters here than just you." Then he left Khendric alone to his thoughts, fears, and past.

* * *

Ara's head had been pounding since Chronor's elevation. The immense pressure had given her the worst headaches of her life. She laid in Darlaene's bed, trying to function. Adenar had dragged her back to the hideout, or so he had told her, as she had no memories of it.

Adenar had filled Viessa, the general's widow, and Olenna, his mother, in on what they knew, seeing no reason not to. The more who knew, the better. Perhaps one of them could spread the message if someone captured or killed her.

Neither Darlaene nor Topper had returned, which worried Ara greatly. And who knew if they would ever see Khendric again?

Adenar waited for Ara to recover, and Viessa had turned to despair and wallowed in her pain when learning about Chronor. Ara had felt her sinister and hateful thoughts through the headaches even. Olenna had suggested they turn to the Meritocrats, where, apparently, she could 'get them some help'. But so far, no one had done anything, at least not Ara. Evening approached with haste, and she felt despair creep up on her too.

Where is Khendric? What happened to him? Was he the one who shot Ronoch? If so, what happened next? She feared the worst: his capture, torture, and death. And if he had been killed, they were surely compromised, meaning they needed to leave the hideout with the book as fast as possible.

With those worries on her mind, she tried rising from bed. It hurt her head, but she stumbled into the main room of the hideout, where Adenar sat reading the book and his mother looked at a sizeable map of the city.

"—there's nothing concrete in here about it," Adenar said to his mother. "It says he led large wars against those who opposed him and crushed them into submission. I reckon he's never been summoned and gained power through a coronation before. Hence, I think discovering something about his plan from the book can be difficult."

Olenna looked troubled, her hand on her chin. Adenar noticed Ara's footsteps. "Ara, h-how are you?"

"My head hurts," she said, rubbing her temples. "But it's manageable." She'd give anything for one of those green drinks Horana had given her in Cornstead. "What are you doing?"

"Trying to decide what to do next," Olenna said. "Either to make out Chronor's next move or decide our own plan." She looked over to Viessa, who slept on some rugs. "And we need to get her out of here. She needs medical attention and grows crazier by the second. And I don't see much hope either. At least not alone."

Ara sat down on a nearby chair and poured herself some water. "I've been thinking—to the best of my ability, at least—perhaps we should seek out Elrich Obarum. Darlaene worked for him to investigate Ronoch. I met him once, so he'd recognize me. Since he hired a beast hunter 'against' Ronoch, he surely won't follow him with the evidence we can provide."

"Elrich has no backbone," Olenna said. "He's weak. I'm certain that upon discovering the new king is a voreen god he'll try to think of a way to best please him."

"But—"

"Listen, I know Elrich Obarum. He is a Passionist, and owns no strength. He *will* cower when on the losing side. And we *are* on the losing side."

"I think mother is right," Adenar said, meeting Ara's eyes. "Sorry."

"Koradin Banner is the man you want," Olenna said. "He would die a hundred deaths for his people and still fight with what was left. If we can convince him, we might get somewhere."

Knock . . . knock . . . knock.

Ara froze, and so did the others. The knocks came again. They remained quiet. Once more, more insistent this time. Olenna moved gracefully through the room and put out all the lights. Then they waited in silence. Ara knew the upstairs door to be locked, though they all heard the metallic scraping sound it made when opened.

"Someone picked the lock?" Ara whispered.

Olenna nodded, grabbing a cudgel. Without Khendric, Topper or Darlaene around, Ara felt so vulnerable. Her hand went to her side, her fingers wrapping around the sword in her sheath, remembering how devastating she had been to those Warborn soldiers. She felt a little safer, unless a squadron of enemies flowed down the stairs next.

Footsteps echoed as someone walked down the staircase. Only one person, by the sound.

"Hello?" a questioning male voice reverberated into their quarters. "If anyone is down here, please, don't hurt me. I am friend, not foe." His words caused no reaction in any of them. "I'm sent by Khendric, who I'm told is a friend of yours." The man walked slowly through their dark hideout, coming closer.

The Warborn could have tortured Khendric for this information, Ara thought. *We should have moved on a long time ago. I'm so stupid.*

"I am sent by Khendric, through Koradin Banner. If anyone is down here, please don't hurt me. I am merely a messenger."

Ara's heart pounded, uncertain of what to do. The dark shape of the intruder slowly entered their room, moving past her and she grabbed him with her strong hand and drove him down towards the ground. If he resisted, she didn't even feel it with her strength.

"Who are you?" Ara asked in her fiercest voice. "Don't turn your head if you value it."

Viessa woke in a hurry, screaming for help until she realised she wasn't the one in danger.

Olenna lit a candle to reveal the man to their eyes. He wore a roughspun cloak with a hood covering his head. "My name is Jack Relen," he said calmly. "Commander in Koradin's army. Or, the Meritocrat army now."

Ara had no idea if his words were true, but Olenna got down to one knee in front of the man and lifted his chin, examining his face. "It's him. You can let go."

"Are you sure?" Ara asked.

"Absolutely."

Ara let go and he stood back up while grasping his neck. Jack Relen had short dark hair and a slim face, looking like a stern commander with a neatly trimmed short beard and a broad build. "That's quite the grip," he said, still rubbing his neck. His eyes scanned the room. "Is that . . . Viessa Toran?"

Olenna nodded.

"I see." He studied Olenna. "I'm sorry, I know I've seen your face, but I don't remember where."

"You have a strong memory then," Olenna said. "I haven't been in the political game for a long time."

He offered his hand to her. "Seems *your* strong memory saved my life. Thank you." They shook hands before he turned to Ara. "You're the female beast hunter?"

"I am," she said, still not certain as to what she should tell him.

"Koradin told me about you and a red-haired lady . . . Darlaene?"

"We don't know where she is," Ara said. "At the moment."

"Right, that's most unfortunate, but we can leave a note. I'm here on behalf of Koradin Banner, to ask you to come with us. He's most interested in what you've discovered and also a certain book you have gotten your hands on. Khendric is with us, though I regret to tell you that he's imprisoned at the moment—"

"What?" exclaimed Ara. "Why?"

"Well, he shot Ronoch Steelbane. Koradin basically saved his life by locking him up, and now he wants to find out if Khendric is just a madman, or if his claims are legitimate. Khendric told him something horrible, apparently, and Koradin wants to believe him, but is in dire need of proof before taking action. Hence, he sent *me* to get *you*. You, and this book, are Khendric's road to freedom."

Ara thought his words over, trying to find any holes, but Olenna recognized him, which counted for something. And if Khendric could be found at the Meritocrat Headquarters, Ara wanted to be there too.

"We have the book," Adenar said. "I think this is our best shot."

"If he is to be trusted?" Ara asked.

"If we can't trust him," Olenna said. "Then we're doomed."

Adenar closed the book and put it into a rucksack. "We should go right away. I fear the longer we stay here, the greater the chance for someone less interested in our well-being breaking in."

"Fine," Ara finally agreed.

"Great," Commander Relen said.

They made ready to leave, and Ara wore her leather armour, her sword and her concealed dagger attached to her body. In a box on the floor, they'd found enough cloaks for everyone, to help them stay concealed, though Ara feared it would make them more suspicious. Adenar had the book, tasked with keeping it safe, while Olenna and Jack helped Viessa.

Ara wrote a letter with their new location for Topper and Darlaene and put it on the table.

Then, they took to the streets. Light rain fell upon the city as the moon hid behind a carpet of black clouds. The back alley they entered smelled like excrement, and Ara breathed through her mouth to avoid gagging.

"The city is in a state of crisis," Jack said. "Especially here and in the Warborn District. People are starving; crimes and murder rates are higher than ever before in Ashbourn's history." He stopped at a corner before the alley opened into a wider street, examining the road ahead. "It looks empty, but different gangs are patrolling many parts of the city, and they're dangerous. We're going to go through as many side streets and alleys as we can, but we need to cross here."

In the mud that covered the street, something looked an awful lot like a body. The longer Ara's gaze lingered, the more certain she grew. Her stomach threatened to empty as her mind made out the man laying deep in the mud, slowly unveiled by the raindrops. Her breath stilled. She swallowed dryly and noticed weak pressure on her mind coming from the houses around her. Countless vague emotions emanated from within the houses surrounding them, and she realized how many people actually hid in their homes.

"Is that a man?" Adenar asked.

Jack threw a glance around the corner. "Yeah. There are . . . many like him."

"Ronoch destroys this city already," Viessa said, shaking her head.

Jack scouted around the corner again, before signalling for them to move with haste. Olenna and he walked as fast as they could across the street, but Viessa slowed them greatly. Once they reached the other side of the street seemingly undetected, he said, "Later today Ronoch will give an announcement that will *supposedly* solve all these problems. He's had *a discovery,* apparently. Also, be ready to fight. If any gangs of starved citizens spot us, they might attack."

"Why?" Ara asked as they dove further into the alley, still feeling pressure on her mind from all around.

"In case we have valuable items or food on us. We're all wearing expensive cloaks after all."

The group moved slowly through the bowels of the district, occasionally meeting lonely people, shivering from the cold of the rain, wearing once beautiful clothes now wet and dirty. Ara felt sorry for them, especially the way they cowered as her group of five hooded figures slid like deathwalkers through the misty alleys. *The best way to help them is to defeat Chronor,* she told herself, having trouble moving on without taking the people with them.

They walked for hours, staying close to the outer wall of the city, before finally reaching two large gates between the Passionist District and the Meritocrat District, separated by a wide main road and a bridge over a canal. The Passionist gate remained open, but the Meritocrat one had been shut.

"We have to go out of the main gate," Jack said. "But then I have a key to a smaller entrance into our safer district."

"I don't see any guards," Olenna noticed.

"No. Elrich Obarum had them removed. It became too dangerous here, and he easily welcomed more soldiers around himself."

"That doesn't surprise me," she responded.

Jack scouted the area and motioned for them to move into the street, but Ara laid a hand on his shoulder.

"Wait," she said, a look of deep concentration on her face. A sense of hatred and violent thoughts came from further up the main street, moving down towards them quickly. A low rumbling sound of several mudded footsteps grew louder.

"Hide," said Jack, and they glued themselves to the wall, hoping the darkness would conceal them as angry shouts accompanied the many footsteps.

A young man ran down the main street and past the gate, but close behind him followed a large group of crazed people, shouting for his death, throwing rocks and wielding hammers, pitchforks, and crude weapons.

The fleeing man ran faster than the horde, and Ara begged he would outrun them, but a rock struck him in the back and he stumbled. Ara gasped as he tumbled into the mud and almost ran out to help him, but Jack grabbed and stopped her. He shook his head with a sad expression. "It's too late," he whispered.

The group gathered around him, hiding the poor man from view as they beat and stabbed with hammers and sharp edges. Ara's hands trembled with anger and fear. The street quieted as one of the violent attackers searched the dead man's pockets, before they all left the scene. Adenar's face paled, and his mother shielded his view with her cloak.

"It's the end of us," Viessa whispered. "He's going to kill us all."

"Stop that," Olenna said.

"Events like these are growing more common," Jack said with silent anger written over his face. "We need to keep moving. Is the street clear now?" he asked, looking at Ara.

She nodded, barely feeling the horde's pressure on her mind, and he led them out into the open. They rushed through the large open street, and Ara begged that no one would chase them. They neared the body of the young man, and Jack checked his pulse. A shake of the head let Ara know what she needed.

"Come on," he commanded.

Together, they crossed the rest of the street, through the gate of the Passionist District, and hurried over the bridge to the Meritocrat gate. Once near the gate, they traversed down the narrow road off to the side, leading to a thick steel door. Ara hoped Jack and Olenna wouldn't trip and fall into the river with Viessa. The door had been hard to spot, as it blended nicely into the tall wall around the district. Jack searched for his key, while Adenar supported Viessa.

This close to the outer wall of Ashbourn, the river exited the city close by, through a grating. While waiting, something caught Ara's eye: a group of trashers jumped into the river and swam through the grating. She counted ten of them, but there were more. *Why are they leaving?* she pondered. *Do they sense a coming storm?* She turned to face the castle, barely visible in the distance, except for its many lights. Chronor's presence loomed over Ashbourn, and it seems the beasts could tell. Shouldn't people be out celebrating after a coronation? Shouldn't the streets explode with people living life?

The others entered through Jack's door. "You coming?" he asked.

She cast a final glance at the trashers, seeing far more of them now, diving into the river and leaving Ashbourn. *Is it because of the food shortage, or something else?*

"Ara?" Jack pressed.

She snapped out of her thoughts. "Sorry, I'm coming."

The group wandered through narrow tunnels until reaching a locked door at the end with no keyhole. A couple of soldiers stood guard close by, and Jack called them over by name. One of them stuck a key into a keyhole on his side of the door, and let them into the district. Ara felt instant relief at leaving the Passionist District behind, and her headache didn't pound as hard as it had. As she had expected, the rest of the way to the Meritocrat Headquarters was uneventful.

"She is strong," Chronor's voice spoke into her mind.

I hope he can't hear anything that I'm saying, she thought, understanding that if he could, Ara could reveal some of their future plans to him.

"Her will is strong. But she will break."

She tried not to let his words manifest, though at least her will seemed strong to Chronor.

Jack led them through a back entrance into the headquarters, and down a level to the dungeons. He opened a door into a large and nicely furnished room, with a long wooden table with more than enough chairs around it. Ara's jaw dropped upon seeing the food on the table and felt her hunger set in.

"Koradin prepared this room as best he could," Jack said. "If you would please stay here while I inform him of your arrival. I'm sure he'll be extremely pleased with the news."

The group nodded, already seating themselves to eat.

"This might be slightly uncomfortable," Jack continued. "But this *used* to be a large cell for extremely troubled prisoners and the fewer people that know you are here, the better. Which means I'm going to lock the door. If anyone notices it unlocked, they might open it and see all of you. You're okay with this?"

A few glances of uncertainty passed between the group. "It's fine," Olenna said, obviously placing a lot of trust in him.

The door closed and locked, and Ara hoped she could break it open if the need arose.

They gorged on the food, except for Viessa, who ate like a normal person, and it didn't take long before the door opened again, and none other than Koradin Banner entered. Behind him followed Commander Jack Relen, and . . . that was it. *No more guards?* Ara wondered. The former king wore a sword, but other than that, only a blue tabard with the Meritocrat icon on it and some informal trousers. His blonde hair flowed beautifully down to his shoulders. "Welcome," he said. "I hope the meal met your expectations." His eyes examined the people sitting around the table, and a look of befuddlement dawned on his face upon seeing Olenna, but within a moment, he regained his seriousness. "Olenna? I didn't expect to see you here."

"I know," she said, remaining cool.

Adenar looked back and forth between the two, as puzzled as the rest of them.

"Anyway," Koradin said. "I'm afraid I want to get straight to business. I have a Master Beast Hunter in my dungeons, who's quite ready to be let out of his cell."

Ara perked up. *He really is here.*

Three people wearing medical uniforms rushed through the door and Jack pointed them in Viessa's direction. They examined her leg and carried her out of the room for medical aid.

"I'm told you have a book," Koradin said as the room quieted. "That book is Khendric's proof."

"Show it to him," Olenna said, prodding Adenar. Still puzzled, he snapped back to the situation at hand and dug out the book from his rucksack.

Koradin walked over and put a hand on Adenar's shoulder. "Thank you," he said, looking at Adenar questioningly.

"Adenar, sir."

The king's lips split into a smile and he squeezed the young man's shoulder. "Thank you, Adenar." Koradin grabbed the book, went back in front of the table, put it down and opened it. Ara rose and went to his side and sat down.

Without turning his head, his eyes locked on her. "Good to see you again, Ara."

"Good to see you too," she said and put a hand near the book. "Just in case you try anything. This book is *quite* valuable."

"I understand," he answered, and started reading with what seemed like incredible speed. Koradin exhaled and grimaced often, occasionally shaking his head while he read for some time. Ara's heart beat hard the whole time, and she jumped as he quickly shut the book.

"This whole book needs to be read," he said. "But I know almost for certain what we're up against. Unfortunately, the Master Beast hunter told the truth."

"Unfortunately?" Ara asked.

"I'd rather be wrong than right in this matter, and him to be a madman. But at least now I have some leverage to present to the council and get them to work with me." He rose. "You may keep the book close, Ara, if that's what you prefer. I need you all to stay in this building. You'll be given food and shelter, and I would very much like to work with you so that we can fight this common enemy." His eyes went to every individual in turn. "What say you?" His eyes fell back on Ara.

"Ehm, I'll talk to Khendric about it. He is sort of the boss."

"Great. He'll be released at once and led to your quarters. I advise you to stay in your rooms for now. After I've talked to the council, you'll be allowed to wander around the building more freely." He strolled out of the room, motioning for them to follow.

He led them up several floors, passing countless soldiers, all of who finely adjusted their posture as the former king walked by. He walked with such an authoritative presence, almost commanding in itself.

Koradin opened a door leading into a huge room, with several smaller rooms inside. "These used to be my personal quarters. Stay here for now, until we get all this sorted out. Then we can work together on how to deal with this."

The group went inside and Ara truly relaxed for the first time in a long time. Koradin closed the door behind him, leaving them alone. She felt a lovely sense of peace wash over her tired body, and found a large bed, falling into its comfortable embrace. All her worries drifted away for a short, wonderful time, sleep finding her more quickly than ever before.

CHAPTER 3

From Advisors to Councillors

Chronor leaves death behind, even after his passing. His most glorious warriors become remnants of this world upon Chronor's demise. The shra'thar remain fearful warriors that can be summoned by mortals—for a sacrifice. Voreen without much to lose, often summons Chronor's fallen champions, using them to murder anyone their momentary master demands. These champions are plagued souls that once fell to Shraz'tah, Chronor's mighty weapon, in a blood oath, doomed for eternity to new masters and puny tasks.

Editor's note: I believe that Vho'rha means what we call shadowwalkers when referring to the shra'thar.

From 'The Dark Traitor,' chapter four on 'The Blood Oath.'

Ara's eyes opened to a cool breeze through a window, laying on a comfortable feather bed. Another crevice in the large bed belonged to Adenar, which made her smile. He slept soundly on top of the bedsheets just like her, snoring softly, and she didn't want to wake him, knowing how excruciatingly tired he'd been. Carefully, Ara rolled out of the oversized bed and entered the large living room of Koradin's quarters.

A familiar shape stood hunched over a table, wearing his large brown coat and hat.

"Khendric!" Ara rejoiced and rushed over to him. They embraced in a tight hug. "It's so good to see you."

"And you too," he said, cheerfully. "I had many worries in trusting Koradin, but here we are again."

Warmth sparked to life in Ara's body.

"And luckily you had the book too," Khendric continued, "proving to Koradin I'm indeed not a madman."

"Well, not definitive proof to completely rule it out," she said with a wry look on her face.

He tapped his index finger to his temple. "At least this madman's goals align with Koradin's."

"He seems genuine," she said. "Right?"

"Indeed he does. Let's pray that is the truth of it."

Ara's eyes scanned the room. "Where's Olenna?"

"She got her own room." He narrowed his eyes. "That woman is peculiar. While you slept, Koradin led me here and I observed them together. She moves and talks around Koradin like he's . . . I don't know . . ."

"A friend?" she asked.

"Sort of, or even something more. She's not intimidated by him in any way, despite him being who he is."

Ara rounded the table, seeing a map of the city with countless drawn lines and circles. "What are you doing?"

Khendric sighed and pressed his palms to the table again, resuming his hunched-over posture. "Trying to figure out where she went, or what happened."

A burden laid itself on Ara's shoulders. "Darlaene's probably fine," she said, trying to sound believable.

"Countless times I've thought her dead, and *every* time she comes back, laughing in my face. But before she miraculously returns, I worry so much I can't function." He faced Ara with a grim expression. "Which is why we split up, or . . . she split up with me. I love working with her, but at the same time, I want to lock her up to keep her safe. She can't be boxed in, and I can't blame her, but it broke my heart." A hint of a smile found its way back to his lips. "But being excellent trackers, we always seem to find each other. The truth is, I really don't want to live without her."

Ara felt lucky to catch a glimpse of their peculiar relationship. "Has she been gone this long before?"

"Yes. Longer even, and with some good explanations too."

"Then she's probably fine."

"I wouldn't be so worried if Topper wasn't missing too."

A knock came at the door and Koradin entered.

"Still glad to be out of that cell?" he asked, extending his hand to Khendric.

"Tremendously so," Khendric replied, taking the hand. "As you know, this is Ara."

Koradin gave her a short bow. "We've met twice actually; one time before this all became a complete mess. I *would* like to keep reading that dark book of yours and explore how to deal with this voreen monstrosity, but I'm afraid time is of the essence. The council has agreed to a hearing, and that hearing is now."

"Now?" Khendric asked. "With more time we can provide better answers. Right now, it'll only be dark tidings."

"So be it. This is to let them know something *is* happening to Ashbourn. Do your best, nonetheless, and we'll work with whatever the outcome may be."

"What exactly is going on?" Ara wondered. Still fuzzy on the details.

Koradin exhaled with a look of annoyance. "In going from king to councillor, the hardest part has been going from having advisors to being equal to the other councillors. The Meritocratic Council doesn't believe anything is wrong with Ashbourn, which is why we have to convince them so that we can get things going."

"I see," Ara said. "And I'm helping?"

"Yes," Khendric said. "I'll do most of the talking, but if you think of anything to provide, don't hold your tongue."

"Good, we must go," Koradin said, gesturing for them to hurry.

* * *

The grand and circular council room had a beautiful marble floor and huge pillars going all the way to the ceiling, with Ara and Khendric in the middle, surrounded by four huge stone chairs. Behind the chairs rose large stone steps for people to sit on, almost like an atrium. Three people occupied the main chairs, Koradin seating himself in the last one. Two guards holding halberds stood to each side of the chairs.

Next to Koradin sat an old, wrinkly and thin lady with ashen hair, cleaning her spectacles. Dressed in voluminous white robes, she looked as majestic as possible, her age adding to the appearance.

Across from the former king sat a plump and round bald man, with a neatly trimmed beard despite his white robes looking more beige from dirt and general wear. His ears stuck out like a trasher's, and Ara thought he looked rather foolish.

Lastly sat an older man, across from the woman. He had his hair combed to the side and a cleanly shaven face. He held his chin high and eyes half-closed, making him look quite arrogant.

"I have hastily gathered the council," Koradin proclaimed, rising from his chair moments after he sat down. "And I thank you for your cooperation. I've concerns that, I believe, affects not just our district, but the whole of Ashbourn, and I urge us to take action."

Ara felt underdressed for the occasion, still wearing her leather armour and a blade-less sheath, as the sword had been removed upon her entry.

"Before you stand two beast hunters: Khendric and Ara. They have been investigating matters within the city and have uncovered something truly disturbing." Koradin turned and addressed Ara and Khendric. "Beast hunters, before you sit Aeba Therkin." The older woman rose from her seat and did a short bow. "Thornar Brassbold." The plump, round man stood and bowed generously. "And lastly, Ponther Caein."

Ponther didn't rise at all; instead, he inclined his head and waved his hand for them to proceed, but opened his mouth before Koradin could speak, "You say 'take action'. Those are dangerous words, especially from someone newly de-throned after a twelve-year rule." His voice struck clear and hard, quite unexpected from such an old face.

"Do you truly think me that transparent?" Koradin re-torted, somehow with a graceful tone.

"It's hard to say," Ponther answered. "It's been so long since we had the *pleasure* of your presence."

"Oh stop it," the woman, Aeba, said with a sharp and nasal voice, waving a dismissive hand. "You're always so de-meaning. We all know you missed Koradin while he was away."

Ponther leaned back with a reserved expression, and his tightened jaw revealed his annoyance.

"It's not like he hasn't been credible before," Aeba con-tinued. "Let's hear what they have to say."

Khendric bowed deeply. "I thank you for agreeing to this most important meeting. For some time, my accomplices and I have investigated Ronoch Steelbane, started by—"

"Of course," Ponther interrupted. "Of course it's Ronoch Steelbane. This is a truly sad display after being beaten fairly."

"Just hear him out, Councillor Caein," Koradin said, keeping his calm, and giving Khendric a gesture to continue.

"—started by an assistant in your very Headquarters," Khendric said without skipping a beat. "I don't think we have that much time, so I'll be blunt. Ronoch Steelbane is *not* who he appears. Ronoch Steelbane is, in truth, an ancient voreen god, named Chronor." Khendric let his words settle, but the council looked unimpressed.

"What?" Aeba asked with a sharp tone. "A what?"

"A voreen god," Khendric repeated, understanding their confusion.

"This is a waste of time," Ponther said, rising. "Let's leave, Thornar."

The plump man nodded, seemingly out of fear and gathered his things.

"In Ronoch's basement," Khendric said. "I personally found one hundred dead bodies—acid used to dissolve them." Ponther and Thornar remained standing, but did not leave. "What's also peculiar is that if you talk to the homeless in the Warborn District, they can tell you about a terrible event where coincidently around one hundred people were kidnapped, never to be seen again. Send someone over there if you must, to validate my accusation." Khendric lifted his eyebrows as if posing a challenge. The councillor licked his wrinkly lips, meeting his stare, and calmly sat down.

"These are indeed wild accusations," Aeba said. "Do you have proof?"

"Of the bodies?" Khendric asked. "Sadly, no. And I believe they have all been dissolved by now, though the poor homeless will undoubtedly confirm it. We infiltrated the Warborn Headquarters on the day before the coronation—"

"Infiltrated?" Ponther interrupted. "That's illegal."

"Not when I am on a case," Khendric said. "*If* the infiltration does not lead to any deaths, a beast hunter, and their associates, have the right to investigate restricted areas. This right is recognized by the Sangerian Grasslands, granted to official beast hunters." Khendric flashed his medallion.

"And were there any fatalities?" Ponther asked.

"Have you heard of any?"

The elderly man exhaled. "I have not."

"During our infiltration, we did uncover something of monumental importance." Khendric hinted for Ara to hand him the book. "This book was written by a voreen woman, and translated by a human woman named Avina. The voreen woman, whose name I'm not going to try to pronounce or pretend to remember, writes in this book about their god: Chronor. Ronoch—or rather, Chronor—protected this book fiercely, and it was only with luck we managed to steal it away from him." He held out forth for them all to see.

The elderly woman, Aeba, rose her hand in the air. "If this book is your direct evidence that Chronor exists, why wouldn't he simply destroy it?"

"I can't be completely sure," Khendric said. "But the book mentions something along the lines of 'Chronor cannot destroy the book, because of some performed voreen magic.'"

Aeba leaned back on her mighty chair. "Well, we know the voreen dwell in rituals and magic we've never understood."

"Don't tell me you believe any of this," Ponther said with an accusatory tone.

"Calm down," she answered, waving a dismissive hand his way. "I'm keeping an open mind, as should you." She gestured for Khendric to continue.

"Chronor can gain the appearance of someone else by consuming their blood. He turned into Ronoch and has now won the coronation."

"Why would a god seek to win a coronation?" Ponther asked, sceptically.

"The more people that follow him the stronger he gets," Ara said, all eyes falling upon her. "It's true, all of this is true." Ponther stared daggers at her, but Khendric's resolution lent her bravery and she stared right back.

"I'm afraid it is," Khendric said. "Winning the coronation boosted his powers immensely. The book says he operates in seven different phases, right?" He looked to Ara.

"Yes, seven phases," she confirmed. "We believe he's either in phase six or seven, meaning he's hard to kill."

Khendric put the book on Aeba's desk and she began shuffling through the pages.

"This is preposterous," Ponther exclaimed. "Ronoch is a voreen god who becomes more powerful when people follow him? Koradin Banner, do you take me for a fool?"

"I've never taken you for a fool," Koradin replied.

"You lost, fair and square. Now take your loss home and stop bothering us with this nonsense!"

"This book looks otherwordly," said Aeba. "I would read more before making a decision, but this certainly isn't something to just blow away." She gave Ponther a knowing look.

A small smile allowed itself to grow on Ara's lips.

"How can the book look legitimate?" Ponther asked as if every word he uttered was the embodiment of truth itself. "You surely don't believe any of this, Thornar, right? Please don't tell me this council has descended into idiocy."

The plump man, Thornar, shook his head with a dumbfounded look. "Uhm, no . . . I don't believe it."

"Good," Ponther said, chin raised high again. "At least we still have two people with their senses intact."

"You should take a look at the book," Koradin told Ponther in a polite, but firm tone.

"Keep your cheap book away from me. You've had enough time to plot this terrible and pathetic plan to get back on the throne."

"I *don't* thirst for the throne—"

"Oh, spare me. Like every man, you thirst for power, and after twelve years of having it, believe me, I understand how hard it must be to lose it."

Koradin's hands tightened on the handles of his marble chair and he clenched his jaw.

"You said a hundred people had been abducted?" Aeba asked, breaking the tension between the two men.

"Yes," Ara replied.

"I'll send someone to ask the homeless of the Warborn District," she said and waved one of the guards over. Before long, he left to do her bidding. "It says here that to summon Chronor, the blood of a hundred souls is needed, amongst other things. We'll have to read this book through, as it will help us determine whether it's credible or not."

"We have to hurry," Koradin said. "I fear we cannot dabble too long on what to do."

"I will have my most trusted scribes make a copy of the book through the night and hopefully be done during tomorrow. If that's alright with you of course?" She looked at Ara and Khendric.

"As long as one of us can oversee the work," Khendric said. "To see that no words are twisted, and most importantly, to ensure the book's safety."

"Naturally," Aeba agreed and snapped her fingers for a servant.

"And do what exactly?" Ponther broke into the conversation, rising dramatically from his chair. "First of all, you need the majority of votes to act on this 'issue,' and even if you got that, what would you do? Wage war against the king? Start a civil war?"

"That's what we have to decide," Koradin answered, his knuckles having returned to their natural colour. "We would first read the book, to see what can hurt an old god."

Ponther snarled. "I won't read your book. And it doesn't matter anyway, as you'll never get a majority. Thornar and I will be damned before we start a civil war. I'll keep that blood off my cloak."

"What if he is right?" Aeba asked.

"You believe them? How do we know they're not just actors?"

"I didn't say I believe them. I'm giving them a fair hearing and so far, what they've put up is enough to at least be investigated."

Ara had trouble keeping her emotions in check, feeling anger manifest in her guts. Ponther had no idea what they had gone through to get the book.

"Do what you will," Ponther declared. "But for now, you don't get anywhere with this, isn't that right Thornar?" Thornar nodded submissively to Ponther, the coward underneath as clear as daylight.

"We will meet again tomorrow, at sunset," Koradin said before Ponther left the large room. "To discuss further and perhaps come to a different conclusion."

"I have better things to do."

"You cannot dismiss my calling," Koradin said. "Unless it is something of grave—"

"Yes-yes," Ponther answered, waving a hand and leaving the room with Thornar tracking his every step.

Aeba shifted through the pages, a look of interest and worry on her face.

"He hasn't changed," Koradin muttered.

"And he never will, but Thornar might," Aeba said.

"So you believe us?" Ara burst forth.

"Hold your horses. I haven't settled yet. Always in such a hurry young people."

"Time is of the essence," Koradin reminded her.

"It always is." She shut the book. "I'll read the copy tomorrow and write down possible questions before making up my mind. Sounds good?"

Both Ara and Khendric nodded.

"Thank you, Aeba," Koradin said, and they shook hands.

"No problems at all, King Koradin." She shook her head. "Councillor Koradin. Old habits die hard."

He offered a reminiscent smile and bowed. Ara and Khendric followed him out of the large room and back to their quarters.

"That didn't go too well," Ara said after she closed the door. Adenar had left, probably to find his mother's room.

"I didn't expect it to go any better," Koradin said. "But now they know of the possibility that something is going on. Beast Hunter Khendric, may I ask you a favour?"

"You can always *ask*," Khendric answered.

"We need to know what Ronoch says in his announcement at the castle. Rumours say his words will bring an end to all the city's plights. I have my doubts, so I want to know."

"And you want me to go and find out what it is?" Khendric asked.

"Precisely. Can you go without being recognized? I can't go as—"

"I have a wig and different clothes, I'll be fine. Bestow upon me the title of 'Saviour of Ashbourn' and we got a deal."

"Naturally, as a councillor that is of course within my power."

Khendric raised his eyebrows questioningly. "You are being sarcastic, right?"

Koradin held his stern expression.

"No?" Khendric questioned. "Yes, you are."

"Complete this task for me and find out."

Khendric huffed and left.

✳ ✳ ✳

A mass of starved, tired and broken people stood at Castle Square, waiting for Ronoch's long-awaited announcement. The heavy bags under their eyes and bent backs revealed their miserable state, and their new king hadn't saved them yet. Khendric guessed the king should be allowed some leeway since he'd only been king for a short time, and in that time, been shot . . . by Khendric. The poor souls at Castle Square hoped he would save them, but Khendric doubted any gift from Chronor would be in the best interest of the citizens. He sat on top of a nearby rooftop, leaning against a slanted panel.

"You let them hurt us," the voices of his past whispered in his ears, and all his worries about Darlaene returned into the plaguing mixture. His heart pounded in his chest and his breathing intensified. *Calm down, Khendric, it's nothing to be afraid of.* The whispers in Khendric's mind grew louder as if he felt Chronor approach. *"You let them cut us apart."* He shook his head clear. "Stop it," he whispered. "Stay focused."

He lifted his gaze as Ronoch took the stage, appearing amid all his guardsmen, all of whom wore large helmets with narrow eye slits and held huge halberds. Khendric rolled his eyes when Chronor used a cane due to his recent 'injury."

"I stand before you again," Ronoch said with his powerful and resolute voice. "The attempt on my life has left me injured, but I will not let it hinder me. The needs of the city are vastly more important than my health, and I have news for you. News that will fill you with hope, and sadly, contempt." The square filled up with people as criers spread his words to the masses.

Khendric fought an internal battle to keep his past from consuming him. Terrible memories tore at his walls, and they threatened to break. *I am better than this,* he tried to convince himself. Terrible moments of his childhood flashed in his mind, and he lost focus on Chronor and the speech. *I should've never agreed to this.*

"Upon gaining full access to the castle," continued the false king, and Khendric forced his attention back to him. "I have learned that Koradin wasn't the good king we all thought he was. Upon inspecting the emergency food storages, Eranna Carner found several of them to be full of food, enough to keep us going long enough to set up new caravans!" He held his hand out to his audience and closed it into a fist.

The crowd booed their dismay with the news, though Khendric didn't believe it for a second. *What are you playing at?* he wondered, his curiosity giving him a respite from his thoughts.

"But don't waste your precious energy with hatred for Koradin Banner. His time is gone and it is our time now. I will fill your bellies with this food, starting immediately. In all districts, we will supply you with large carts of food and give it out to all who go hungry! Soldiers will share the food equally with all who wait their turn!"

The crowd cheered wildly with happiness, but Khendric narrowed his eyes questioningly. *He's feeding them all? Why?* A part of Khendric thought Chronor would want them hungry and suffering for some malevolent reason.

"I will not waste more of your time," Ronoch said. "I am not as strong as I had hoped after the attack, and you are all hungry. I shall leave you to it."

He turned and, with the "help" of his cane, walked back into a waiting carriage amid his guards. Soldiers on stage redirected the crowd to food carts stationed, while others handed out maps with more locations in other districts. As Chronor moved further away, his trauma faded, feeling like a constricting rope around his chest loosened. His thoughts still loomed, and he wanted to keep himself busy to push them away, so he decided to wait in the food cart line.

After some time, and after a lot of people had gotten their batch of food, Khendric received his share; three rolls of bread.

"Share it with your family," the soldier said, his eyes hidden behind the helmet. Khendric turned to leave, but he grabbed his arm. At first, Khendric thought the soldier had recognized him as the assassin despite his wig and new clothes, but he just said, "Make sure *everybody* eats it. Do you understand?"

Khendric nodded quickly and left. *Better bring this back to the others,* he thought and hoped he'd get back fast with a carriage.

* * *

Night slowly enveloped Ashbourn, and Koradin watched his city grow dark from his large room high atop the Meritocrat Headquarters. His family had moved with him after he lost the coronation. It had felt strange to move out of the castle, as it had been their home for twelve years. He owned a large house in the district near the wall, but it had stood empty for so long that the thought of living there felt awkward. *Though using both properties will be smart,* he thought, feeling safer with his ability to be unpredictable.

His three daughters both relaxed and had a blast in their new home, but his wife had a harder time, sensing his troubled mind. Her beautiful arms hung around his neck as she watched the night with him, admiring the stars far above.

"Will you come to bed tonight?" Lenda asked with her soothing voice. "You have barely slept since losing the coronation. I can't understand how you're still functioning."

Lack of sleep barely affected him as much as it would a normal person, though it *did* sound lovely to get a full night's rest. "I'm waiting for the beast hunter to return."

She let out a breath and removed her arms, walking around in front of him, making his view ten times better.

"How about you get some sleep and I'll meet him." The sincerity in her voice revealed her worries.

A smile spread across his lips, and he lifted his eyebrow. "Are you really *that* eager to spend time with him?"

The left side of her lip curled into a clever grin. "Well, he was rather handsome and . . . you don't have the time to enter my bed despite my begging."

"Neither will he with all the work I'll give him. And second, I'll have him hanged for . . . potentially attracting my lustrous wife."

"You're not the king anymore," she reminded him in a playful tone, putting her index finger on his lower lip. "You can't just have the man hanged."

"Right, I forgot. It probably wouldn't kill him either." In the following silence, Lenda sat down beside him and rested her head against his shoulder as the moon gave them enough light to vaguely see the streets of Ashbourn far below. "You know," Koradin said. "We're fortunate those beast hunters came around. Without them, we would be doomed."

"I heard an aspiring young man began it all," Lenda said, a hint of something in her voice.

Koradin exhaled, knowing too well what she wondered. "It was him."

Lenda rose elegantly and walked away. Koradin understood her, but had no words or time to think of a way to comfort her.

"Of course, it *had* to be him," she said from somewhere. "It's like the past coming back to chase us."

Koradin prided himself on saying what he felt to be right, despite knowing it could cause a storm, and tonight would be no different. "I'm actually sort of proud." He tensed his hands, ready for anything.

"Of course you are," Lenda said. "I know you too well, and if I choose to put aside my emotions; I understand you."

Koradin released the tension.

"But with Olenna and him walking around the Headquarters, I don't know," Lenda said. "It's painful."

"I know. I do understand. It feels wrong to apologize again for something that happened so long ago, but—"

"I don't want you to apologize," she said. "We're past it, I'm just airing how it feels. And I know you cannot focus on something of such little importance now."

He walked over to her, finding her residing on the large bed they shared. "Lenda, I love you, for so many reasons. When all this is over, I'll shower you with amazing gifts and we can bury that hatchet once more."

A faint smile dawned on her gorgeous lips. "I'm too weak against the faint promise of gifts. You're lucky you're wealthy, or I'd be gone in a heartbeat." Some of her playfulness returned.

"Faint promise? Fine, I deserve that," he said. "But there's another matter I need to discuss with you. I want to move Nirala, Kora, and Lenara out of the city to our estate in Stormfall."

She creased her brows. "Move our daughters?"

"Yes. Ashbourn isn't and won't be safe for some time, and with you all gone, I won't have to worry and can think more clearly."

"Do you really think it will be that dangerous?"

"Yes," he said sincerely.

She looked away, not pleased by the suggestion and deep in thought.

Koradin glanced at his sword, Mattronia, feeling more certain they had a chance against the might of Chronor. Despite Chronor being a god, Koradin felt certain his blade could kill him, but he wouldn't tell anyone in case the god had a spy.

"Don't be afraid," Matt whispered in his mind. *"I will stand with you."*

"They'll leave tomorrow," Lenda finally said, stealing back his gaze. "Lay down with me now. The beast hunter will wait." Her lustrous eyes mesmerized him and he wrapped his arms around her.

***

On the verge of falling asleep, Ara sat up abruptly as Khendric opened the door to their quarters, rubbing her eyes.

He looked tired and a little manic, as fluctuating thoughts emanated from him.

"You're back," she said with a sluggish voice

"A grand observation," he pointed out, mockingly. His dark thoughts receded with every spoken word, hopefully because of her presence.

"I need more followers," Chronor's voice siphoned into her mind, but she pushed it away, not wanting to bring him up in conversation.

"What did you find out?" she asked.

"It appears Chronor is feeding his citizens," Khendric said, bringing the god up anyway, and threw a small bag of food on her bed. "And he's telling them Koradin kept this food hidden from the public. I doubt that's true, but you never know."

Ara opened the bag to find three small pieces of bread.

"Don't eat that."

"Wasn't planning on it," she said, smelling it instead. "Doesn't smell suspicious."

"We should take it to someone with gnurgles," Khendric suggested, undressing and yawning. "Maybe they'll react to it. But I'm way too tired to deal with that now." Khendric shut the door to their rooms and went to his bed. She laid back down on her own.

"Think you'll be able to sleep?" she asked.

"I hope so. I'm tired, but my mind is plagued. No point in hiding that from you."

She didn't know how to respond, almost feeling caught. "Earlier today, when we were with the council, that Ponther guy was envious of Koradin. It emanated from him so strongly I think I could make out the emotion."

"Really?"

"I feel something else now. Something new. It's like a low distant humming. I've questioned if it's really there, but it definitely is. As if thousands of people whispered in unison, but from afar, and I can barely hear it."

Khendric frowned, but said nothing.

"More and more join in the whispering, making it stronger and stronger, though still remaining faint."

His eyes fell to the ground as he contemplated her words. "There are many things wrong at the moment. We're going to knit them together piece by piece. But I'll be honest and say that I hope we're not too late. I hope we can actually do this. I've never dealt with a god before. But we'll attack that issue tomorrow when we're refreshed," Khendric said. "For now, let's try to catch up on some much-needed sleep. And though we are in Koradin's care, we shouldn't necessarily trust him completely just yet. It's healthy to remain sceptical and not become blind to possible giveaways."

She wanted to do what he said, but Koradin did seem like a guy they should trust. "Good night, Khendric."

"Have a good night, Ara."

But Khendric's words rang in her mind for hours, sprouting tendrils of different worries. After sitting up and laying back down many times, her exhaustion overcame her worries, and sleep finally found her.

CHAPTER 4

The Crumbling Cliff

In later phases, Chronor will, by nature, prolong the night.
From 'The Dark Traitor', chapter six.

Light rain fell over the city, creating yet another grey and murky day. The humming in Ara's mind had grown worse. The magnitude of each pressure stayed the same, but she felt more of them spring to life. It felt like waiting for your doom to arrive, sensing it growing worse, but with nothing to combat it. She wanted to share her concern with Khendric, but he couldn't help either, so she kept it to herself.

The two had eaten breakfast, and sat reading in the book they had gotten back from Aeba's transcribes, both in deep concentration.

"She resists me," Chronor's voice echoed, interrupting her reading. *Should I say anything?* she wondered, but a glance at his concentrated face helped her decide. *Am I resisting him? How?* If true, she felt a little better at least.

They both shot up from their chairs as a young man with freckles and pimples barged through the door. He breathed hard, putting both hands on his knees, wearing the blue pointy hat belonging to official messengers.

"M-master Beast Hunter Khendric?" he finally asked, rising with sweat running down his forehead.

"Yes?" Khendric answered. "Are you okay?"

"Yes," his squeaky voice said, his breathing as laboured as before. "You have a visitor. Or someone who claims he knows you."

Ara and Khendric shared a glance, before joining him out of the door. The messenger led them to the main entrance on the first level. "He is out here," he said and gave a courteous nod.

They opened the door and found a massive man surrounded by four guards, holding spears warily to his chest.

"Khendric!" the man exclaimed. "I'm back!"

Khendric went down the stairs. "Tell me something familiar," he asked of the one who claimed to be Topper.

"Really?" Topper asked, huffing. "How was that terrible saying again? Oh yeah. 'The secrets of the past, are always hidden in the future.'"

"It's alright," Khendric said to the guards. "He's with me."

One soldier leaned closer. "And you are?" he asked in a non-threatening way.

"Koradin's beast hunter. He'll vouch for me. If you wish, send someone to inquire with him and I'll wait here with you."

The man considered Khendric's words, narrowing his eyes. "Stand down," he ordered his fellow guardsmen before turning back to the beast hunter. "I'll inquire with Koradin and find you if it becomes necessary. I have other things to do than to stand around here."

"I understand," Khendric said and nodded respectfully. "Thank you."

The soldier returned the gesture, and they took off.

Topper walked toward Ara and Khendric with a giant smile.

Ara sprang forward to hug him. "It's you." He returned the long-lasting hug.

"It's me."

"I'm happy to see you," she said, letting go.

His huge new body seemed to block out the sun as he towered over her. "You're a brute," she said. "A little plump, but a muscular brute."

"I know," he said with a deep voice, flexing his muscles. "Isn't it great? And I like to think that it fits being bald." He wore a faded green tunic accompanied by white linen pants and no shoes.

"What happened?" Khendric asked impatiently. "Is she alive?"

Topper's happy face turned sombre. "I don't know. I didn't see her die, though the situation was bad. I'll tell you more inside."

The reunited group went to their quarters, where Topper told them about finding the real Ronoch in a cell, which came as no surprise. He went on to their futile escape and the gate closing on Darlaene and him. "She's gotten out of worse," Topper finished, but Khendric threw a mug of water across the room in anger nonetheless.

"She's so stupid!" he roared, clenching his fists tightly, kicking the table.

It didn't look good for Darlaene, especially with being missing for so long. Ara could offer no comforting words and didn't know how to stop his tantrum.

Ultimately, he fell into a nearby chair and buried his face in his hands, emanating dark thoughts like steam rising from his head. "If she's dead, I'll never forgive myself."

"How did you get here so fast?" Ara asked Topper in hushed tones to be respectful to Khendric, though it seemed he thought her dead before knowing for certain. "It's been three days or so. It took you longer the last time you died."

Topper's eyes stayed on Khendric's brooding form for some moments, before he leaned closer to Ara. "I was clever. When Darlaene got me killed at the gala, I felt we were in over our heads. So I dug up my black heart and brought it with me to a village closer to Ashbourn. Hence, I managed to get here quicker."

"Clever. What do you know so far?"

"I know Ronoch won."

The pressure Khendric's thoughts exuded on her mind made holding the conversation harder, but she tried her best to focus. "He's also an ancient voreen god."

"What?" Topper's eyes grew wide.

"He takes blood from the Ronoch you found in the cell and inherits his appearance, posing as him to win the coronation."

"And how do we kill him?" he asked.

"We haven't gotten that far in the book yet, but we need to as fast as possible."

"So you got the book?"

"We did."

Khendric got back to his feet and walked closer with fewer dark thoughts surrounding his mind. "I'm being irrational. She's probably fine, just like every other damn time. Also, bigger things are at stake here, things I'm not sure we can handle."

A knock came at the door and the same freckled messenger entered. "Uhm," he repeated. "Koradin wants to meet you in his quarters."

"What for?" Khendric asked.

"To forge a plan, and you have to bring 'the book.' I don't know which book that is, but he said you would know."

"Alright then," Khendric said and they followed him to Koradin's quarters. Ara felt better with Topper at their side.

* * *

They all stood around a large square table inside Koradin's room. Koradin had trusted Khendric that the new body in the room was the reincarnated Topper, luckily. Next to Ara stood Adenar, and she felt some sparks flutter through her guts at seeing him again.

Next to Koradin stood his wife, the previous queen Lenda, looking tall and gorgeous with her usual determined look, and Commander Jack Relen, looking sharp as always in his uniform.

"Later today," Koradin said. "The council will decide whether or not to take action regarding our ill news. I'm fairly certain Thornar will yield to Ponther's mighty grip." He turned to the three beast hunters. "Thornar married Ponther's daughter—before he was elevated to a councillor. This made him even timider than before to Ponther's oppressive aura."

"That explains why he barely uttered a word," Khendric said.

"So we need to make a plan," Lenda broke in. "For how to approach this problem without the consent of our council, and therefore without an army."

"We need to find out how to kill him," Koradin clarified. "And I hope that book can tell us something useful. For those who do not know, Chronor operates in phases, becoming considerably harder to kill with each phase, right?" He looked to Ara.

"Right," Ara said. "And when he won the coronation, I fear he became *a lot* harder to kill. The book said something about"—she found the page about the phases and read it aloud—"'but any weapons forged from anything divine can kill him. Our voreen blades are forged from voreen blood and shadestones, which are also used to summon Chronor. Therefore, our blades can still be used to kill him. This is the only weapon I know that can be used.'"

A deep silence rested over the room.

"We don't have voreen blades laying around," Koradin said. "Since we can't carry them."

"What?" Adenar asked. "What do you mean?"

"From legends and stories, I've heard that only the voreen can carry them," Koradin explained. "I think it's true, or else we'd have a few people running around with powerful blades and we would all have heard about them."

"It's true," Khendric said. "A voreen blade usually marks a voreen's resting place."

"Well," Lenda said. "What do we do then?"

"There is something else," Ara said, reading a few more lines of the book. "Avina, the human editing this book, talks about other potential things that could help in defeating Chronor. She wrote about a metallurgic dust left by dead doombringers, that can be forged into a weapon, believing that doombringers were divinities or part of a divinity. She thought they could at least harm him."

"We don't have that either I'm afraid," Koradin said. "At least not that I know of. I've heard of rare exhibitions displaying dust said to stem from a doombringer, but where we could potentially find it, I do not know."

"What about any other . . . divinities?" Adenar asked. "Do we know of any?"

Ara fell silent, looking to Khendric and Topper, praying any of them would open their mouth. A short glance passed between them, but they said nothing, for some reason.

Koradin said, "Even this Avina-woman wasn't sure if doombringers counted as divinities. For all we know, boulderbeasts, trollmen or even the giant skywhales of the sea could be divinities in this sense."

Ara raised her eyebrows, surprised by his knowledge. *He would make a good beast hunter,* she thought. *I don't even know what skywhales are.*

"And all of those are hard to come by," Topper added with his deep voice.

"Can't we just storm in and kill him?" Jack Relen suggested.

"I'm afraid not," Koradin said, exhaling. "Are we sure he's in phase six? How do we know he's not in his seventh phase?"

"We haven't read about that phase yet," Ara admitted and remembered something from last night. "But I do believe he hasn't reached it."

"How so?" Koradin asked.

She let out a breath, not wanting to utter these next words. "I have a connection to him. Sometimes I . . . hear his thoughts—or sentences he speaks—in my mind. Last night the words 'I need more followers' came to my mind. That might indicate he's in phase six and hasn't reached phase seven yet. Why else would he need more?"

"How do you have this connection?" Lenda inquired, eyes narrowed inquisitively.

"She was attacked by a minion of Chronor," Khendric said sternly. "Miraculously, she survived. We believe it was through that survival she somehow earned a connection with him."

Lenda almost glared at her, massaging her temple with one finger. "And how do we know this is not a two-way communication?"

Ara opened her mouth to protest, but no words left her lips. Khendric and Topper looked at each other uncertainly too.

"Great," Lenda said. "You don't know."

"We don't know for sure," Khendric admitted. "But there is reason to assume that if Chronor heard fragments of Ara's thoughts or words, he would have known a lot more than he has shown so far. He was oblivious to our infiltration, though I heard him say he could feel her presence. But you are right, we cannot know for sure."

Lenda turned to Koradin. "She should not be here."

"Perhaps not," he agreed, and Ara's heart dropped. "But for now we're not laying a plan, merely acquiring information. Perhaps Ara should leave once we try to establish one."

Ara wanted dearly to protest, but it made sense.

"What's the difference between phases six and seven?" Koradin asked. "How much harder does he become to kill?"

Ara snapped her focus back to the book and started reading:

Phase seven: somewhere around a million followers.

Chronor has to be stopped before reaching his final phase. He lusts for this so he can conjure forth his ultimate warriors through the oath of blood. In phase six, he controls all voreen, humans, and creatures that have drunk his blood.

A cloak woven with green fire and black smoke surrounds his large body, and a burning crown hovers above his head.

The blood oath

In phase seven Chronor may finally perform the blood oath. It's through this ritual that he gains his most feared champion, the rosh'gar. Upon reaching the seventh phase, Chronor can challenge, or be challenged, to a blood oath. The oath of blood requires Chronor's and the challenger's blood to be mixed before or after the oath has been verbally agreed upon, as long as the blood is fresh. Then they duel to the death. If Chronor wins, the challenger will not die, but transform into a rosh'gar.

The rosh'gar are Chronor's ultimate servants, as they cannot die unless Chronor himself is killed. Violent black smoke erupts from the loser's body, enveloping and transforming them into something unnatural. Once the darkness around them abates, their former self is gone, replaced by a molten version of themselves, belonging to Chronor. Smoke swirls around their black and red-hot figure, and a terrible blade forms in their hand. They cannot be stopped—cannot be killed—unless their anchor to this world breaks by ending Chronor. They are his unstoppable force to conquer and destroy all who oppose him.

Furthermore, Chronor can only be killed in a blood oath, which is why he must never reach this phase. He is impossibly skilled, and a loss for the challenger results in catastrophe for the world. Even in a blood oath, he must still be killed with a divine weapon.

The blood oath must be entered into willingly; Chronor cannot force or intimidate anyone to duel him. A blood oath entered into through fear won't result in the creation of a rosh'gar, nor his death.

Editor's note: These rosh'gar do not yet have a name, so I will call them moltens.

She finished reading and looked up at the others, seeing concern on their faces. Occasional waves of grim thoughts emanated from Khendric, but he fought to control them.

"Great," Adenar said. "So we're going to have to duel an ancient voreen god with a weapon we don't possess in hopes of winning, or else turn into his most destructive force."

"Assuming he's in his seventh phase," Koradin said. "I told the whole of the Meritocrat army not to trust Ronoch should he win, and all the noble families I know. They swore to keep their scepticism of him and spread it to all within their reach. It started a cascading wave through the district, destroying his reputation, or so it seems. If we're lucky it was enough souls to stop him from ascending to his final phase."

"I think so," Ara said, honestly. "Why else would he need more followers?"

"Then we *only* need a 'divine' weapon," Khendric said. "But we don't really know what divine weapons *are* at all—except for voreen blades."

An uncomfortable silence fell over the group.

"I think this is when we must try to forge a plan," Koradin finally said.

"She must go," Lenda said without hesitation.

Ara choked up at her sharp words and tone.

"I'm afraid that is what's best," Koradin agreed.

Khendric and Topper gave her apologetic looks.

She couldn't help but feel betrayed, but knew they were right. She turned and walked towards the door.

"And why is he here?" Lenda asked, nodding at Adenar.

"Why shouldn't he be here?" Khendric quickly asked.

"He's an assistant. Is he not?"

"He started all of this," Topper said defensively. "Without him, Ashbourn would have been lost."

"I hate that we have to expel Ara from this room," Khendric said. "But at least that makes some sense. If you send out Adenar, then we're going with him."

Lenda lifted her arms apologetically into the air. "You're right. My apologies, Adenar." She couldn't look into his eyes while uttering the apology, but at least she said the words. A meaningful glance passed between her and Koradin, of which Ara did not know the meaning, before all eyes fell back on her. She sighed and left, though it stung.

She sat in a chair outside the room and such a long time passed, her annoyance turned to anger at not being a part of their discussion. Then it turned into understanding again, and for some time the two feelings duelled within her mind, before her eyes ultimately shut and she got some much-needed rest.

* * *

The door to the great room opened, awakening Ara. Khendric, Topper, and Adenar left the room, and she sprang up from her chair. "So, what happened?" she asked excitedly, but grim expressions met her. Some dark thoughts emanated from all of them.

"We shouldn't tell you," Khendric said sternly. "But there *is* no plan."

Ara deflated. "W-what?"

"We don't know what to do," Topper said. "We talked and discussed, but couldn't formulate a plan."

"So what did you say?" she asked.

Khendric walked down the hallway, dark thoughts buzzing around his head. "We ended up discovering there isn't much we can do."

"Wait, stop," Ara said, but he just kept walking. Topper too walked down the long hallway. She wanted to follow, but had to ask everyone in that room if this was true.

"I'm sorry," Adenar said. "We did agree to investigate and try to find a solution, so not all hope is gone yet."

His words did not comfort her. She hadn't seen Khendric or Topper like this ever before; as they had just given up. Worry spread through her veins, her solid cliff beginning to crumble.

"I need to talk to Koradin," she said and went back into the large room. Adenar didn't follow.

Koradin talked with Lenda and Commander Relen, and the bread Khendric had brought yesterday laid on the large table.

"Ara," Koradin said as a welcome.

"I see Khendric brought you the food," she said, annoyance and frustration bleeding into her voice.

"He did. But we don't understand why he fed the citizens. We took the liberty to read in your book for clues, but couldn't find anything. If you have any thoughts, I'd like to hear them."

Ara narrowed her eyes, her built-up anger simmering down somewhat. She had been prepared to bring a storm with her, demanding answers, but perhaps Khendric and Topper's words had gotten a little too close. Koradin seemed to still try to formulate a plan. "Maybe," she said. "Maybe he needs to feed his 'followers' so they won't starve. If the citizens die, there's nobody left to follow him."

"I thought the same thing," Koradin said.

"But I think there's more to it," Commander Relen said. "Why else would he allegedly cause Ashbourn's supporting villages to break down, starting this famine and blaming Koradin for keeping food hidden? I think he wanted the people to go hungry, so that when he presented the food, they *would* eat it. There's something sinister going on here—I can feel it in my guts."

"Don't we have someone we can try it on?" Ara asked.

All three looked at her with discomfort. "I don't know how ethical that is," Lenda said. "Unless you volunteer?"

Ara glanced at the food and realized what she had said. "I see your point. What else?"

"Not much," Lenda answered, walking over to another smaller table and pouring herself a drink. "Not anything, really."

"I'm afraid it's true," Koradin confirmed. "For now, we're stuck. We should try to find solutions, but I don't see any as of now." Ara vaguely felt some thoughts from him and Commander Relen for a short moment.

"Koradin is . . . mine," Chronor's voice said, making Ara freeze. *What? What did he mean by that?* Suddenly, she became more critical towards the former king, finding it peculiar that such a resourceful man had ended up without a direction. Perhaps it was on purpose, or perhaps Chronor meant something entirely else. *No,* she redirected her thoughts. *What am I thinking? He's been nothing but helpful.* Perhaps Khendric and Topper's pouting had made her mind conjure up straws that simply weren't there. But she still found herself less trusting of him, as Khendric had originally told her to do.

"The girl has a point," Lenda said. "Though she didn't say it directly, at some point we have to feed that bread to someone and observe the effects. I know it's dark, but . . ."

"No," Koradin contradicted her. "I won't do that. If almost all of Ashbourn's population is eating it anyway, I'm sure any effects will become clear soon enough."

"We should keep it," Commander Relen said. "So we have the option. Some Chronor sympathizers might end up in our jail."

Koradin ground his teeth. "We'll keep the bread."

Ara grabbed the pouch, afraid he'd switch it with regular bread. "I'll take care of it."

Koradin frowned, but didn't object.

Stop it, she told herself. If they couldn't trust Koradin, then who could they trust?

Through the doors to the great room stormed three young women a little older than Ara's age, looking distraught. She recognized Koradin's daughter, Nirala, from the political gala.

"Father!" she exclaimed. "It was horrible!"

"What?" Koradin answered, embracing them with great concern together with Lenda. Tears welled in their eyes.

"They wouldn't let us go," Nirala said, seeming to try to keep her cool. "They beat up our guards! It almost ended in bloodshed."

"What almost ended in bloodshed?" Lenda asked.

Nirala let out a slow breath and said, "We were about to leave the city, but when we got to the gate, the guards stopped us." Tears pressed behind her eyes again, but the younger sister took over.

"They told us we weren't allowed to leave. Captain Vara tried to speak to them, but they didn't even answer. They barely behaved like humans, faces hidden behind helmets. Vara tried moving past them, but they struck him down."

"What!" Koradin asked. "They killed him?"

"No, just one punch, but swords were drawn. We shouted we were your daughters, but they didn't care. Before we knew it, soldiers swarmed us from behind and they mercilessly beat our guards. S-so . . . we fled. We don't know what happened to them." Her hands shook, but Lenda clasped them.

"That was good, Kora," she said to her daughter. "And of you too, Lenara." Lenara nodded with red eyes.

"I think they arrested them," Nirala said. "I saw them handcuff Captain Vara."

"I'm glad you're not hurt," Koradin said, his voice seeming to vibrate with anger.

"They weren't human," the youngest daughter said. "They didn't listen to what we said. I'm so scared they're going to come for me."

"Don't worry about that," Koradin said, putting a hand on her shoulder. "Nothing can get to you here. I think they were more interested in not letting anyone leave the city."

"Chronor is in charge of these soldiers?" Ara broke into the conversation. "Right?"

Koradin nodded. "But they're good men, disciplined soldiers with the best of intentions towards Ashbourn's citizens."

"Chronor?" Nirala wondered and it became clear how little they had been told.

"I'll tell you later," he told them.

"Perhaps it's new soldiers?" Ara asked.

"Could be, but I don't think so. Where would he find them without causing a massive uproar? Especially if newly hired soldiers behaved like this." He stopped to think for a moment. Lenda gathered her daughters in her arms and led them back out of the room, leaving Ara with Koradin and Commander Relen at the table.

He looked troubled and let out an exasperated breath. "There's so much I don't understand. I want to know how we can deal with Chronor and I was hoping that book would bring more answers."

"I hoped so too," she said. "I think the book was written when Chronor operated in more obvious ways. Not in this covert manner. But at least we know how to kill him."

"Yes. I'm worried about what plan he's concocting to earn his last followers. How he will break our will?"

Ara remained silent, lacking words.

"Well, I have to attend this farce of a meeting and get rejected to actually do something about this mess."

They withdrew from the room, Ara's frustration at the lack of a plan slowly returning. She felt alone walking the large halls of the Headquarters. Nearing her room, she felt Khendric inside. *He is not good,* she thought, wondering how to tackle this on top of everything else.

Despite being such a great, talented and skilled beast hunter, he had a strong emotional side, and became reckless and bold when it took over. At least he did better than after Cornstead.

She entered their rooms, but stopped halfway through the door, eyes wide open. Both Khendric and Topper packed their bags, fully dressed in their coats.

"W-what are you doing?" she asked, her eyes drilling into Khendric.

Khendric stopped packing. "Don't look at me like that," he said with sadness in his voice.

"What?" she prodded, stampeding through the room, taking the backpack out of his hands. "What are you doing?"

He took a step back and looked everywhere but her eyes. "We're . . . l-leaving," he croaked.

Shocked, Ara's mouth fell open as she stiffened, her heart the only moving part of her, and it pounded.

"We're leaving Ashbourn," Topper said, not able to face her.

Ara shook her head free from the stunning words. "Leaving? You *can't* be serious? We can't leave. We have to deal with Chronor!"

Khendric put his hand on the backpack, but she pulled it further away.

"No! I won't let you," she protested, feeling anger and fear set into her soul, her voice trembling.

"This is too much for us," Khendric said, meeting her stare dead on. "We can't fight a voreen god. I wish we could, but the truth is . . . we can't, okay? Is that good enough? Is that what you want to hear? He's already too strong."

"Don't you dare do that?" She said, biting her teeth together.

He looked away, but his angered expression didn't fade.

"What about the city?" she shouted, stepping in front of him again. "Are you just going to leave them to this grim fate?"

"They are beyond saving," Khendric told her, forcing the words through his teeth. "Their fate is sealed."

Ara's legs almost faltered and she took two steps back, wounded to the core. "You . . . coward. You're not even going to try? You're just going to quit? Where will you go? He won't stop with just Ashbourn. This is just the start, and when you *can't* outrun him, he'll be too powerful to stop!"

"I don't know," Khendric answered, shoulders raised and neck bent. "Across the sea?"

"You cannot be serious?" she asked, tears welling in her eyes. "*You* can't leave. I don't believe what I'm hearing."

"Ara," Topper shouted. "We have to face reality. Chronor is too strong. He has the entire city."

"Not the *entire* city," she shouted back, not scared of either of them.

The great rock cliff they represented in her mind crumbled, swallowed by an ocean of fear and hopelessness. She felt Khendric's thoughts strongly. None of them said anything, the sound of Ara's heavy breathing echoing through the room. She searched their faces for some answer, but they couldn't face her. "You can't do this, you know that right?"

Khendric licked his lips, and Topper shuffled his feet, but no response left their mouths.

"You're too involved in this. We uncovered it all, and for what? To just leave it in the dust while the whole of humanity is swallowed?"

"I'm sorry, Ara," Khendric said, picking his backpack up from the floor. "I know this isn't what you want, but there's nothing we can do. We're just regular people."

"You are not just regular people, and I don't care if we can't do anything!" she shouted in protest.

"If we stay here, we'll just become more corpses beneath Chronor's foot."

"So you run with your tail tucked between your legs? You leave it behind like cowards?"

"Yes," Topper said sharply back. "That's what we're doing. It's hard and goes against our nature but it's futile to—"

"Oh, please," Ara interrupted him. "Don't give me that speech. If it truly goes against your nature, then stay! Please, I need you!"

Khendric faced her and put his backpack on. "You're right. We're cowards and this stings. But dying is a worse alternative."

"You've given up before we've even tried."

"We have tried. Now we can still run."

"This isn't you," she tried, feeling her wall of anger breaking, threatening to let the river of sadness flow through.

Khendric swallowed audibly. "So, are you coming?"

Ara's breath caught in her throat. "Am I coming?" she asked, greatly offended. "Unlike you, I won't leave these poor people."

"Ara, think clearly," Topper said and stretched out a hand to her. "Come with us."

She batted it away. "Get your hand away from me." Tears cascaded down her reddening cheeks. "Please, don't go. I don't want to do this alone, but I *will* if I must."

"You'll just be another skull to crush," Khendric said. "We can't force you, but you have to understand this is no place to die."

"At least I'll die for something!" Her voice cracked, biting her teeth together with every ounce of strength in her to keep her from breaking completely.

"But you *will* still die," he said.

"STOP! Please don't go?" she begged in a soft voice.

"We have to," Topper said.

"Please, come with us," Khendric suggested with a saddened look.

Ara's knees almost buckled. "How can you ask me that? I am too involved. I'm connected to him." She let out a sharp breath.

"You can just run away."

"What about Adenar? He'll never leave Ashbourn."

They shared a concerned glance. "We know."

"I can't just leave him," she said through her sobs. "He won't understand and it will devastate him."

"He's just some guy," Khendric said, closing his eyes as a tear rolled down his cheek. "Y-you'll . . . forget him."

Her hands trembled. She had trouble breathing, and she fell forward into Khendric's chest, just crying. He grabbed her and held her tight. "Shh," he said. "Come with us, and we'll forget about all of this."

Her hands wrapped around him, and Topper joined too. She felt the warmth coming off them as they enveloped her. She loved them. They had given her life, and she almost said yes, but images of Adenar flashed in her mind. He would never forgive her, and she would never forgive them. "I-I can't . . . go," she whispered.

"Such a stubborn young woman," Khendric whispered, pulling away the hair plastered to her face. "Ara, you have to come with us."

She clenched her arms around him one last time. Knowing her final moment with them couldn't last forever, she violently pushed them away while she still had the strength to do so. "Fine then! Go!" she screamed before her mind forced her to give in to their wishes.

"Ara, please calm—"

"Go! I won't leave the people of Ashbourn to die."

They stared deep into her eyes. "Ara—"

"Don't say another word."

Khendric's eyes fell to the floor. He found three pouches. "Take these. They're filled with my blood. *Please* stay out of trouble, but use them to regenerate if the need arises."

"Go," she said, her jaw shaking with anger. "I . . . I can't believe you."

"I'm sorry," he said, voice cracking. "I'm so very sorry, Ara."

They had to leave now, because she couldn't stand this for much longer. If they went through that door, she'd never find them again in this big world. The two men that lifted her from ruin would walk out of her life. "GO!" She shouted before her feet forced her with them.

They turned and closed the door, and as the handle rose, Ara knew she had lost them.

Her knees finally gave out and she crashed to the ground, weeping as she had never wept before. She hammered the floor, cracking the floorboards as she screamed until her throat turned hoarse. She felt betrayed, and they left her broken and alone. The tears stopped as her mind numbed, and for what felt like forever, no thoughts crossed her mind, leaving her a blank husk on the wooden floor. She didn't have the strength to think, wanting not to exist without them. Then the tears and thoughts returned like a tidal wave, breaking her heart apart.

CHAPTER 5

Sowing Seeds of Doubt

*Our voreen culture is a lid on Chronor's power. The more voreen,
the more deadly blades to end his search for power.
From 'The Dark Traitor', chapter one.*

Ara's eyes grew heavy from looking at countless pages thick
with text. She had been at the library for hours upon hours,
trying to read up on anything she could find about divinities.
It had been the best way to distract herself from being abandoned by Khendric and Topper. She could never forgive
them, but it probably didn't matter—the chances of meeting
them again were slim at best.

When these thoughts sprang to mind, she felt the sting
deep in her guts. Those two had been the most important
people in her life. They saved her, took her with them, and
helped her become the person she was today. Despite being
connected to a dark ancient voreen god and sensing dark
thoughts, *and* having an immensely strong arm, there was
truly more to her than that. Her mind had become strong
and her resolve even greater. She'd done things she would
never have dreamed about in her past: faking her way into a
large political party, chasing a shadowwalker, fighting dozens
upon dozens of soldiers—not to speak of the whole ordeal

in Cornstead. It had all moulded and shaped her into who she had become today. Hopefully, that would somehow be enough.

Except for her and Adenar, the library was empty. Luckily, he had come with her, also determined to find a solution, despite losing hope when hearing of the beast hunter's decision. She saw it in his eyes, but still, he pressed on.

They yawned simultaneously and tried shaking their heads awake after spending hours searching to find anything useful. She had read through the entire red book too, but to no help. Khendric hadn't asked for it back, which puzzled her. He wouldn't forget about it, or so she thought at least. Perhaps it had been a parting gift? She shoved the thoughts away as well. It seemed no matter what she contemplated, her thoughts would always lead back to those two.

"Nothing in this book either," Adenar said, sighing. His voice echoed through the grand room containing more books than Ara had ever seen.

"There used to be more people in here, right?"

"A little more, yeah. But I don't think it was ever packed."

Ara leaned back on her chair. "The city has transformed. Everybody can feel that something's up, but we don't know what."

"I've heard reports of citizens acting maniacal, force-feeding or murdering their neighbours."

"What?" Ara asked, swallowing dryly. That put straight fear in her heart. It also worried her that the humming in her head had grown stronger too. It felt like a multitude of tiny fractions of Chronor's presence pressed on her mind from around the city. "I think divinities might be from an age before mankind," Ara said, hoping some dialogue would draw her attention. "I mean, there's barely anything about it. Someone thought gorewings are descendants of divinities, and for all we know, that could be true. That's the *only* thing I've found about anything divine."

Adenar rubbed his hand on his forehead. "Maybe we're looking in the wrong place, but the other library is in the Royalist District. And we can't go there. It's not safe."

"This district is barely safe," Ara said.

Adenar shook his head. "With the shortage of food, people seem to almost be in an uproar. I don't think many in the Meritocrat District believed Chronor when he said Koradin kept food hidden, but that doesn't matter when they starve. I've heard more and more take their chances in other districts, finding guards to get their handout of bread. And of those, almost none come back, based on the reports, at least."

Ara's motivation waned, feeling powerless against a god. Adenar's tired eyes stayed glued on the table, and he didn't react when she opened another tome heavy with text. She exhaled in protest, but knew it had to be read.

He suddenly rose. "Let's go to the museum."

"The museum?"

"Yeah. We're only reading about possible divinities, but maybe a curator has some thoughts—or some ancient items could be of use."

"You don't think you would know about that?" Ara wondered.

"No way. It's been ages since I was there. Who knows what kind of boring exhibit could be useful."

Ara huffed out her nose, and a quick smile grew forth on her face. "I'm not going to object." Going to the museum sounded a lot more fun than having to read more of these awful books.

The duo left their books on the table, not bothering to clean up after themselves, as they would probably be the next people back at the empty library anyway. A group of boys ran around and played in the otherwise empty streets, adding some much-needed laughter lacking too often these days. A few merchants inhabited the market in the vain hope that at least one customer would stroll through, but none would. People stayed inside, scared to go out, scared of the unknown, despite Koradin's guards patrolling constantly.

In the far distance, the large gate in and out of the district rose high, with the lattice down, luckily. She knew Koradin had been trying to get reports from the outside districts, but few could offer anything of use. The low pressure in her mind felt like it came from the other districts—past that gate.

They found the museum as empty as the library, yet far more interesting. Anything else than books would excite Ara now, and a huge museum with countless exhibits of various beasts made her blood bubble. A wretcher skeleton with some valuable talons attached made her realize how large the undead wolf-like creature really was. Other displays showed gorewing bones, varghaul heads, dolls from a puppetmaster, and at the end: a taxidermied duskdevil on display. They searched the building vigorously for anything possibly divine, passing hairs from different creatures, dead beetles and bugs, paintings of the lumberer, and gruesome statues depicting people turned into abominations caused by mimeit eggs. Ara hoped for any remnant of a doombringer, but not to her surprise, it wasn't there, not even in the restricted section, which they broke into by simply ducking below a rope hopelessly hoping to bar their entrance.

"Give me her blood," Chronor's voice whispered into her mind, but she ignored the truly terrifying sentence. *He wants my blood? Why?*

The thoughts vanished when Adenar put a hand on her shoulder. "This isn't looking too good. Maybe Koradin has news?"

It worried her how much he trusted Koradin. Chronor's words about how 'Koradin was his' cast a new light on the man, and she couldn't simply ignore it. She would continue to work with him, but at the same time remain cautious. "Yeah, maybe," she finally answered.

They left the museum with disappointed faces. It all felt so futile without Khendric or Topper by her side. Khendric would always say *something* to make the day brighter, but now she had to do that herself. *Maybe I should have just gone with them,* she thought, but it was too late. She wouldn't even have an idea of how to track them down, and the connection between her and Chronor made her feel she had to stay. She could never outrun it.

"What do you think Chronor's plan is?" Adenar asked as they left the museum behind, once again venturing through empty streets.

"I don't know," she said honestly. "I hoped the book would provide more answers, but Chronor is playing a different strategy than it describes."

"I'm pretty sure that what's going on in the other districts has to do with the food he's handing out."

"Yeah, it may seem so."

"I don't know, though," he said. "But we have had some insight that tells grim news. No one walks the streets, except for in large violent groups, killing people on sight. I've even heard rumours they have dark eyes."

"Dark eyes?"

"Yes, but that could easily be exaggerations to add some spice to rumours."

"Let us hope so," she said.

"I will lure them out," Chronor whispered. *"With false hope."*

Ara scrunched up her face at the plaguing voice inside her head, but these words seemed important, and she found her small notepad and added them. Khendric had told her to do so. A stab of sadness hit her as she thought of him, and fought to keep her tears at bay.

"I don't like that," Adenar said, reading from her notepad.

"Me neither."

After walking the almost empty streets of the Meritocrat District, they reached the Headquarters, walking up countless stairs straight to Koradin's quarters. She knocked on the beautiful and hard door, feeling awkward and privileged at the same time.

Lenda opened, her eyes souring when seeing them. "I'm not sure this is the best time," she said, glaring at Adenar.

"It's alright," Koradin's voice came to the rescue. Hunched over in a chair sat a frustrated former king, rubbing his temples while staring at a table.

"Any news?" Lenda asked them, sitting down across from her husband.

"Sadly, no," Ara said. "We've been trying to find anything about divinities and even went to the museum for possible items."

"Clever," Koradin said, not breaking his everlasting stare.

"Do you have any news?" Ara asked, expecting bad news.

Koradin let out an exasperated breath and Lenda looked away. "The meeting today did not go well," she said curtly. "If you have to know."

"Not only could we not sway Ponther to our side," Koradin said. "But he had also found out, somehow, that Khendric was the one who shot Ronoch on the day of the coronation. I don't exactly know what he accused me of, but it wasn't far away from treason and harbouring a murderer of the new king."

"What?" Ara and Adenar exclaimed. "So, what happens now?" she asked.

"Well," Koradin said. "Luckily, Khendric was already gone and couldn't be questioned. I didn't admit to the charges, but did not refute them, either. I won't be arrested, but I lost credibility. It's going to be next to impossible to turn people over to our side from now on."

"Perhaps the two of you," Lenda said, nodding at them. "Can convince my dear husband to just overrule the council. We can't wait until it's too late before we do something."

Koradin remained motionless, not answering or reacting to her words.

"What about Aeba?" Adenar asked.

"She's actually convinced we're right," Koradin said, raising his eyebrows. "Which was a surprise. She read her copy of the book and believes we're under attack by Chronor."

"That's good," Ara said, happy for *something*.

"Yes, but I'm not sure how much good it will do."

Nobody spoke, and it turned awkward. Ara just stood there, waiting for more good news that would never arrive. She felt the world's problems crush down on her, anxiety threatning to break her.

"Oh." Koradin lit up, hopefully as a saving beacon of light. "I almost forgot. Someone is waiting for you in your quarters, Ara."

"Who?" she asked.

"Who do you think?"

She wanted to blurt out, "Khendric and Topper," but knew it wasn't so.

"Darlaene, of course," Koradin said, and Ara immediately felt better. Not what she dreamt of, but far better than much other news.

* * *

Ara and Adenar rushed to their rooms, bursting through the door, panting heavily as they met a familiar figure sitting upright on a chair with long red hair. Ara's eyes widened; both joy and hope flaring to life within her body.

"Darlaene!" she exclaimed. "You're alive!"

"Of course I am," she replied nonchalantly with a shrug, barely looking up from the book in her hand.

"But-but . . ." Adenar stuttered. "How?"

She shut the book and rose, walking over to the table. "It's a long story. I'll try to shorten it, and then I want to know what you've been doing. I hope you know Ronoch is not actually Ronoch."

"Yes," Ara said. "He's an ancient voreen god, named Chronor."

Darlaene raised her eyebrows. "Oh?"

"You didn't know?"

"No. Koradin didn't tell me anything, too busy with meetings. He shoved me in here and told me to wait."

"So, how did you know Ronoch wasn't actually Ronoch?" Adenar asked.

"Because Topper and I found the real Ronoch Steelbane in a cell. We tried to get him out, but . . . it got complicated. Topper was shot dead and I surrounded by guards, having to use Ronoch as a bargaining chip for my own life."

"Hence Chronor could use his blood to transform himself into Ronoch for the coronation," Ara said. "Imagine if you'd successfully stolen him. Chronor's reign would have never begun."

"A little too late for that now," Darlaene replied, huffing. "Unfortunately."

"But where have you been?" Adenar asked.

"In hiding. I didn't dare come back here, in case I was followed. I fled to Elrich in the Passionist District and stayed there, still employed by him. I gave him information, keeping myself valuable. After a couple of days, whatever tail I had was surely gone, and I came back here."

"Khendric and Topper left," Ara said, the words jumping out of her mouth before she could stop them.

"What?"

"They said the task was too big and . . . just left."

A frown clad Darlaene's face, and her nonchalant mask dropped. "Oh." Her gaze fell to the ground. "That makes this considerably harder." A tear manifested in Ara's eye. "But, we got to work with what we have." Darlaene put her hand under Ara's chin. "It's okay. We're going to do this." Darlaene smiled widely, but Ara didn't know how to feel about it. Darlaene took it better than Ara had thought, but she had left Khendric many times before, so perhaps it didn't scare her as much.

"How are things in Elrich's district?" Adenar asked.

"Not good. Not good at all. As soon as he noticed everything going wrong, the coward retracted all his soldiers to the Headquarters, protecting himself."

"When did it go wrong?" he followed up.

"Just like everywhere else: with the starvation. Desperate people even attacked soldiers for scraps. More people joined criminal gangs and robbed warehouses, taverns, and storage facilities. They started killing everyone in their way, blaming anyone untouched and in power for the famine. Then this Chronor handed out food, and it all got even worse."

Ara and Adenar shot each other a glance. Finally, someone who knew *something*.

"People who ate the bread changed," Darlaene said, her eyes staring out a window.

"How?" Ara asked.

"They became dormant or ferocious. Sometimes they'd attack other citizens, or stand about doing nothing, alone. Their eyes changed, turning dark with orange irises. I even saw them assault other people, forcing that damn bread down their throats. And they ended up just like them."

A possibility puzzled itself together in her head.

The humming in her mind—the people who had eaten the bread, now turned by Chronor. The book mentioned him corrupting those he conquered, so they wouldn't turn on him. Ara took a step back, her hope sinking just at the chance of this being true. She felt *a lot* of people under Chronor's influence, if she was right. Every single individual put pressure on her mind, forming one large bulk. Hundreds upon hundreds of thousands had eaten his food. *How will we fight this?* The small hope Darlaene had sparked in her snuffed out and she fell back in a chair.

"Ara, are you okay?" Adenar asked.

"Uhm . . ."

"Did you gain anything else from your infiltration?" Darlaene asked, seeming not to notice Ara's hopeless expression.

"We did," Adenar said. "We found Chronor's book. Or, a book written by a voreen about Chronor, and how to defeat him."

"Really?" she said, intrigued. "So how do we kill him?"

"He has to be killed by a divine weapon," Ara said monotonously, eyes on the floorboards.

"Divine weapon?"

"Like a voreen blade," Adenar said. "A theory suggests that dust from a doombringer could work too."

"That's it?" Darlaene asked, frowning.

"As far as we know," he answered. "If you know of any other divinities, let us know."

"But that is only if we're correct in our assumption that he is not in his final phase," Ara said.

"Phase?" she asked.

"Chronor operates in different phases, gaining strength as he progresses through them."

"And how does he progress through them?"

"By gaining followers."

Darlaene narrowed her eyes, before they widened in understanding. "So that's why he needed to win the coronation."

"Exactly," Adenar said, snapping his fingers.

"And," Ara added. "If he has ascended to his final stage, he can only be killed in a duel, called a blood oath. Whoever challenges him can kill him, but if the challenger dies, they become a molten; Chronor's immortal warriors."

Darlaene simply looked into her eyes for a long time, as hope seemed to dim inside her mind too. "That's . . . a lot. I'm beginning to understand why Khendric and Topper left. Do you by chance have this book still?"

"Yes." Adenar found it from under the large bed.

"That is a terrible hiding spot," Darlaene said as the book fell into her hand, and she sat down. "Has anyone read the book besides you two?" Her eyes ran over them.

"Yes," Ara said. "Khendric, Koradin, and Aeba Therkin, an older woman on the Meritocrat council. She had a trusted scribe write a copy of it, so she could read it."

Darlaene let the book fall to the table. "A copy?"

Ara nodded.

"Then I'll read it myself when I have the time. For now, we'll continue with what you know. What have you been doing up until now?"

"Tried to gain *some* knowledge," Ara said. "By reading books at the library and we visited the museum as well, but learned nothing of value."

"It seems we don't know much about divinities," said Adenar, "or anything from that long ago. Chronor called it a 'time of divinities,' but we don't have any information on that period, I think."

Darlaene rubbed her temples. "A theory suggested that doombringers could be divinities?"

"Part of a divinity," Adenar corrected. "I think."

"Well, a museum won't have dust from such a powerful being, because it would probably put the museum at too much risk and be stolen."

"Why?" Ara asked. "Is it known to be powerful?"

"No, but it's incredibly rare, so people *want* it. There's no guarantee it would work or do anything though." She rose.

"Anyway, I'll do some research in the dark underworld of Ashbourn. There might be hope still."

"I'll come with you!" Ara quickly said, following in her footsteps.

Darlaene chuckled. "No, you won't. I won't drag you down into that underbelly unless I have to." She went for the door.

"Please, don't go." Ara's heart pounded hard, not wanting to let the experienced beast hunter leave.

"Don't worry about me." Darlaene turned. "I've survived everything up until now, I'll be back. I still work for Elrich, so I have to spend some time in the Passionist District too. Hopefully, it will lead to some good two-way communication, and I'll come back whenever the chance offers itself."

"Can't you just stay with us?" Ara pleaded.

"Though that sounds nice, having these two districts communicating will be a huge advantage to fight this monster." She put a hand on Ara's shoulder, then turned and left out the door. "Oh," her voice rang through the door. "Don't trust anyone wholly—especially Koradin."

Ara opened the door immediately. "Why?"

Darlaene stopped her stride and faced her. "I don't know. I just have a bad feeling about him. Stay cautious." She turned and continued down the hall.

Ara closed the door and lingered on the former king's name. *Koradin. Why didn't she trust him?* It bugged her immensely. Ara's gut feeling told her to trust him, but then Chronor's words came to mind . . . and now Darlaene's too. She had way more experience than Ara, so perhaps her intuition had caught onto something.

"I'll go tell Koradin about Darlaene's connection to Elrich," she said to Adenar, who looked a little confused. "We should do that, right?"

"I think it's for the best, yes," he answered. "I'll go check on mother." He also went out the door, giving her an awkward glance before leaving.

The walk to Koradin's quarters felt too long, especially with empty hallways, leaving them too silent.

"The girl," Chronor whispered into her mind. *"She will fall to . . ."* The words drifted out of her hearing. She stopped and leaned her head against the wall.

"Stop, please," she whispered. Ignoring his words became harder, and one part of her wanted to make the most of the potential, but she didn't know how to do that, and the other part just felt tired and tormented. Every word tired her out, feeling like he had total control, and it all went according to his ominous plan.

"Keep her alive . . ." more of his whispering words seeped into her mind.

"Stop!" she screamed in the hallway, hammering her hands into the stone wall. "Stop it!"

His whispers went still. She waited, but it didn't return, enveloping her in silence, making her feel more alone than in a long time . . . against a voreen god. *Damn Khendric and Topper,* she thought, grinding her teeth together. She resumed walking up the stairs to his quarters, reaching his rooms, but stopped. A conversation leaked out his slightly open door.

"This is madness," a croaky old woman's voice said—Aeba. "I don't care if that beast hunter tried to assassinate Ronoch, and it won't matter to our soldiers when we tell them what we are up against! I read that book and I dread what is about to happen to our city if we don't act now!" A silence followed. "That beast hunter was a hero who unfortunately failed in killing the greatest threat against Ashbourn in its history. Don't let Ponther's smearing affect you, we have to act. You must seize control of the district and fight!"

Ara let out a relieved breath, Aeba's tone and words causing energy to stir in her bones.

"If it turns out we're wrong," she continued. "Then we'll take the punishment, even if it's death. I believe you, Koradin. I've seen the way you talk about this and how it consumes you. And you know the army will follow you. They'd lay their lives on the line for you time and time again. You must overrule the council!"

"No," Koradin's cool voice replied.

Ara's jaw dropped. *What?*

"What?" Aeba exclaimed. "What do you mean 'no'? Don't you believe your own words and warnings?" The following silence unnerved even Ara outside of the room. Rapid footsteps approach the door. "Unbelievable," Aeba muttered as she left.

"I see the need, but . . ." Koradin said and Aeba stopped her stampeding. "I'm not a king anymore. I can't let the people see me still try to act as king when I clearly am not. It would—"

"What?" interrupted Aeba. "It would ruin your reputation? Does that matter now? Does any of what you just said matter? We don't know what's happening in the districts. We don't know what Chronor is planning or how he will strike. Where is that strong resolve I saw just yesterday?"

"I'll give Ponther more time," Koradin said with a still calm voice. "Then, at some point, I'll seize control."

"How vague. We need you to take control *now*. Ready the district for war and find some way to fight this monster!" Silence befell them yet again.

"Some more time," he answered.

Aeba stormed out, not spotting Ara hiding behind a pillar.

Ara felt confused, and even betrayed by the former king. Finally, someone chose their side and wanted to fight alongside Koradin, but he rejected the option, why?

Chronor's words drifted back to mind. *"Koradin is mine."* Tears pressed behind her eyes. She needed Koradin to be the rock she could lean against, but she realized he might be a spike instead. It felt like she fought alone. *Perhaps I can get closer to Aeba,* she considered. *I hope Darlaene comes back soon.* She began walking down the hallway, having trouble with her resolution to the cause.

"Ara?" a strong voice sounded behind her.

She turned to face Koradin, who did look genuinely troubled.

"Do you have any news? It would surely help right about now."

Her mouth opened slightly, but no words left her lips, disgusted with him. Dark thoughts emanated from his mind, pressing on her. She wished desperately to read them. "No."

Koradin's eyes fell to the ground. "If you find anything, *anything* at all, please let me know."

Ara breathed hard, her mind a torrent of emotions. Perhaps it would be better to work closer to Darlaene and Elrich. "Sure," she lied and turned, leaving. Koradin closed the door behind her.

CHAPTER 6

The Collector

List of voreen who have killed Chronor before his final phase:
- Thrak'sha of the Thu'ta clan: no record of how it was done
- Morida: Won a duel against him, after Chronor had beaten
sixteen other opponents with no break between fights.
- Pon'ba, Slayer of Men: Assassinated Chronor.

List of voreen who killed Chronor in a blood oath after he as-
cended to his final phase:
- Rhakta, The Master of Skulls.
*   From 'The Dark Traitor', chapter fourteen.*

Ara stood atop the large wall surrounding the Meritocrat District, staring out over Ashbourn. Koradin had instructed all soldiers to let her walk wherever she pleased, which felt freeing. The wind blew strong, and light rain fell over the enormous city. Adenar stood by her side, seeming to be in a similarly sombre mood. They shared a glance, but Ara felt awkward and looked to the ground just as a patrol of guards passed by.

Chronor's voice had been silent since the day before, which felt like both a pleasure and a curse. Despite his voice being tormenting, it also gave her vague insight into his thoughts and actions. Perhaps Chronor had revealed vital information about Koradin's allegiance? Or maybe not? She sighed as the conflict coursed through her mind, not even knowing what to do with the information should it be true. Lately, she'd felt that other presence on her mind too, mostly from beyond the wall. As if thousands of small dots in the distance slowly connected and grew stronger, and she felt fairly certain it was people under Chronor's control.

"The city is really changing," Adenar said, breaking their silence and the monotonous sound of the pitter-patter of the rain. He gazed at the giant castle in the middle of the city. "The streets are so quiet. Normally, you'd hear chatter from the Passionist District all over here. Now . . . nothing."

"I feel so lost," Ara said. "The only person I feel like I can truly trust . . . is you."

Adenar smiled quickly. "And I don't feel I can do much." He sighed and shook his head. "I wonder what's coming. I wonder how Chronor will play this out. Will there be war?"

"I hope not," Ara said, resting both her elbows on the wall.

"At least you have your arm. I've barely held a sword, and my quill won't do much."

"Without you, the city wouldn't even have had the opportunity to stand a chance."

"Do we?" he asked, making her frown questioningly. "Do we stand a chance?"

The wind blew her hair in all directions as rain tapped on their faces. The grey day got darker already as Chronor's presence had its effects on Ashbourn.

"I don't think so," she answered. "If Chronor walked in here and started killing us, what could we do?"

"So, why isn't he?" Adenar asked.

She opened her mouth to answer, but realised she didn't have one. *Why isn't he?* she wondered, the question bothering her. "I don't know. Perhaps he wants something from us?"

"What good are dead followers?" Adenar offered. "Maybe that's why."

Ara considered his words. "It makes sense. Dead, we have no potential. Alive, we can help him reach his final phase if we're right about which one he's in."

"So, he needs us to follow him. How will he do it?"

"I think those who ate his bread somehow turned into mindless followers. I've somewhat seen it before in a village named Cornstead."

"But the food wasn't distributed here," Adenar said. "At least not widely."

"Maybe he first had to gain total control over the other districts, where his plaguing influence was stronger, but I'm sure some from this district accepted the bread too."

Ara went into deep focus, allowing herself to feel the adding presence on her mind. The dark whisper of the city she thought to be the people who ate Chronor's bread grew ever stronger, but she tried separating them—it felt impossible. A few of them felt to be inside the wall of the Meritocrat District, and she grasped one strand with enormous concentration. With her eyes almost closed, she started walking.

"What is it?" Adenar asked, but she couldn't answer. "Ara, what are you doing?"

She waved her arm at him to stay silent and kept her concentration up. The presence wasn't that far away. With eyes half-closed, she went down from the wall and into the large street. Adenar's footsteps followed her closely. She walked through the empty street, past a market, and the presence grew stronger. After passing through some smaller streets, they entered a dilapidated neighbourhood and ended up in front of a house with no lights, a ruined chimney and broken windows. Someone or something moved inside, she felt it.

"Someone is in here," she said. "And I think their mind has been corrupted from Chronor's bread."

"We should get the guards."

"We could try, but I doubt they'd want to do this, being busy with other matters."

"What? But that 'someone' could be deranged and kill us."

"Most likely deranged, yes, but we got to find out what's going on." She ascended the slanted steps and pushed the door open. It screeched, making Adenar back away, but Ara unsheathed her sword and handed it to him.

"Me?" he said, surprised and scared. "Shouldn't you have it?"

"I have my arm."

Adenar took a deep breath, shook his head in disapproval and grabbed the sword.

She stepped inside the dark house, lit only by the weak light of the grey day streaming through the windows. A broken chair lay in the short hallway in front of them, besides a staircase and two doors leading to different rooms.

"I think it's coming from upstairs," Ara whispered, sensing the presence. She led the way and Adenar followed cautiously. With barely any light, Ara's foot slipped on something at the top of the stairs. She caught herself on the railing and stilled, listening.

Nothing.

Adenar let out a relieved breath.

Thud . . . thud . . . thud . . .

Vague footsteps sounded from down the hallway to their right. Ara ran her fingers under her boot and sniffed them. The metallic smell of blood filled her nostrils. She snuck her head around the corner and gazed down the hallway. The hallway ended with a large window, and in front of it stood a tall, silhouetted person wearing ragged clothing. He faced away from them, standing in an unnatural position with arms and neck bent at weird angles, wavering back and forth, but didn't appear to hold any weapons.

Turning her head to Adenar, she glimpsed something round laying still on the floor across the hall. The darkness made it hard to see, but it could be a corpse. She silently snuck closer and confirmed her suspicions when grabbing onto hair attached to a cold head. A yelp almost escaped her mouth as the little light inside reflected in the dead eyes of the woman.

"Is t-that . . .?" Adenar whispered, but she motioned for him to stay quiet.

Trails of dried blood ran down the woman's cheek.

Anger roared into life within her. She felt Chronor's weak pressure emanating from the figure at the end of the hall, and the god's blood had caused this. Even in this district, Chronor's plague had spread, and she felt so powerless to stop it. At least here she could do something, though; something that *had* to be done. She put the woman's head calmly down on the floorboards, rose, and walked straight towards the corrupted man.

He snapped his head toward her as her footsteps rang through the hallway, his head twitching as he barred his teeth and growled.

"Ara!" Adenar shouted behind her. "Watch out!"

The ragged man's eyes shifted to Adenar and he sat off toward him, hands outstretched like a deathwalker.

Adenar screamed, but Ara pulled her arm back and released the unmatched strength residing within her cursed limb. The corrupted man flew backwards and crashed into the window. It broke and half of him dangled outside in the rain, his strained breaths bringing a tear to Ara's eyes. This poor person had become a monster and killed his family, all because of Chronor. He slumped to the ground, still alive, but hurt badly, seeming unable to move his legs. His head twitched and his eyes looked in all directions.

Ara towered over him and he tried grabbing for her, but without functioning legs and one broken arm, he was barely a threat. The dim light from outside lit his pale face. In his eyes remained nothing of his former self, a dark presence occupying them instead. Complete darkness surrounded his orange irises.

"Can you understand me?" she asked, but he only growled in between laboured breaths. "Did you eat the bread?"

"Whoever he was," Adenar said when he caught up. "He's gone."

Ara breathed heavily and bit her teeth together. "Give me my sword."

Their eyes met, and after a moment he nodded and placed the sword in the palm of her dark hand.

She aimed at his head, and exhaled slowly. "I'm sorry we couldn't save you." The blade penetrated his skull and he stopped moving. To get the blade free, Ara had to place her foot on the dead man's head and drag it out, which took away some of the seriousness of the moment. She felt foolish, until Adenar started laughing.

"I know it's wrong," he said, trying to stop. "It's just so bizarre. I'm so sorry."

She chuckled softly, glad for the emotional respite until she realized she'd been right. "The pressure I feel on my mind are all the turned souls," she said grimly, facing Adenar. "And there are . . . *many.*"

At first, he mirrored her expression, but he waved her words away with a hand. "Well, we're many too."

She furrowed her brows, but he went and opened a nearby door leading to a bedroom with a window providing some light. He found a satchel on the floor and opened it, pulling out bread, sighing. "It's that damn bread."

"Adenar," she said, putting a hand on his shoulder. "Look."

In the corner of the room stood a young boy looking straight at them with empty dark eyes. Adenar jumped back, but Ara stayed calm. The boy didn't react to Adenar's movements at all.

"Oh no," she said, sighing heavily. "He ate the bread." The boy looked pale and starved, with brown hair in all directions. She calmly walked closer. He didn't shift his gaze until she stood some inches away, but that was all he did.

"Hello?" she said, but it caused no reaction.

"He can't be more than eight years old," Adenar said.

She gave him a small push. No response at all. "We have to tell Koradin," she said. "And we have to bring him."

"Yeah," Adenar agreed with a sombre tone. "Let's hope he stays calm."

She pushed the boy forward and his legs sluggishly followed. He waddled on with no objections. They carried him down the staircase, and luckily he didn't go into an animalistic rage.

They left the house of darkness behind and led the poor boy through the streets. Ara held his hand, and he followed with little resistance, seeming as if his mind had been whisked away. She tried not to let hopelessness eat away at her mind, and stay focused, but feeling his cold hand in hers made it harder. Chronor had no limit. Nobody would be safe. They *had* to stop him.

They walked through the district and ended up in front of the Headquarters, entering through a back gate to cause as little commotion as possible. The courtyard and building crawled with people, but it seemed they let her do what she wanted. A lot of eyes stared at them, but none approached, seeming to know who she and Adenar were. They took the boy to Ara's momentary quarters and, surprisingly, Koradin entered not long after them with his royal and authoritarian demeanour, yet kind and warm eyes.

"Ara, Adenar," he said with a nod of his head which they returned. "I've heard you brought a . . . visitor?"

Ara showed him to the large bed, where the boy sat motionless and emotionless.

Koradin frowned. "Is that a boy?"

"Yes."

"What's with his eyes?"

Both Ara and Adenar explained what had happened: the house, the maniacal man, the dead wife, the corrupted bread, and finally the boy.

"I knew something was wrong with that bread," Koradin said, leaning closer to inspect the boy's eyes. The boy snarled as the former king neared.

"That's weird," Adenar pointed out. "He's never done that before."

Koradin leaned back. "So, everyone who ate Chronor's bread turns into this?"

"I don't think so," Ara said. "The man attacked us. I don't know why this boy is calm. Maybe he'll lash out later."

"We'll lock him up," Koradin said. "And force-feed him. Poor child is as thin as an arrow." He faced Ara. "And you think more citizens in this district are like this?"

"Most likely. Others accepted his bread for sure."

"We must find them," Koradin said. "It's too big a risk to have agents of Chronor roam freely. Who knows what kind of army he has within our walls already? I'll organize parties of soldiers to search every house in the district."

His seriousness impressed her, but she tried stifling the feeling. It would be mighty suspicious if he brushed this away, so perhaps this was a ruse.

"You might have dulled the edge on Chronor's blade," Koradin said. "How did you find him?"

"Oh," she answered, her eyes falling to the floor. "My mind could . . . uhm."

"Can you help us track down more corrupted people?" Koradin asked before forcing her to say more.

She let out a relieved sigh. "Yes, I can."

"Great. And before I forget: Darlaene has arrived."

Ara's eyes shot up.

"I'll send her to your quarters immediately, and I'll call upon you when the search parties are ready. I need some time to organize it." Koradin took a step back and ran his eyes over them. "Good job, both of you." His eyes lingered on Adenar for a moment too long, before he cleared his throat and went out the door.

"He really listens," Adenar said with a smile, but he seemed to forget that Koradin was also a politician. "We couldn't have hoped for a better response."

He idolizes him, she thought, but could she blame him? Koradin seemed the perfect example of everything one should aspire to be. "Yeah," she said, grinding on the word.

A knock came on the door and Darlaene entered, looking as vigorous and gorgeous as ever; the kind of woman Ara wanted to become.

Ara exhaled in sweet relief and embraced her. Darlaene had some moments of awkwardness before wrapping her arms around Ara.

"You're back," Ara said before letting go.

"Of course," she replied, glancing at Ara before examining the room. "Can't let you handle this alone, can I?"

Ara smiled warmly at having an experienced beast hunter to help push the despair and hopelessness away.

"How are you?" Adenar asked.

"Good. Do you have a certain book?" she asked, straight to business. "I'd like to read about our threat."

"It's not here," Ara said. "It's in Adenar's room. We change its location frequently."

"Clever," Darlaene said, a hint of a smile slashing across her face. "Mind getting it, Adenar? I've got a feeling we might need it."

Both Ara and Adenar frowned, but she waved an impatient hand at him. "Come on, move along."

"Fine." He went out the door.

"I have news," Darlaene said and sat down elegantly in a wide chair. Ara felt a fire spark to life. *Finally, we're getting somewhere,* she thought. "I might have a way to get us a weapon against Chronor."

"Really?" Ara almost shouted.

"Yes, but it'll only work if your sources are correct. There is a man in Ashbourn known as the Collector, who lives and rules the underworld of the city. I've been able to gather some information that he might have something from a doombringer."

"What?" she asked.

Darlaene nodded. "This information cost me dearly, and I can't be sure it's reliable."

"Something from a doombringer?" Ara asked.

"That's all my informant said. But it has to be dust, right?"

Adenar entered the room and put the book on the large table.

"We have to do it," Ara said eagerly.

"Do what?" Adenar asked.

"I have sources claiming we can get some doombringer dust from a man in Ashbourn."

"What?" he asked, eyebrows rising.

"Someone called the Collector."

He frowned. "I know of every noble in this city, but I have never heard of any 'Collector.'"

"He's not that kind of person," Darlaene assured him. "He keeps to the dark, so we have to find him at night." Darlaene went over to the table Adenar had placed the book on and rolled out a map over the city. "I have a lead on his whereabouts tonight, but only tonight. Believe me when I say this guy is hard to track down—or even get people talking about him."

"Where do we meet?" Ara asked, feeling her sliver of hope.

Darlaene's finger fell inside the Warborn District. "Unfortunately . . . that's where he is."

"Oh," Ara said, her shoulders sinking. The location looked like a regular street, but she did not want to enter that district at all. She had hoped the Collector stayed within the Meritocrat District, but what was the chance of that? She sighed, but knew it had to be done.

"We'll meet back here when night has befallen the city," Darlaene said. "We'll use the small exit out of the Meritocrat District and walk straight through the main gate of the Warborn District."

"That sounds unsafe," Adenar said.

"There's barely any activity and no guards," she answered. "If it looks unsafe, we'll turn right around."

"Alright," Ara said, knowing they had to take some risk.

"I'll come to," Adenar chimed in.

Darlaene frowned at him. "Why?"

He shrunk a little under her gaze. "Well, I mean, maybe you need some protection."

"I didn't expect you to want to come," Darlaene said, no malice in her voice. "It may get dangerous. How well do you handle a sword?"

Adenar licked his lips and looked to the ground.

"If something happens," Ara said, leaning towards him. "I don't think your quill is going to do much, and you don't have the unfair advantage I do."

He did not look pleased.

"It's okay. We'll be fine."

"You better be," he said, exhaling deeply. "I wish I was of more use."

"Without you, we wouldn't even be here," Ara said with a cheerful smile. "And if we survive, I'll teach you all the little I know of sword-fighting." She felt even more thankful for Adenar's presence than she expressed. Without him, she would have lost her mind after Khendric and Topper left.

"Then we have a plan," Darlaene said, and headed for the door with the book in hand.

"Where are you going?" Ara asked.

"And why do you have the book?"

"I'm going to Elrich to inform him of our plan, in case something goes wrong. And then I need time to read as much as I can. I will bring it back for the meeting with the Collector. I think we'll need it." And then she darted out the door, gone—again. But Ara didn't feel as lost as the last time she left, for at least now they had a plan.

* * *

Before evening would arrive, Koradin had Ara help his soldiers track down multiple people afflicted with Chronor's disease in the district, and it left her exhausted. Crumbs of bread had been present in all houses and all inhabitants had dark eyes. Hopefully, they had found them all, but Koradin wanted her to continue tomorrow, and the thought alone made her muscles ache. If she would be able to help more, came down to the meeting with the Collector though. Would she even be alive to watch the sunrise?

She leaned against the massive wall around the district, feeling safe as it towered over her. The realization she would soon go to the other side of the wall threatened her feeling of safety greatly, and she fidgeted her hands. Darlaene hadn't shown up yet, but Ara hadn't waited for long. Just as her eyes almost fell shut, footsteps approached, and Darlaene's slim figure walked down the street towards her.

"Did you bring the book?" Ara asked as she neared, feeling uncomfortable at the prospect of bringing it.

Darlaene nodded.

"Why do you think we'll need it?" Ara wondered.

Darlaene stopped in front of her. "I'm afraid we might have to trade it." She put a hand on Ara's shoulder. "But you had that copy made, right?"

Ara sighed and nodded. The book felt so valuable, but the words inside held the true importance.

Ara used the keys she had 'borrowed' for the door and they went through the small passage. She knew where Commander Relen usually hung them and they had been easy to snatch. Having the keys on her created a huge security risk, but she had a good hiding spot planned that Adenar knew about. If they did not return, he would retrieve the key—and hopefully shed some tears for her.

They came out the other end and into the large street between the two district gates. Ara locked the door and clutched the key hard with an irrational fear of losing it.

Darlaene led the way fearlessly in the dark of night, and Ara mustered her courage, which paled in comparison. They reached the large imposing, yet open gate of the Warborn District, with not a soul in sight. Ara put the key under the partially ruined barrel leaning against the wall, along with other rubble. She felt like someone else than Darlaene watched her, but no pressure appeared on her mind. The silence unnerved Ara to the core. No chatter rang through the air of the abandoned marketplace, and no feet hammered on the cobbled streets. Even at night, countless people used to roam about, but not anymore.

"Where is everybody do you think?" Ara whispered. She thought those afflicted by Chronor perhaps hid indoors like the ones in their district, but she felt nothing at all.

"I don't know," Darlaene answered, taking the lead through the street. "In hiding somewhere, maybe?"

"Is the Passionist District like this too?"

"Sometimes. Sometimes groups of people walk about and attack random people or places. Once, a tremendous mass of people gathered outside the Passionist Headquarters and just stood there, staring at the building throughout the night."

"Really?" Ara asked, eyes big with horror.

"Yeah. It was terrifying. Elrich was scared out of his mind."

"I feel like Chronor has almost everyone in his grasp," Ara said.

"They didn't attack though," Darlaene said. "I don't know why. Perhaps Elrich's soldiers kept them away."

"I think Chronor is trying to break the will of the few people still opposing him, gaining followers instead of leaving corpses."

"That sounds reasonable," she agreed.

They finally reached the small and completely dark tavern marked on Darlaene's map.

"It's supposed to look empty, right?" Ara asked.

"I guess. The Collector is not a public person, so this looks about right."

They went to the door and Ara pried it open with her hand, hoping the owner wouldn't be too mad.

They searched the empty tavern, but found nothing. The upper floors yielded the same result, but something still felt off. No sheets laid on the bed and the drawers had no cutlery. No dirty dishes in the sink, or any waste in the bins. The cooking pots weren't even dirty.

Ara felt something press on her mind and she turned sharply to Darlaene as understanding dawned on her. "They're under us."

"What?" she asked, frowning.

"I can feel thoughts coming from under us."

"Right now?"

"Yes," she answered. "And they are moving." Ara followed the pressure on her mind as best she could. "It's coming from under the kitchen, and it's moving . . . upwards?

"Someone's coming up then," Darlaene said. "We got to hide." She motioned for Ara to hide behind a desk with her. Muffled footsteps reached their ears. Ara peeked over the edge of the desk, seeing a large shelf slide along the wall. Darlaene pulled her head down before she could see more.

"I gave him what he asked for," an angry voice said. "This isn't right! He told me he would get me out of the city!"

"We're just the muscle," a much deeper voice answered, and two sets of heavy footsteps walked across the floor. "Just doing what we're ordered."

"Do you know who I am?" the first voice said again as the group disappeared out of the kitchen. "I am Ser Rhoyel Hvander! Unhand me!"

"Fine," two thick voices answered in unison and a thud followed.

"Ouch, you mongrels!"

A door closed and the two people calling themselves 'the muscle' returned to the kitchen. Ara stayed hidden, but Darlaene shot out from their hiding place and elegantly sat down on the desk.

"Hello boys," she said with a cool voice.

The footsteps came to a halt abruptly. "Who are you?" the low, thick voice asked.

"My name is Darlaene, and I'm here to have a chat with the Collector."

Ara had no idea what to do and the silence hanging in the room almost made her vomit.

"Ara," Darlaene said. "You can get up now."

For some reason, relief flooded over her. She rose, laying eyes upon the two largest men she had seen, both the size of Topper's new body, taut with muscle. One scratched a hairless head, but they both had a lot of earrings and piercings, and arms covered with tattoos. Their sleeveless shirts and chains around their necks made them look fierce and brutish.

"That's not really how it works," one of them said, looking uncertainly at the other.

Darlaene sighed dramatically. "I don't care," she said, putting her sword and various daggers on the counter. "Are we going?"

"Uhm," they both said, searching each other's faces for the answer.

"What are you waiting for? It's not like we're threatening."

The hairless one pointed to Ara. "She still has her blade."

"Oh," Ara exclaimed and clumsily removed her sword.

"So?" Darlaene prodded. "Let's go."

"Uhm," the one with hair said again, turning to his friend. "They haven't got a deal."

"It's not easy to make a deal with a person hidden in shadow," Darlaene said. "But we have something that will interest him."

"What is it?" the bald one asked.

Darlaene rolled her eyes. "Oh please. Like we're telling *you*."

"Fair enough," he replied to Ara's surprise. "Well, sure. You're unarmed and we'll just hurt you if you're a waste of time. We still need to pat you down, though."

Ara swallowed dryly, feeling like her magically enhanced arm couldn't match up against these brutes.

"Fine with me," Darlaene said, holding her arms out. They approached and patted them down surprisingly professionally. He didn't touch her anywhere inappropriately, even apologizing for being rough.

"Alright. Let's go, but try to be quick. The Collector has a lot to do on his last day in Ashbourn." They walked toward the moveable shelf, but stopped. "Oh, and let us see your eyes."

Ara frowned at first, but realized the reason a moment later. She opened her eyes and let the large man inspect her.

"She's clear," he said.

"This one too," the other one replied. "Come."

The two men led them through the secret door and down a spiral staircase. They came to the bottom where a metal door greeted them. One of the brutes knocked and a hatch opened with two gleaming eyes peeking through.

"Ah," a thin and squeaky voice said. "Brotus and Baldar! My two favourites!"

"Will you just open," Brotus—or Baldar—replied. The hatch closed, and a series of locks sounded through the door before it opened quickly and a skinny man greeted them with open arms. He wore a tall, bright blue hat with a long, dark-blue suit that went to his knees. His long curly and orange hair made him look absolutely insane.

"Welcome ladies," he said, exaggerating a bow.

"That's just Lou," the brute closest to Ara said. "He's . . . kind of loopy." They guided them past the greeter and through a small hall, where they opened another thick door and beautiful music met their ears.

Ara had never thought she would lay her eyes on such a strange scene in her life. The huge underground hall looked lavish enough to be inside the castle. A large orchestra played fantastic music for a large number of people spread out over countless tables and a bar. However, it seemed the hall was split into two sections. All the people closest to the orchestra wore noble-like clothes with glorious fabric, playing card games and sipping drinks of various colours. On a smaller stage danced four dancers in exotic outfits. These kinds of extravagant people stretched out to the middle of the hall, where the lighting suddenly dimmed. The people on the other half sat on stools around smaller tables, or leaning against a bar counter, wearing more traditional and darker wear, playing cruder games like knife-throwing, or even participating in a small fighting pit. Chatter and noise echoed all around and servers ran about serving drinks. The contrast between the two groups of people was like night and day, but they seemed to coexist easily. The marvellous sight almost made Ara burst out with laughter, and she couldn't understand how something like this could exist underground, hidden away from the public. *There's more to Ashbourn that I know,* she realized.

"It's usually not this bad," one of the brutes said. "But we're having a 'doomsday celebration' tonight, and tomorrow, everyone's getting out of Ashbourn."

"Really?" Ara said. "So they're celebrating the end of the city?"

"Nah," he replied. "Some are just trying to have a good time before it all blows up, while others are attending and squaring up deals, hopefully not getting violent in the process."

"This way," the other brute said, and guided them into the hall, through the middle of the divide between people.

"I'm betting my right eye," one very questionable man said, pointing a knife to his eye.

"You're on," a slim woman with a large scar across her face answered. A part of Ara wanted to listen in, but the nice brute behind her ushered her forward to the luxurious part of the large room, which had better lighting.

One man with a white silk shirt and a monocle, raised a hand towards them while still keeping his eyes on his cards. "Not now, Brotus," he said with a sharp voice.

Brotus exhaled and waited patiently, motioning for Ara and Darlaene to do the same.

The man was handed another card and a die. He looked displeased after turning the card and rolling the die. "Ah, I'll never win this anyway."

The other people around the table threw some coins into the middle of the table, but Ara didn't understand why.

The man with the white silk shirt turned to them and looked at his brutes. "What?" he asked with a light-hearted voice.

"These two wanted to talk to you," Brotus said.

"I don't have a scheduled meeting with them."

"No," Brotus replied, uncertainty clouding his voice. "They—"

"You have until the next round to pique my interest," he interrupted his goon, eyes drilling into Ara and Darlaene. "Go on, talk."

"You are interested in ancient relics," Darlaene led the conversation.

"Very much so."

"We have something more ancient than anything you own."

"I doubt that," he said with a smile, but kept his eyes on Darlaene.

"It stems from voreen culture, never laid eyes upon by more than a handful of humans."

Ara grew anxious, seeing immediately where this would go. Could they part with the book?

The Collector's narrowed eyes lingered on them. "Everyone, leave," he said. The other people stopped the game and looked at him with puzzled looks. "Find another table . . . now."

They rose without a hint of irritation, but Ara felt a mild cloud of angry thoughts from them. *They're great actors.*

"Have a seat," the Collector said and they sat down. "I am the Collector and I run this establishment, at least for another day. I own one-of-a-kind exhibits, and never part with any of them . . . unless for the right price." Darlaene opened her mouth, but he silenced her with a finger. He looked younger than Ara had pictured, with slick black hair and a handsome face. His cheeks had recently been shaved, and his moustache had been styled by professionals. "Do *not* waste my time." He moved the toothpick in his mouth around almost mesmerizingly with his tongue.

"Then," Darlaene began. "I'll be frank with you. We're only interested if you have what we desire."

He chuckled and stirred his drink. "I'm sure I can provide."

"We need doombringer dust," Ara said.

The Collector raised an eyebrow. "The rapidly decaying dust from a doombringer?" he asked, smirking slightly. "I didn't expect *that*."

"Do you have it?" Ara asked, her heart pounding.

"Slow down, girl," he said. "This is an elegant dance, my dear. And we've just been introduced."

Darlaene kept the seducing smile across her lips and the two looked to be flirting with lustrous eyes, not that Ara was an expert on the subject.

"You descend into my domain and you ask for the world itself," the Collector said.

"Few people can offer the world," Darlaene answered.

"Oh, so very few, and such a rarity is hard to match. What do you bring to the table?"

"We need reassurance," Darlaene said with a sterner tone. "Do you have what we seek?"

The Collector met her eyes with a dangerous stare, obviously wanting to see their relic first. Ara feared he didn't have the dust and wanted to know if killing them for their unknown artefact would be worth it. She flexed her strong hand, feeling a little better.

"Because," Darlaene said. "If we show you, you'll desire this with such a powerful lust, you will do anything to get it."

The Collector, however, looked unimpressed. He sized Darlaene up and down with his eyes before removing the toothpick and flicked it across the table. "Fine. Because I want to see what you think is *so* valuable. And believe me, it better be valuable."

Ara exhaled slowly, her face paling. She tried to keep her composure and stay as cool as Darlaene, but she just couldn't. What if he didn't see the value in the book? Either, they traded away the book and lost it, or they were murdered for bringing a worthless item to his table.

The Collector snapped his fingers, and from behind him emerged a servant. He whispered a few words, and the servant disappeared.

"I didn't catch your names," the Collector said.

"We're beast hunters," Darlaene answered.

He perked up. "Beast hunters, you say." His eyes narrowed as he more closely examined Ara. "You," he said, looking into her eyes. "What have you been up to lately?"

"Ehm," Ara stuttered.

"Anything illegal maybe? I have eyes and ears everywhere and some interesting rumours have caught my attention lately. Some talk about a young woman with . . . extraordinary power."

He knows who I am, she realized, feeling sweat form on her forehead.

"Your eyes betray you, young one." The Collector leaned both elbows on the table. "Such power inside such a *small* creature. I mean no offence, I understand you are *quite* dangerous. What an honour to have you in my estate. I must admit, my interest in what you're bringing is growing."

Behind him, someone rolled up a cart and upon it stood a large glass cage with something displayed on a pedestal. The Collector lifted his shirt, showing an enormous set of keys on a keychain. He grabbed one key seemingly at random and unlocked the lock on the cage. The servant tilted the glass back and the Collector put his hand upon the small pouch inside.

"This is dust collected from a doombringer only hours after its dissipation, coated in slime from centitars to protect it from deterioration. I hope you understand how rare this is." He held the bag towards them so they could peek inside.

Ara got a glance at the green dust before he pulled it away. "I think I've earned to know what you bring."

Darlaene pulled the book out from under her cloak. The Collector looked with great interest as she placed it on the table. "This book," Darlaene said, "is written by the only literate voreen ever in history. It contains knowledge from an age we were barely even a part of. An age of divinities, gods and wars."

The Collector's eyes stayed glued to the book, his fingers ready to caress it. "What is the book about?"

"How to defeat the voreen's ancient god, Chronor," Ara said.

His eyes shifted to her as some thought circulated in his mind before a look of realization seemed to dawn on him. "Am I wrong in thinking that this voreen god is not just a story?"

Ara nodded.

"And I am also right to believe that it is his presence that is sickening the city?"

"Yes," Ara answered him frankly.

"Good thing we're leaving tomorrow."

"It's hard to get out," Ara said.

The Collector chuckled. "Do not worry for me. *I'll* get out, but thank you for your words of warning."

"This book tells of how to defeat him," Darlaene said. "It might be Chronor's most valuable possession."

"And yet you have it right here. I now understand why a group of people broke into the Warborn Headquarters." He pointed to them, and then down to the book, tapping his finger on it. "It was because of this."

Darlaene pushed it towards him and lust sprouted to life on his face.

"You will let me open it?"

She nodded.

"She can easily get it back," Darlaene said, nodding towards Ara.

"I don't doubt that." The Collector tore his eyes away from the book, and to her. "My dear, can you show me your arm?"

"My arm?" Ara wondered.

"I just want to see what the rumours got right. Soldiers talk, you know."

Ara removed the glove and uncovered her arm, exposing the dark veins.

"Marvellous," the Collector said and leaned closer. "It's exactly as described. What I'd pay to keep you as my bodyguard—or *trophy*." His eyes fell back on the book, fortunately, and he started shifting through the pages, reading a paragraph here and there. "This . . . this is something else."

"Does it satisfy?" Darlaene asked.

"I didn't think it would, but it absolutely does. Let me guess: you need the dust to defeat him?"

"Spot on," Darlaene disclosed.

"You get what you need to defeat him," he said, leaning back on his chair, looking at the ceiling. "And I get his most valuable item to flee the city with, making me his number one target should you fail to stop him."

"If we fail, it won't matter," Ara said. "I don't think he'll stop his destruction and the book will have little meaning to him at that point."

"I would be lying if I said I didn't want this because of the associated risk. Because I *do* want this. One can always chance upon doombringer dust, though rarely. But the original book written by a voreen on how to defeat their ancient god? Now *that's* a one-of-a-kind."

"So we have a deal?" Darlaene asked.

"Don't you need the book?" he wondered.

"We know what we need to know," Darlaene said. "And though it pains us, we can dispose of it. It's the only item we have matching the worth of doombringer dust."

The Collector closed the book and pushed it back to her. Then he sat back and rolled his tongue around in his mouth.

Ara's stomach churned with suspense.

He bit his lip, staring at the book, before snapping his fingers. "Fine, let's do it."

"Really?" Ara blurted.

Darlaene curtly grabbed the Collector's outstretched hand and they shook firmly.

"Get the contract," he said to a servant behind him and not long after a single sheet of paper landed on the table in front of Ara, riddled with writing.

"It's a formal document," the Collector explained, "stating that both parties agreed to exchange items and that nobody can claim their former item back. You may inspect the dust until you are satisfied. Should you find anything not to your liking, you may withdraw from the deal without any repercussions." The Collector tossed the bag over on their end of the table. Ara opened the pouch, staring at the incredible substance, hoping it would be enough for a weapon.

"How do we know that this is actually doombringer dust?" Ara asked.

"I would not have the reputation that I have if I dealt in foul deals. But"—he leaned forward, grabbed the contract, and added something in his writing with a quill—"if you somehow discover it is *not* doombringer dust, you may have your book back and five of my other exhibits of your choosing." Some eavesdropping bystanders gasped. "This is highly unusual behaviour from me, and I reassure you the dust *is* the remains of a doombringer."

Ara couldn't believe her ears, but it did make her more certain about the deal.

Darlaene signed the contract and so did he. The Collector shook hands with both of them once more and placed the precious book under his arm. Ara grabbed the bag of dust from the table and secured it on her person.

"I must retire," the Collector said, rising, "to study this new artefact of mine." He gently bowed, and Ara returned the gesture.

"And," he said, eyes on Ara. "Don't be afraid to seek me out again, young lady. No harm will come to you and I am most interested in you."

Ara didn't know how to reply, but luckily, he disappeared into the darkness before she had to answer.

Brotus and Baldar escorted them out of the underground hall without as much as a stare from any of the other people down there. They went back up to the deserted tavern above, but before the brutes let them out the door, Brotus said, "The Collector's rules stop anyone from following you with hopes of stealing your valuable item. Anyone breaking this rule will be executed along with every relative they know."

"What?" Ara asked.

"It's to protect buyers," Baldar said. "It's easy to murder someone on their way back home, after paying an enormous price for an artefact. It would be bad for the Collector's business if his customers had a habit of dying after leaving his estates. Nobody has ever violated this rule, so no need to worry."

Ara felt her shoulders lower and they parted with the bodyguards, who had been surprisingly nice.

The walk back into the Meritocrat District was uneventful. Ara found the key under the same barrel and let out a relieved breath. "I can't believe we made it," she said, knowing she would feel even better when behind the Meritocrat wall. "I wish we could still have the book, but . . ."

"We need this dust more than the book for now," Darlaene said. "And we also have a copy."

It made sense, but it still felt like a loss.

They got back inside the Meritocrat District and walked toward the headquarters. Despite seeming just as abandoned at night, this district felt safer and more like home.

"I have to head to the Passionist District," Darlaene said. "To report to Elrich."

"Will you be back soon?" Ara asked.

"I hope so. Uncertainty grows ever more in these times, but I hope so."

They parted and Ara returned to the Headquarters as quickly as possible. The courtyard and the halls were totally empty of people, but Ara welcomed the solitude, especially with the valuable doombringer dust. Meeting Koradin and having to lie would be painful and hard, so she found her room quickly and hid the precious dust in the closet.

She sat down on the bed, listening to the complete silence, feeling pressure on her mind again . . . feeling alone again. *I wish Adenar was here,* she thought, sitting silently in the darkness. *Maybe he's here in the headquarters.* She slid off the bed despite feeling tired and walked to the door. *Or perhaps he wants to sleep?* she wondered, her hand resting on the doorknob. Her heart beat hard, and it felt like eels squirming in her guts. She wanted to see him because . . . well, because . . . she turned the doorknob.

She barely exited her room before seeing movement in her peripherals. Someone stood outside her door, leaning against the wall. Her muscles shot into action, but a sharp pain entered her neck, like a needle. She gasped and clutched her neck. A man in dark clothing and a mask held a syringe in his hand. *No,* she thought, feeling herself becoming sluggish. *I have to kill him fast.* She grabbed for him, but he stepped backwards, so she darted forward and slammed her hand at his head. He evaded her again, her fist striking the wall, leaving cracks in the stone.

Something kicked her feet out from under her, and she fell to the ground. She rolled around to see another man in similar clothing throw himself on top of her to hold her down.

"Help!" she screamed, but a hand covered her mouth. She grabbed her assailant and tore him off, but her strength faded fast and he stayed on her. *No, not like this,* she thought as her eyes shut involuntarily.

Darkness.

CHAPTER 7

A Waning Sun

It is believed Chronor created the voreen from his own blood fused with that of humans. We don't know the truth of our creation, only that we stem from him somehow. I know, through Avina (the only human I know) that humans also don't know how they came to be. She also told me humans believe the voreen existed before them, yet we believe the other to be true.

Maybe that's why we despise you so much. Perhaps it's because Chronor created us to be better than you, yet you still live amongst us. I think it's an embarrassment that our culture falls before yours, but violence is our nature and our doom, and is how Chronor made us.

From 'The Dark Traitor', chapter eight.

Ara slowly returned to consciousness, her first thought being: *I'm alive? Where am I?* A hood covered her face, but some sunlight streamed through the fabric. Not enough for her to see much, though. Her other senses returned slowly and she realized she sat on a horse from the familiar motions. And she wasn't alone. Multiple footsteps revealed people close to her, but none spoke. She'd been gagged, leaving her no choice but to participate in the silence. The surroundings smelled like trees, and it felt like the horse walked carefully through uneven terrain. Ropes held both her legs firmly to the stirrups of the saddle, securing her in place atop the horse, affording her no wiggle room. Her heart wouldn't stop drumming, and panic threatened to overtake her. *Stay calm,* she tried telling herself. *Whoever this is hasn't killed me yet. There has to be a reason.* However, it became increasingly hard to stay calm when she discovered her strong arm had been locked up behind her back with multiple chains and locks. *They know.* When moving her strong arm slightly, it became clear that forcing herself free would break her normal arm. Could this be Chronor's work? Perhaps some ancient motive eluded her?

But why the forest? Some ritual perhaps? She breathed slowly and kept fear at bay. *I might have to break my arm,* she thought, trying to mentally prepare for such a hurtful sacrifice.

The horse halted and multiple people put their hands on her, and she wanted to wiggle and fight, but the hands were careful, so she decided to stay cool for some more moments. The ropes around her legs released her and several hands lifted her off the horse.

"I know you're awake, stay quiet," someone whispered into her ear. Before she could decide against it, they put her down softly on the ground. "I'll handle this, get to your positions, hurry." Several footsteps skittered away in what sounded like grass and brush, and the restraints around her arms loosened too. "Time to remove the hood."

The hood loosened and was lifted off. Bright light blinded her and she narrowed her eyes until they adjusted to her surroundings. A figure slowly turned from blurry to clear and her heart almost stopped.

Topper?

Topper's large body laid next to her with a guilty smile. He gestured for her to stay quiet and removed her gag.

Ara put her arms around him and pulled him close in a deep hug. After a moment, his huge arms wrapped around her and he returned it. "I'm sorry."

"You stupid stonepudder," Ara whispered as tears left her eyes.

"Listen," Topper said. "We'll explain *everything* later, but for now you're going to have to go along with whatever we're doing. Okay?" He let go of her.

"You didn't leave me," she said as their eyes met.

"We would never leave you and we're both very sorry."

"So, Khendric is alive too?"

"He is, and looking forward to seeing you."

"Where is he?" she asked, needing to provide him with a hug too. She noticed all the other soldiers around her, all grasping bows, laying on the ground, seeming ready for something.

"Not here," Topper whispered. "And we don't have a lot of time. Peak over that ledge."

Ara climbed to the edge and peered over. They were at the end of a forest before great fields of grass. She saw nothing at first, but Topper climbed up beside her and pointed at something in the middle of the field. She narrowed her eyes and saw something that looked like a humanoid figure sitting down.

"You see it?" Topper asked.

"What is it?"

"A voreen."

Her mouth fell open and she whispered, "I-I had completely forgotten about that." She looked him dead in the eyes. "That's genius. We just need to get the blade."

"Exactly. We're about to kill it."

Topper pointed at something close to the voreen; a person walking up to it. One single person with black short hair.

"That's Khendric, isn't it?" she asked.

"Yup."

"He's going to die. What's he doing?"

"Creating a diversion."

* * *

Khendric cautiously approached the female voreen, fighting to stay calm, but her gaze stayed locked on him. As if her hard stare wasn't intimidating enough, her precious voreen blade laid across her lap. She didn't appear concerned, but interested in his foolishness perhaps?

With his blade in hand, he slowly removed his pistol from its holster and swallowed dryly.

The voreen rose, her fierce dark-green blade glimmering in the sunlight, a stark contrast to her grey skin.

"You don't need to beat her," Khendric muttered under his breath. "Just survive long enough for the damn cavalry."

She lifted her blade toward him but kept her frown.

She can't understand my actions either, he thought, exhaling.

She tilted her head to the side and licked her lips. Despite holding the sword pointed at him, her bulging arm didn't shake at all.

In his peripherals, Khendric noticed the cavalry in the far distance, charging through the fields. *Good*, he thought, having a hard time believing he stood face to face with a voreen.

He hoped the company of a hundred soldiers would be enough to defeat her. After all, it had been all Koradin could spare. And hopefully, with Khendric approaching alone, she wouldn't try to flee until it became too late.

"Thrak'thu nu thelaman," she said.

"And a good day to you too, madam," Khendric answered with a shivering voice. It hadn't come out as confident as he had wanted at all.

She lowered her blade and bent her knees, entering a stance unknown to him. In a flash, he aimed and fired, but she dodged with inhuman reflexes. He fired again and again, but before his eyes registered her movements, her voreen blade entered his gut, piercing through his body. *I didn't even see her close the distance.* Unbelievable pain forced him to his knees.

She towered over him, triumphantly, and retracted the blade, making him wail in pain. A devious smile spread across her lips.

His skin stitched itself together, but way slower than usual.

Her triumphant stare turned to confusion; she probably expected a deathwalker to appear soon. Gripping his collar, she lifted him into the air easily. "Shar tha naku!" She raised her blade once more and readied for a swing.

Khendric had dropped his weapons and tried to break out of her hold. He kicked at her, but she didn't even react. The strength of his hands couldn't match a fraction of the force behind her grip, and drawing breath became impossible. He closed his eyes for the incoming decapitation—

A mighty horn bellowed in the distance, taking her attention. Dropping Khendric to the ground, she turned toward the charging cavalry. He crashed to the ground, desperately drawing breath. To his horror, she laughed as the thunder of hooves reached their ears, and charged them head-on.

* * *

"Get up! Fire at will!" Topper's words rang across the ridge. "Fire, fire, fire! Slow her down!"

Grasping her surroundings, Ara realized the full contingent of archers dispersed behind rocks and trees, notching their arrows. The voreen ran across the grassy fields with speed matching the incoming horses. The archers released and a volley of arrows rained down around the voreen, but none hit her.

"It's too fast," Ara said. "Way too fast."

The voreen came to a stop, her eyes tracking the arc of the projectiles. Another volley rained around her, but she gracefully avoided every tip.

"No way," Topper said hopelessly. "Hold your fire. The cavalry is too close. Infantry, with me!" The archers put their bows down and drew swords, falling in behind armoured soldiers getting into formation behind Topper and her.

The stampeding cavalry clashed with the voreen and her mighty sword spun around impossibly fast, sending soldiers into the air, slicing and dicing her foes with inhuman strength. The massive blade she wielded decapitated a horse while she flew above its rider, before she landed on her feet with ease, dodging a lance coming for her head.

"Here," Topper said, putting a large battle-axe in Ara's tainted hand. "Help us kill this thing."

The hairs on her arms rose and fear settled in her stomach. *Fight that?*

She opened her mouth, but Topper cut her off, saying "We need you."

"But, I can't—"

"Stop thinking. We're all afraid. Get angry! Get brave!" He walked in front of the soldiers. "This creature in front of us is but a mere minion of the monster trying to demolish your city! Ashbourn bleeds, but we'll staunch the wound and kill that which harms it!"

Some surrounding soldiers nodded and slammed their swords on their shields, and it worked. Ara felt braver, her blood beginning to boil.

"We are going to kill this voreen and send a message to Chronor that the people of Ashbourn will NOT bend!"

The soldiers roared in unison, and Ara couldn't help but join. They hammered their swords into their shield rhythmically and roared like beasts.

Topper lifted his sword toward the voreen. "CHAAAARGE!"

Ara tightened her grip on the axe and ran at full speed ahead, feeling vibrations under her feet as all the soldiers followed. The voreen slaughtered the cavalry, dancing around the battlefield with such athletic prowess it put humanity to shame. As they neared, the day mysteriously darkened, as if night approached. *Voreen magic,* she realized, *not good.*

She spotted Khendric sprinting to join the battle as well, but he had a long way to go. Ara couldn't believe how much ground the voreen had covered, given how far away Khendric was, but they would surround their adversary with the remaining cavalry and infantry.

The voreen spun circles in the air, slicing four soldiers apart, before landing solidly on the reddening grass. There she stood with bloodied blade in hand, barely winded, as the surrounding darkness thickened . . . the dead began to rise.

"Deathwalkers!" Ara shouted.

"Prepare yourselves!" Topper bellowed as they closed the final distance and the soldiers roared mightily.

The voreen prepared herself for them, but a bullet ricocheted off her blade and stole her attention. Khendric fired his remaining shots, but the voreen dodged inhumanely quickly, and surprised Ara as she leapt towards the infantry. Their shields braced for impact, but her mighty swing carved through the steel and wood—and the men themselves. Ara ducked, saving herself with sheer reflex. She wanted to retaliate, but had no room to use the massive axe.

The voreen barely landed before barrelling through three soldiers with her shoulder, and delivered a massive strike, killing too many. Her sword kept going, severing flesh from bone—Topper's shield survived the impact and he forced her sword to the grass. The voreen's eyes refocused on him, gritting her teeth and—Khendric came in flying, planting both boots in the voreen's side. The soldiers had enough time to flock her and came in for the kill.

Before any sharp edge could harm her, she lunged high into the air, flipping backwards out of her certain doom.

The soldiers and Ara seemed perplexed for a moment at the insane athleticism, which cost them dearly, because as soon as her feet touched the ground she darted forward and killed several soldiers. A rider came in for a swing, but she dodged and spun out of the way, her massive blade reaching the man on top—his armour saving him by an inch.

An opportunistic soldier saw his chance and stepped forward with a chance to maim her, but a deathwalker grabbed him and tore his stomach open—a dangerous reminder for Ara to keep her eyes focused. More and more deadly red eyes roamed the grassy fields. She tried following the voreen's movements, but so did every other soldier, and she had trouble keeping her balance.

Topper charged the voreen, but she thrust her blade through his shield easily, and he narrowly avoided the edge of the weapon; based on the look on his face, he seemed surprised.

Taking advantage of the lodged blade, however, Topper pushed the voreen's weapon into the ground again, giving a soldier an opening to stab her in the thigh. Ara rushed forward to strike as well, but in the chaos Khendric stepped in front of her, blocking her path. His sword bounced off the voreen's apparently tough skin.

She wanted to push Khendric aside, but he spun around and put his arms around her, turning her gaze toward the ground. "Deathwalker!" he screamed. The voreen blade could split them apart at any time, but didn't and the deathwalker passed through them. More and more horrendous screams rang through the air as soldiers lost their lives to the risen dead. Nobody could help them, and the longer this continued the more there would be. *We have to stop her fast.*

Khendric let go and Ara's eyes found the voreen in the thick of battle, slicing soldiers apart. They ran towards her, but she threw her blade in their direction, suddenly disappearing out of sight with a blast of smoke. Her hands re-formed around the hilt of the spinning blade and her whole body followed in a flash of black mist. Ara and Khendric had little time to react to the unknown voreen magic, but her attention and blade fell on her closest prey.

"We must kill her quickly!" Ara screamed. "She's only going to get more dangerous."

Deathwalkers sprung to life with every soldier falling to the voreen blade, their numbers dwindling. Ara hadn't done *anything* this whole fight, outmanoeuvred at every step, but finally she joined the ring of soldiers surrounding the voreen.

"Don't look into their eyes!" Khendric yelled, as he tried a useless stab.

The voreen looked at him, and then at Ara, narrowing her eyes. "Thentah'an tu Chronor!" she yelled, dashing forward and striking down the soldier right next to Ara. "Thentah'an tu Chronor!"

Ara had no idea what she meant and lifted her axe for her first strike, but the voreen stepped into the attack and grasped Ara's forearm, pulling her closer. Ara stumbled to the ground at the voreen's mercy. *I'm going to become a deathwalker,* she thought despairingly. But . . . nothing happened to her. The battle raged around her, metal splitting apart, soldiers screaming as life left their bodies, but no harm fell upon Ara.

When she dared to look, the voreen stood above her and fended off any attacker. Broad and wide swings made it impossible for anyone to close the gap as she seemed to protect Ara. *My arm?* Her eyes fell to the dark veins and she wondered if they had saved her life. *Stop it. Act,* she reminded herself. Her axe laid too far away, but a dozen swords littered the ground. Her fingers wrapped around a handle and she got to her feet behind the voreen. With no hesitation, she drove the tip in between the voreen's shoulderblades with every ounce of strength. It dug through her flesh and protruded through her chest.

Everything stilled. No scream from her. No cry. Nothing except for a wide open mouth as she looked to the sky. Her mighty weapon fell to the ground.

"They found her," Chronor cried from the recesses of Ara's mind.

The voreen turned to Ara and fell to her knees. She looked confused. Betrayed perhaps? Her eyes pierced Ara with anger. She tried to form words, but spat dark blood instead. Ara met her stare until the voreen fell limp to the ground, dead.

A breeze rolled over the battlefield of red grass and ghosts. None cheered at their foe's downfall. Instead, they all breathed hard. Their army had been severely reduced, but they had made it at a large cost.

"Look to the ground!" Topper's deep voice echoed across the field. "Look to the ground. Don't make eye contact with the deathwalkers. No one will save you if you do."

Khendric approached Ara next to the voreen. "Are you alright?"

"Chronor knows," she said. "Khendric, he knows we killed her. We have to go."

He chewed his mouth in uncertainty, his eyes searching hers. "Alright," he said, nodding. "Everybody get back to Ashbourn! We are out of this forsaken place. Keep your eyes down." Tired and sad soldiers began walking away, their pace slow. Too many had died to get this blade, and Ara hoped it would be worth it.

Ara and Khendric remained and Topper joined them, while soldiers passed by. The darkness receded and sunlight broke through.

"You couldn't tell me," Ara said.

They shook their heads. "We couldn't," Khendric said. "In case he would know of our plan, so we had to deceive you."

"I thought I'd never see you again."

"We were terrified you'd do something foolish and get yourself killed," Topper said with a half-smile. "We'll talk about it when we get back to Koradin."

"He's a part of this too?"

"Of course," Khendric said. "These are his troops."

She felt foolish for wondering if he was a traitor.

"Ara. I need you to pick up that blade." Khendric pointed to the green dark voreen weapon on the ground, stained with blood. "*That* is the reason you are here. None of us can carry it and we're *really* hoping you can."

The vicious blade laid at her feet and she got down to a knee. She closed her fingers around the handle. The huge sword stretched as far as Ara's body. She sucked in a deep breath and lifted the sword from the ground with her dark arm easily. It felt light in her hand, and she raised it towards the sky.

"Yes!" Khendric punched the air with one hand. "It actually worked!"

She pulled them both into a crushing hug. They returned it, and the familiar warmth spread through her body.

"We've got to go," Khendric said. "Keep your eyes down." They joined the rest of the soldiers, Ara with the massive blade in hand. She couldn't believe how hopeful she felt after reuniting with Khendric and Topper. They left the grassy fields behind in a worse condition, with countless deathwalkers roaming around. She hoped she could make the terrible price they'd paid worth it.

* * *

A growing worry festered in Koradin's stomach. Had his small army prevailed over the voreen or had they all been slaughtered? If they were all dead, Ashbourn would be lost. It was past midday and the sun actually shone, though nightfall came earlier every day.

He should be out there fighting by their side, but Chronor would probably know if he went missing. So he hoped his small army could bring home the precious blade. *If Ara can even carry it.* A stab of guilt made him scrunch his face. He had helped deceive that poor young woman. Hopefully, she had been reunited with Khendric and Topper and they could stop lying. *As long as they're still alive.*

Koradin had skipped the last council meeting because they would ask about the missing troops and uselessly berate him. For now, he hid in the massive tower of his estate with an excellent view over the city. His mansion resembled a smaller castle and had been built into the wall of Ashbourn, placing him exactly where he needed to be. All three of his daughters and wife were with him in the tower. He stared out over the city, while the others discussed what to do if his plan failed, and the more time dragged on, the more his gut feeling told him they were right. And he knew the only sensible thing to do if this plan failed was to flee.

"Together," Matt's voice said. *"We can beat him."*

Koradin sighed, thankful for the pharlanax's words, but couldn't answer. If he let them know about the conscious ancient being inside his head, they'd think him crazy.

The door burst open and Koradin turned sharply to see Garys, his most trusted messenger, completely out of breath. "They're back," he shouted, panting. "They're back!"

Koradin and his family all followed the messenger through the guarded hallways of his mansion. Every soldier they passed left their station and joined the growing ensemble as they reached the terrace overlooking the vast fields outside the city. In the far distance, an army approached.

"They're waving just one torch," Garys said and pointed.

"What?" Koradin grabbed the spyglass from him.

"Over there!" Garys pointed and Koradin saw easily only one torch with his enhanced vision, next to a large dark-green voreen blade. *They made it.* It had come at a heavy cost; the army greatly reduced.

"I don't believe it," Koradin said, astonished.

"Give me that," Lenda said and looked for herself. "I don't believe it either."

"We have to initiate the plan now," he said to Garys. "Tell Commander Relen to take out the guards." Garys nodded and ran off to find the commander. Koradin turned to his wife and three daughters. "Don't leave the Headquarters, okay?"

They nodded, and Lenda grabbed his chin and gave him a gentle kiss. Her eyes said, "Don't let it be our final one." He leaned in for a real passionate kiss, and embraced her in a hug. His beautiful daughters joined. "I love all of you," he said. "And whatever happens, know that I'm forever proud of you all."

They didn't want him to go, and in truth, he didn't want to either, but he was a king. His eyes ran over them one final time and he left, running down all the levels of the building, grabbed a horse and rode to the barracks. He stormed through the door to the main hall, drawing everyone's attention. "It's on! We're initiating 'Operation Dark God'. Captains, get your men to positions, NOW!" The captains saluted sharply and began shouting orders of their own.

"You heard him! Move! Get up on that wall!" Captain Husk barked.

"Get to the gates!" Captain Meavers roared.

Koradin ran through every barracks until all soldiers had been informed. In little time the whole area had transformed from silence into the clanking of armour from thousands of soldiers. They used no bells or horns to alert the initiation of Operation Dark God, wanting to keep a low profile and not alert the other districts.

Koradin travelled with the soldiers and before long ascended a wall beaming with people. Orders rang through the darkening day. He looked at his oncoming reduced army as they neared the gate to the city.

"That was easy," a familiar voice sounded from beside him—Commander Jack Relen.

"Jack?" Koradin asked. "But what about—"

"As I said: that was easy. We chained and gagged the guards and my men are keeping the entrance safe."

Koradin breathed a sigh of relief. Chronor had posted Ashbourn soldiers outside all gates to the city to keep anyone from leaving. Koradin hadn't done anything about it to keep the malevolent god from posting more soldiers just for this occasion.

He faced the Headquarters, which rose proudly in the distance in the looming darkness. He knew the council would know something was happening by now, but he would deal with them soon. He turned to stare deeper into Ashbourn, and the quiet concerned him. He'd hoped to see some reaction from Chronor, but perhaps the god didn't know yet.

The clatter of armour dampened and soldiers stood proudly at their stations. The Meritocrat wall looked fiercer than ever.

Jack found him again and said, "They have successfully entered the city. They're on their way to the Headquarters as we speak."

"Perfect. You take control here and I'll attend to the headquarters. If anything should happen, you know what to do."

Jack saluted and took control of the wall.

Koradin rode hard to the Headquarters, accompanied by Jack's most trusted people. He took a direct route through the empty streets, hoping not to pass the beast hunters and the brave army. He had other business to attend to first.

The gate of the headquarters opened as he arrived, and he and his party dismounted at the entrance. Koradin walked determined through the halls and hallways, his trusted guard at his heels, their armour clanking together. The people inside offered a wide berth, clearly seeing he had somewhere to be. He felt better now that the gears of resistance finally turned, and swung open the doors to the council room. All members were present—with an audience, too. Koradin strode inside.

"Finally!" Ponther exclaimed. "There you are, just in time to answer for this-this act of WAR!"

Koradin walked to the centre of the room, his guards waiting by the door. "Ladies and gentlemen. I am hereby taking control of the Meritocrat District and all its assets."

Audible gasps reached his ears and the people in the council room looked at each other, confused.

"Who do you think you are?" Ponther shouted down at him and many others raised their voices in protest. "You can't do that!"

"I am doing it. Our armies are following my commands and we're initiating the defence Ashbourn needs against Chronor, the ancient voreen god."

"There is no proof—"

"Sit down, Ponther!" Aeba commanded, rising from her seat. "The evidence is clear. You're willfully blinded!"

Taken by surprise, Ponther and his followers fell silent.

"Thank you Aeba," Koradin said. "Chronor is a very real threat to our great city and I am taking necessary action."

"You are not king anymore!" Ponther pointed out with a calmer tone, and his zealots agreed with him, booing Koradin.

"That is true," Koradin replied, turning to Ponther's supporters. "But the soldiers have a habit of following me, having been king for such a long time. So you are without an army, and I am with one." He fished out a sheet of paper from his pocket. "This is a contract, written by myself and approved by officials of the Meritocrat Party. If I am indeed wrong and we can say so with certainty, I am to be jailed for ten or more years—with no chance of reducing the sentence—for seizing control of the district. You may take it or not, but I assure you I *am* in power, at least for now. Let us hope we can defend this city." He looked around the room. Aeba smiled wildly. Some faces stayed scorned, while others seemed hopeful and excited.

"For Ashbourn," Koradin said.

"FOR ASHBOURN!" all the soldiers in the room and at the door shouted. Aeba hammered her fist on the table in front of her and joined the choir. Ponther had been deflated, knowing no power rested at the whims of his fingers anymore. Koradin turned and left the room, feeling a fire burning within him that had been dormant for years.

* * *

Ara sat on a chair in the same planning room she had been shunned from before, deep within the headquarters. The army had dispersed and only she, Khendric and Topper were there. An unsettling feeling within her mind wouldn't let go. It had grown ever since they entered Asbourn, but she couldn't put her finger on what it was. The door stayed closed, but countless feet shuffled past outside, voices screaming and shouting. *Something is definitely happening,* Ara thought, hoping it was a good sign.

The doors opened and Adenar, Koradin, Lenda and Aeba entered. Koradin and his ensemble stopped in front of the table where Ara had put the voreen blade. She had cleaned it, but it still looked menacing with its deep dark and green pattern that faintly glowed, making it look almost alive. She still couldn't believe they had such a weapon. Soldiers closed the doors to the room.

"Ara," Koradin said. "I must apologise to you. We laid the plan to seek out and find the voreen. While Khendric and Topper did so, I snuck out small units of soldiers that would help bring it down. When I got word the beast hunters had tracked it down, we had to get you out there, but we couldn't tell you anything about the plan, in case Chronor could somehow find out. And . . . I take it you know the rest. We all hated having to leave you in the dark. I am sorry."

"It's alright," she said, smirking at him. "It was a good plan and I'm glad you did it."

Koradin lowered his shoulders.

"And while wallowing in my pain I did something useful too," Ara said. "I got my hands on doombringer dust."

"What?" they answered in unison, all raising their eye brows.

"I went with Darlaene and—"

"Darlaene is alive?" Khendric interrupted.

"Yes. She's working with Elrich and me, hence she's probably in the Passionist District."

"Good," Khendric said, trying to hide the large smile on his face.

"Anyway," Ara continued, "I got my hands on doombringer dust with Darlaene from a man known as the Collector."

Koradin seemed even more surprised and chuckled. "The Collector?"

"Do you know of him?"

"I do, but I didn't think he was still in Ashbourn. Originally, I thought I hanged him, but it turned out to be some unfortunate look-alike. I only found out years later and didn't think he'd come back to the city, but perhaps the regime shift gave him courage. He's a slippery man."

"We had to trade the book for it," Ara said.

"What?" Topper asked.

"But we have Aeba's copy," Ara quickly answered.

"That's great," Koradin said, making Ara relax. "I'll have my best blacksmith forge a weapon with the dust. Good job. I have initiated Operation Dark God. The district's army is on high alert and we're prepared for war. Ara, do you know if Chronor knows what we have done?"

"I'm fairly certain. He knows we killed the voreen at least. I heard it."

A solemn silence fell over the table before Koradin said, "That's why we are on high alert. My soldiers are ready for an attack. We have to wait and see what he'll do, but we have to lay our plan of action too."

"We won't win an all-out war," Aeba pointed out. "Our army is somewhere around one-third the size of theirs."

"You're right," Koradin said. "We can't lead an assault. We have to defend ourselves."

"An assassination?" Khendric offered.

Koradin narrowed his eyes. "Could work, but it's risky. If failed, we'd lose the weapons and have no chance of winning."

"Besides," Adenar said. "Chronor has eyes all over the city—or so we can assume. All those people with dark eyes must have *some* link to him."

"Right now, we're blind," Koradin said.

"There's got to be some reason he's not attacking outright," Ara said. "I think he needs us alive for—"

Knock-knock-knock-knock-knock.

Adenar rushed to open the door and in stormed another soldier, breathing heavily. "Koradin," he said through breaths. "Something . . . something is happening . . . at the wall. You have to come."

"Are we under attack?" Koradin asked.

"No, but . . . it's easier if you see for yourself. Quickly!"

✳ ✳ ✳

They rode hard through the night towards the wall, Koradin leading the way, followed by Khendric, Topper, Adenar, Ara, and a sizeable group of soldiers.

They reached the wall, dismounted, and rushed up the nearby stairs. Ara did her best to follow, thankful to have left the blade at the Headquarters. Hopefully, Chronor wouldn't attack too soon.

Commander Relen waited at the top. "What is going on?" Koradin demanded, not even winded from the ride, while Ara fought to keep her breathing under control.

"It's peculiar," Commander Relen said, motioning Koradin to step closer to the wall. "Listen."

Not a single light beyond the wall was visible, playing a trick on Ara's mind. It looked like Ashbourn ended beyond their wall; a giant void. How could *every* light source be off? No moon aided them either.

It was unnerving, making every hair on Ara's body raise. Chronor's control became apparent.

A sound emanated from the darkness; the sound of thousands of feet creeping closer to the wall. Every pair of eyes on the wall faced the darkness, peering beyond to see anything. Ara felt just as uncomfortable as all the other soldiers, their faces pale.

"What is that?" Khendric asked the commander.

"Sounds like . . . an endless horde of people walking closer," he answered, and Ara knew he was right. She felt it. She felt *them* coming closer.

It came from everywhere beyond the wall. Koradin grabbed a torch from a nearby soldier and tossed it out into the darkest night. It soared through the air and landed on the ground, lighting up exactly what Ara had feared: a thick crowd of barely lit people walking toward them like a heard of sheep . . . then, it was snuffed out.

"It's people," Koradin said.

"It's *all* the people," Ara said. "It's all the people of Ashbourn."

The light of the torches on the wall lit up the nearby area and from the darkness below emerged the endless mass of dark-eyed people along the whole wall around the district. Ara's mouth fell open. Khendric and Topper's eyes widened and Koradin placed both hands on the wall at the staggering sight.

The previous king barred his teeth in anger. "Not all of them," Koradin answered.

"I think Chronor's plan has begun," Ara said. Her insides churned, but Adenar grabbed her hand. He looked worried too, but it offered her some strength. She squeezed his hand back, and a weak smile spread across his lips.

"We are ready," Koradin said, staring out over the supposedly endless sea of dark-eyed citizens.

CHAPTER 8

Remnants of Ancient Warriors

Rhakta, The Master of Skulls, detested Chronor with his entire being, envious of Chronor's divinity. Rhakta, The Master of Skulls, wanted to become a god and devoted his life to discover how to ascend to godhood.

Rhakta, The Master of Skulls, was the fiercest fighter of all the voreen, besting every opponent that posed any challenge. Seeking mastership in duelling and handling the blade became dangerous, because Rhakta, The Master of Skulls, would seek out any skilled voreen and put an end to them, and was feared by all. His tribe became dominant until Chronor was summoned.

From 'The Dark Traitor', chapter sixteen.

The sun finally rose from behind the mountain, proving Ara's worst fear to be true. Every citizen from the three other districts stood outside their wall, all with dark eyes, all under Chronor's control. Her heart ached, and her mind tried to tell her to flee. Their angry, animalistic expressions made them all the more terrifying. She couldn't believe the number of people stretching into every street as far as the eye could see, packed to the absolute fullest. She ran her fingers over the voreen blade, the mighty weapon granting her some strength.

Koradin looked horrified too as the sun cast light over the city. These were his people—or had been.

The dark-eyed people stood so close together that manoeuvring through them would be difficult. Bakers, smiths, street urchins, bankers, soldiers, sailors—everyone. All with hungry eyes fixated on the Meritocrat wall. Ara's hope of living through this paled as endless stares drilled into her. *How can we stand against this?*

She wasn't alone in her despairing thoughts on the wall. Soldiers slumped their shoulders, standing in hunched-over positions and gazed upon their doom. *This is what Chronor wants,* she thought.

"How many do you reckon there are?" Khendric asked Koradin with a calm voice.

"More than seven hundred thousand," he answered. "Chronor is using everyone, not just soldiers."

"He's trying to intimidate us," Ara said. "He's trying to break our spirit."

Koradin shot glances at his surrounding soldiers. "It's working too."

"How many do we have?" Topper asked.

"Soldiers? Around twenty-five thousand."

"And residents?" Khendric wondered.

"Somewhere around two hundred thousand. We're devastatingly outnumbered."

"Arm any who can carry a weapon," Khendric said. "We need every soul."

"Few of them have weapons," Ara pointed out, looking at the endless horde. "If we arm every capable person, we're going to stand a better chance."

Koradin gazed out over the city. "Commander Relen, see to that it happens. Also, clean the square in front of the gate and set up pavilions and tents. We're going to need a base closer to the wall."

"Yes, my King," Commander Relen saluted and hurried off.

Koradin let out a deep breath. "I didn't think he would use the citizens. There are even children down there." He clenched his jaw, gazing down at all those people he'd been king for all these years.

"What are we going to do?" Ara asked.

"I'm open to suggestions." He turned away from the threatening sight. "It's thanks to you that we have a fighting chance. I cannot ask any more of you."

"You can be greedier than that," Khendric answered with his sly smile. "I mean, you clearly need more help."

To Ara's surprise, a tiny smile spread across Koradin's lips. "Thank you."

"I've seen Ara fight with a hammer," Khendric said. "I can't wait to see what she can do with that fierce blade."

"But that does bring up a problem of morality," Koradin said. "These are my citizens, my people. I don't want to kill them."

"I understand," Khendric said. "But they *will* kill you and everyone else in here."

Koradin gave him a hard look, but Khendric returned it and stood firm. "You're right," the king said. He turned towards his soldiers in the square. "This is Chronor's strategy! To scare you! To make us feel small, but we are not! We are taking a stand against him and he *will* feel our strength! He will come to understand the might of our army. Stand tall! One day, this will—"

"Koradin," Khendric interrupted. "Look."

Koradin turned around and laid his eyes upon a dreadful sight.

Like fish around an octinara, the massive crowd dispersed around a figure. Ara's eyes widened as the tall voreen god strode towards them. The sound his dark otherwordly armour made as he walked reached all the way to where they stood on the wall. The armour burned with green flame on each separate piece, moving slower than natural, dancing lazily on the edges of the black mystical metal. His eyes also bore a green, flickering flame. He stopped a good distance from the wall, and a dark-green blade slowly materialized from black smoke in his hand—Souleater. The huge weapon had a long shaft with a spiked cross-guard and a dark green stone at the pommel. A large menacing helmet hid Chronor's head, his voreen spikes protruding through the helmet somehow.

Ara stood frozen in place, stunned. Khendric and Topper seemed as paralyzed as her.

Koradin held his hand around the hilt of his sword, but it remained in its scabbard. "We let Ashbourn fall to this?" he said through gritted teeth.

No answer escaped Ara's lips, her eyes glued to the monstrosity before them.

Four seemingly random people with dark eyes walked into the circle around Chronor; three women and one man, all holding knives or similar weapons. They stood with their backs to the voreen god. In front of them, magical green fire burned lines into the ground, forming various symbols that made up a ritual Ara recognized. They looked just like what Viessa Toran had made to summon the shadowwalker. The circles lit suddenly with fire and a sinking sensation hit Ara's stomach.

"Tell me that isn't—" Topper began.

"The shadowwalker ritual," Khendric answered.

"Shadowwalker?" Koradin asked.

"You're about to see," Khendric said.

One of the women began cutting off her arm with the crude knife in her hand. No screams left her mouth as the knife cut deep into her flesh and blood spattered the ground. Her arm fell into the dark fire, and black smoke burst forth from the circles in a violent torrent, spinning around the woman before forming the dark figure that made up the terrible shadowwalker. It knelt on the ground in front of the woman.

Chronor pushed the small woman away and took a step closer. Once the shadowwalker noticed him, it lunged backwards, but Chronor's quick fingers locked around its neck. He lifted it off the ground as it fought to break free. "It is good to see you," Chronor's deep, unnatural voice rang through the air. "King Thindar of the Storm Mountains. These humans will never understand the courage you proved to me on that day ages ago. And now you are back to serve."

A leash seared itself into existence around the shadowwalker's neck. It writhed in agony, twisting and clawing at it with its arms. Chronor held his former servant until the fiery leash fully formed around its neck.

"Welcome back to servitude," Chronor said, dropping the dark figure to the ground. "King Thindar of the Storm Mountains." The shadowwalker landed in a kneeling position. Chronor walked to the next person in line with the same circles ahead of her.

"How do we fight them?" Koradin asked Khendric.

"Any weapon damages them," Khendric said. "But they can withstand a lot of damage, and they don't slow. You have to attack and attack until they vanish."

"You!" Koradin commanded three nearby soldiers. "Did you hear that? Spread the message along the wall, scream it at the top of your lungs!" The soldiers did as commanded. "Archers!"

Bowmen approached rapidly, lining up on the wall.

"He's about to summon three more isn't he?" Koradin asked Khendric.

"Yes."

"Archers, knock arrows!"

Chronor dropped his second servant, a leash forming around its neck. "My greatest challenger." His dark voice still rang above all the clatter on the wall. "Rhakta, The Master of Skulls." He towered over the kneeling shadowwalker. "You took it all from me, all my greatest creations. But there can only be one god and his *servants*. You are the latter."

"Aim at the leftmost shadowwalker," Koradin commanded. "Fire!" Arrows flew through the air.

"Go," Chronor commanded, waving a dismissive hand, and walked to the next dark-eyed victim. The horde split to give the shadowwalkers a clear runway.

Both of his warriors sprang into action, charging the wall with incredible speed. Arrows embedded themselves in their bodies, but they didn't slow. The nearby citizens were slaughtered though, but others took their place.

"Swords out!" Koradin roared, pulling his huge sword from its scabbard. The metal had a weak orange hue, and Ara noticed engraved glyphs along the fuller of the sword.

The shadowwalkers didn't head for them though, instead running further down the wall before scaling it with ease.

"Ara!" Khendric yelled. "Go with Topper and deal with them!"

Ara clutched the long voreen blade in her hand and nodded. Topper unsheathed a greatsword himself, and they took off running.

* * *

Koradin watched the two beast hunters run towards the shadowwalkers, which slaughtered his soldiers. *Why aren't they attacking here?*

The poor man in front of Chronor sawed his leg off; a third shadowwalker would be upon them soon.

"It's a show," Matt said in Koradin's mind. *"He wants to prove his superiority."*

"Step aside," Khendric roared, shoving an archer aside and pulled out his pistol. He aimed and squeezed off three shots in Chronor's direction, none striking the god.

The man in front of Chronor slumped to the ground, abruptly ending the summoning of the next shadowwalker.

Chronor's gaze fell upon Khendric, and as if a sign of respect, inclined his head. He reached out a hand towards the crowd and a young boy wandered to the dark fire.

"No," Koradin said aghast, feeling like a stone dropped in his stomach.

"You monster," Khendric said.

The little boy picked up the bloody saw.

Chronor took a step back and gestured towards the boy with a challenging expression.

Khendric took aim, clenching his teeth.

"Khendric," Koradin said. "Don't—"

"Shut up!" Khendric held his pistol up, but lingered. "Damn it!" he yelled and lowered his weapon. Koradin put a hand on his shoulder, but Khendric shrugged it off. "Don't touch me!" He turned to Koradin, eyes red with tears and dropped the pistol to the stone. He put both hands to his temples and screamed maniacally, falling to his knees. "He's in my head!"

Koradin didn't have time for this and sent Khendric flying down the staircase and away from the battle.

"*He will heal,*" Matt muttered in his head.

The little boy sawed off his hand, and Chronor leashed the new shadowwalker.

"*We must kill this monster.*"

"Fire at the new shadowwalker," Koradin commanded.

All the archers took aim.

* * *

Ara and Topper reached the shadowwalkers, which had slaughtered countless soldiers and mercilessly continued their brutality. Ara ran over corpses trying not to stumble with her massive blade. She neared the most hurt shadowwalker as it spun and slashed its dark weapons into two soldiers. It had its back to her, bleeding smoke profusely, as she stabbed her sword through its back. It exploded into smoke and vanished

The other one turned sharply and lunged away from Ara and Topper while taking a spear through the calf mid-air.

Landing in a spin, it struck a soldier dead and continued fighting, placing a wall of soldiers between itself and Ara.

"It's scared of you," Topper shouted as he barreled forward through the people in front of them, and Ara truly appreciated his size.

The shadowwalker pushed further away at the cost of more weapons piercing its being, but Ara and Topper caught up. It kicked away a soldier and turned to her, raising both swords to parry Ara's mighty slash, stopping her voreen blade, but wavered under her strength and had to push her blade aside as multiple swords stabbed it. Topper darted forward and slashed his huge sword right through its leg.

Unfazed, it charged Topper and slashed at his chest. Topper grunted and threw himself backwards. Ara stepped in front of him, but the creature used the opportunity to slice at the soldiers behind it.

Ara did her best to follow the shadowwalker, but it jumped and landed perfectly on the edge of the wall, battering away swords as smoke gushed out of its injured body.

A mighty kick from the shadowwalker sent a soldier flying, creating a path for Ara and she caught up, but her swing missed entirely as the creature moved too fast, dodging and sidestepping out of the path of her assault, yet taking other blades to its body. Ara followed with another downward strike, but the creature sidestepped her and slid across the stony ground, slicing its shadow-daggers over her chest. She staggered to the ground and checked to see if she bled, but the armour took the blow.

The creature slid into a cluster of soldiers, continuing the killing spree.

Ara got back up on her feet. She caught up to the shadowwalker and attacked desperately, but it parried or dodged every strike, pushing away from her. The smoke trails it left behind made it hard to see exactly where it was, but she just kept moving forward. "Face me!" she yelled, growing tired of the evasiveness.

It turned and looked her dead in the eyes—a spearhead shot through the shadowwalker's chest and took it by surprise, sealing its fate. Ara's blade separated its head from the rest and it released its final wave of smoke.

As the dust settled, one frightened man became visible behind the shadowwalker with a part of his helmet cut off—Commander Relen. He removed the helmet and ran his hands over his scalp. "Guess I should be happy I am not a tall man."

She'd been inches away from killing Koradin's most trusted ally, and she exhaled slowly. "Are you okay?"

He nodded and turned around. "There are two more. You go, and I'll take care of your friend." He got down on a knee next to Topper, who clutched his chest.

"Topper are you okay?" she asked.

He gritted his teeth together and waved her away. "Yes-yes, now go! I'll live."

* * *

Koradin stormed the two shadowwalkers with the rest of his council guard, but he outran them all with ease, and held his blade, Mattronia, tight in his hand. She felt good in his hand, lending him courage. "For Ashbourn!" he roared as he attacked the closest shadowwalker, which blocked his sword, but it struggled beneath his strength and staggered, suffering several stabs in the back from surrounding soldiers. It side-stepped and darted towards Koradin with a blade heading for his bowels, but with supernatural speed, he grabbed the creature's shadowy hand and twisted it. It felt like grabbing something solid and fluid at the same time. For a moment, the shadowwalker appeared shocked, before Koradin pummelled it in the face. It crashed into his men and Koradin followed quickly, his long sword entering the creature's stomach. It combusted from where his blade pierced it, leaving behind a blanket of smoke.

Koradin didn't waste time and scouted the area for the second one, but his soldiers had killed it. "Great job! Now get the wounded out of here." Too many had been killed, and they seemed battered by the fight. Blood made the ground slippery, and they had to clear the area quickly before it got worse. "Get strollers for those brave souls who gave their lives for our freedom."

Medical personnel with strollers ran up the stairs to get the wounded out, while the survivors helped carry the dead. Some shed tears, others put on brave faces, and some leaned against the wall and stared into the sky.

Koradin stared out over Chronor's army to spot new threats. The god still stood in his circle. His sacrificial bodies laid dead at his feet, their blood staining the cobblestone.

Anger welled deep within as he stared evil straight in the face. Fresh soldiers lined up beside him, forming another line. A captain with a trimmed brown beard stood by his side, eyes narrowed and focused. Koradin had seen him many times, but did not know his name yet.

"How are you?" Koradin asked."

"I've been better, King Koradin."

"Tell me honestly, do you think we can win?"

The captain pursed his lips and mulled his question over. "I didn't. But seeing how we killed those . . . monsters, perhaps we got a chance."

"Good. Let's hope the rest of the soldiers feel the same way."

"They do," he answered. "This is a good lot."

Chronor walked back through his army, but didn't go far before he turned back. He raised his hand and four new innocent citizens approached, the same circles on the ground bursting to life. They stopped in front of each circle and picked up the bloody weapons.

Please no, Koradin pleaded, letting out a strained breath.

One of the sacrifices hacked his hand off with an axe, and before long, Chronor burned a new collar into his deadly new shadowwalker.

"Now I'm not so sure anymore," the captain said. "*That* does waver my spirit."

"He can just keep them coming, and coming," Koradin whispered, noticing the wave of hopelessness wash over his soldiers. "His supply is endless of sacrificial bodies."

Chronor summoned the second shadowwalker and leashed it too.

Koradin tore himself away from the sight and found the nearest archer. "You. Knock an arrow and see if you can hit from this range."

The archer did as commanded, took aim, and fired. The arrow flew through the air and plunged itself into the body of a dark-eyed citizen, reaching short of the fresh shadowwalkers.

The archer scratched his chin uncertainly. "I'm sorry for that, and I don't think we can hit them from here."

"Get the archers on the first row," Koradin bellowed. "Spears on the second, and stay ready to take them out should they attack!"

The soldiers reacted to his orders, but too many faces revealed the truth.

"We can only get better at taking them down!" Koradin shouted. The archers lined up and drew arrows, while spearmen stood ready behind them.

Koradin watched the horrible sight and the whole city seemed to quiet. The four new shadowwalkers didn't attack. Instead, they faced the wall with menacing poses, smoke shrouding their imposing figures. *It's a mental game,* Koradin realized, and seeing the look on his soldiers, he knew it was working.

Ara arrived with her enormous blade, the captain by Koradin's side giving her his spot. "What's he doing? Why are they just standing there?" she asked, breathing heavily.

"To put fear in our hearts."

"We can't fight them forever," she said. "If that was just the first wave—"

"Then we're in for the longest fight of our lives."

Someone ascended the stairs behind them—not padded boots, but leather. Koradin recognized the deep sigh.

Ponther pushed the soldiers aside and put his hands on the wall, eyes wide as he surveyed the terrible sight. "You were right. I didn't believe you, but you were right."

Koradin felt no joy at hearing those words. "And I'm afraid we're outnumbered," he said.

"What are we going to do?" Ponther asked, terrified, his face the palest on the wall.

"We're working on that," Ara said, but Ponther fled down the stairs and Koradin let him go.

The four shadowwalkers faced them, blades out. Chronor expanded his circle and walked closer to the wall, holding a chain in his hand. The chain wrapped around an unwilling person's neck. Chronor stopped and yanked the man forward. With his arms chained behind his back, he crashed hard into the ground.

Koradin's enhanced vision helped him see that the man's eyes weren't dark. "Who is that?" he asked aloud.

"The Collector," Ara said, a grim expression on her face.

"I must thank you!" Chronor's said, making some of Koradin's men take a warding step back. "You returned my book." From somewhere beneath his menacing armour, Chronor pulled out the dark volume Ara had traded for the doombringer dust. "I know my district well."

"We have the copy, right?" Koradin asked, leaning close.

"I don't know," Ara answered. "Ask Aeba."

"Messenger," he inquired, and a young man came forth. "Find Aeba Therkin and make her check whether her copy of 'The Dark Traitor' is safe."

"Yes, my King," he answered and took off.

"He was easy to find," Chronor continued. "When I am done with *all* of you, nobody will ever lay their eyes upon this most wretched thing again." He tucked it back under his armour.

The Collector wore grey rags and looked pathetic. Koradin had never seen him, but had heard a lot of him and knew this wasn't his usual attire. He had lost everything and was in terrible danger, but he did not cry for mercy.

Chronor laid a huge, tentacled hand on the Collector's back. "You've been most useful." His other hand grabbed the man's face and pulled the head clean off. With a gut-wrenching crack, blood sprayed from his torn neck, and the body fell limp to the ground. Ara and many soldiers gagged as blood pulsated from the corpse, but Koradin just felt his disdain for Chronor grow.

Chronor dropped his head and walked away. His followers ran and tore the collector's body apart, feasting on the fresh body. Many on the wall vomited at the horrific sight, but the king steeled his stomach. "Tomorrow," Chronor said with his huge back turned to them. "You meet your end."

CHAPTER 9

Puppets of a God

When Rhakta, The Master of Skulls, heard Chronor had been summoned, he wanted to kill him and find out how to claim his divine powers. Chronor stayed far away from Rhakta, eluding him. Rhakta, The Master of Skulls, named Chronor a coward and claimed to be of equal stature.

But then, Chronor did seek him out. The god made sure to reach his final phase first and planned to make Rhakta, The Master of Skulls, into one of his most dangerous warriors.

- From 'The Dark Traitor', chapter sixteen.

The rays of the sun didn't shine as much as they used too, dimmed by some invisible force. The weaker light added to the sombre mood in the district, where every head hung low, and every sigh seemed too audible. Sitting atop the wall and staring at their impending doom, Ara struggled to find positive thoughts amidst the rubble of darkness hanging over her.

She'd been reading her red book about different beasts, and it helped calm her down. Aeba had reported that the copy of the black book was intact, so it didn't really matter if Chronor had the original.

"Your time has come," Chronor's voice spoke, causing Ara to flinch. *"Die."*

Her heart rate rose, but she tried breathing calmly, keeping her eyes on the hoard outside to see if anything changed. Blocking out his words was hard as they were literally inside her head, so she let out yet another hopeless sigh. Being alone didn't help either, but Topper helped Koradin with planning in the newly set up pavilions. She'd been certain his wound would kill him, but he shrugged it off and got it stitched shortly after.

Her hand subconsciously tried grabbing the hilt of the voreen blade, but it had been hidden from her. Topper had blindfolded and walked her to some unknown location to stow the sword away and lead her back, in hopes of Chronor not knowing where it was either. If she carried it with her, chances were too great that he would find and kill her. Topper promised it was close, though. Khendric and Koradin knew its location too, apparently, in case he died.

Someone walked up the stairs behind her and sat down next to her. "Thought I'd find you up here," Khendric said, wearing his large hat and coat again. He didn't look entirely defeated.

"I heard what happened," Ara said.

Khendric chuckled. "Great. So everyone knows Koradin threw me down the stairs because of . . . well, it's not important."

"Did it hurt?"

"I don't remember."

"It's your past, isn't it?"

Khendric looked forlorn as he nodded, eye straight ahead, his tongue picking at some phantom thing between two of his teeth.

"He used your past when we fought him the first time too. Chronor took one sniff of your arm and then—"

"I know. Alright?" His eyes fell.

Ara sighed before saying, "For being so tough and so incredibly capable, you're the most emotional person I know."

Khendric furrowed his brow and looked at her with an offended expression. "You have *no* idea what I've been through."

She shook her head slowly. "No, but *he* does. Chronor knows, somehow, and he's using it against you."

No answer escaped his lips.

"No one else is reporting: the past coming back to haunt them," Ara said. "I don't understand why it happens to you."

He leaned back and put his hands against the ground. "I think it's because I've had his venom in me." His thick voice tried to hide something. "You had your nightmare in Cornstead, and then you were done. I don't know how it works, but being near him now . . . I can see them, as clearly as I remember them."

"Your parents?" Her eyes searched his face.

Khendric opened his mouth to reply, but no words came.

"His venom probably has different effects on different people. We don't know which phase Chronor was in when his venom entered you, but he's using this as a weapon to turn you into a reckless fighter. I'm terrified that it's going to get you killed. I've seen how you get when—"

"STOP!" Khendric bellowed, a dangerous fire behind his eyes. "That's enough from you. This certainly won't help me, except now *you* make me think of them too."

"Maybe if you talk about what happened—"

"I can't relive it in my head, don't you understand? T-the shame, the . . ." He bit down on his lip.

Ara hated this. She felt his thoughts clearly and they tormented his head. He stood out like a flame in the night. Who would be able to fight with such a plagued mind?

He was about to stand up, and she exhaled heavily. "Hey, I have a question," she said, hoping he wouldn't leave her. "It's not about this, I promise."

Khendric hesitated, but remained. "What?"

"I've been reading in the red book."

"And?"

"Who's Alec? He's signed the bottom of almost every page."

Khendric said nothing, and he stared blankly at her before his rocky expression softened into sadness. Tears welled in his eyes, but the darkness faded. A short teary-eyed smile fluttered across his lips. "Alec," he said, voice breaking. "That's . . . funny." He cleared his throat and took the book into his hands, running a finger over the signature. "It's not Alec. It's short for . . . A-Aleccina." His blank eyes produced a tear as he inhaled heavily. "Aleccina was . . . my mother."

Ara's eyes widened, but she remained silent, feeling her heart beat hard.

"She was a beast hunter." A smile expanded on his lips amidst all the coming tears. "I haven't thought of her like that in . . . many years."

"As a beast hunter?" Ara asked.

"Yeah. It is actually a pleasant memory of her." He wiped his tears away.

"She wasn't pleasant?"

"She was perfect," he said, looking into the sky. Sadness clad his mind, one of pain from a time long passed. "I've just placed those good memories somewhere . . . somewhere where I haven't visited in a long time." Khendric flipped through the pages of the book. "*She* wrote this. It's her actual writing, and it's the only thing I have left of her. Can't believe I was crazy enough to give it to you." He chuckled shortly, but the sadness didn't retreat. "This was from before my time. Before she met my father."

Ara kept quiet, listening intently.

"They were so happy."

"Your father was a beast hunter too?" she asked without thinking.

"No," Khendric answered with a soft voice. "He built houses. My mother gave up the life of a beast hunter when she got pregnant with me. I still have fond memories of them. Father built us a house in the forest . . .” His smile soured and painful thoughts sprouted in his mind again. “A remote house . . . too remote,” he said sharply.

Ara put a hand on his shoulder.

“It was foolish of him . . . because then *they* came.”

“Who?”

“The bandits.”

“Your mother could fight,” she asked, hoping to divert his thoughts. “Couldn’t she?”

“Better than most. I begged her to teach me, but she always said no.” His hands clutched his thighs, and he exhaled heavily. “But they were too many and they caught us while we were eating. I still remember that meal. It won’t let go of my mind.”

“Did your mother and father fight?”

“To live her whole life as a beast hunter, only to be killed by lowly, evil men.” His lips shook, but instead of anger, Khendric started crying uncontrollably. He hid his face in his hands and hunched over where he sat, sobbing loudly.

Ara put her hand on his back and let him cry. Surrounding and passing soldiers said nothing.

Khendric bawled for a long time, Ara staying vigilant by his side, feeling water press behind her eyes too at seeing him ruined like this. These tears were of sadness and longing, not anger, shame or hate. She’d never seen him express these feelings, but it was about time.

His crying turned to long breaths and he sat up again, face red and wet. He put a hand on her thigh. “T-thank you. I haven’t cried for them in . . . I don’t even know if I have. Those thoughts have always been fuelled by anger, hatred and . . . fear at the very core.” Khendric let out an exasperated breath. “Now, on the other hand, I thought about mother and father and our past together. And . . . I’ve never cried like that, but I feel . . . better.”

"Would you tell me what happened?" she asked, staring into his dark eyes.

"I'll try," he said, taking a deep breath. "Those bandits, we heard them coming, but mistook them for travellers. They attacked and tied us up." His voice vibrated, but he took a short break. "One of them, the leader, cut me loose and gave me a knife. I'll never forget his name: Landry the Instigator, they called him. He asked me which of my parents I loved the most."

His mind clouded, but he seemed to want to push through.

"I didn't answer him, but he . . . started cutting and forced me to answer. I said 'mother!' Then he laughed and grabbed her chin." Khendric stared forward, eyes hard. "He forced the rusty knife into my hand and he told me that my mother would die so my father could live, knowing he was number two. He grabbed my head and told me to prepare to watch my mother die—over and over, screaming it to my face. How can anyone prepare for that? Mother and father screamed and pleaded. I cried until Landry forcefully moved the knife back and forth in my hand. Then my mind just stopped. He made me—" His words failed him. His mood changed to anger and he drew a sharp breath. "He made me . . ." He let out a primal scream which actually stilled him. "I won't let his deed go unsaid: Landry made me behead my own mother with that knife. I felt her blood run over my fingers. I remember the exact moment life left her eyes, but the knife kept going and going and going . . . even though I begged for it to stop, he kept going and going. He let me sit there, stunned, looking at my mother who would never talk again and then he beat me savagely. He put her head next to mine the entire night, and my father held me tight, telling me over and over that it was going to be okay. But then came morning and they killed him too, stabbed him in the back over and over. He held me tight, clutching me until his arms lost strength, but he held on as long as he could to protect me."

Dark thoughts flowed through his mind, but they felt different, as if he saw his parents' sacrifice and love, instead of the gruesome acts of the bandits. "Then they cut into me. Deep cuts, so I would bleed out. 'No survivors,' Landry said and took off, leaving me to bleed to death."

"How did you survive?" Ara asked. "You have no scars."

"As my blood left my body, I fainted. Maybe I could still hear, or perhaps I hallucinated the heavy hooves approaching me. I awoke and slowly got better. Sensation returned and a large tongue licked my body. When I opened my eyes I saw a huge green beast treating my wounds."

"A green beast?"

"Yes, an emeron. It took me years to find out what it was, but I was saved by an emeron. They're large beasts with thick stone-like skin and three horns at the end of a long snout, but they're believed to be a myth. Tales tell of emerons finding people brought to death's door by merciless evil and saving them, making sure no wounds can hurt them again."

"So, that's why—"

Khendric nodded. "That's why I've survived as long as I have."

"That's amazing!"

"I cursed the emeron for so long," Khendric said with a grim tone. "The damn creature kept me alive so I'd relive these horrible memories night after night."

"Where did you go?" Ara asked.

"Master Yanavar found me. An old man, who was killed by a gorewing right in front of me. But before that, he found me in the gutter of a village and fed me in exchange for aid. He took care of a lot of orphans until we grew up. Master Yanavar saved us all and taught us how to fight. After the gorewing killed him I decided to hunt beasts. I still had my . . . my mother's book. Because of the bandits, I swore to stay away from dealing with people." Dark thoughts returned to his mind and he wrinkled his nose. "You want to know what is the worst?" He faced her. "The shame."

"What?" Ara asked, frowning.

"I couldn't save my parents. I wasn't strong enough, and the shame is . . ."

"Are you serious?" she asked, but Khendric seemed lost in thought.

"I should have done more. If I knew then what I know now," he mumbled.

"Are you an absolute moron?" she asked.

"What?" He seemed dumbfounded.

"For being such a rational person, that's the most irrational thing I've ever heard you say."

Khendric blinked his eyes, confused. "What did you just say to me?"

"You said the worst was the shame, right?"

Khendric gave a small nod.

"The shame of being a little boy against a load of bandits? You couldn't have saved them Khendric, not even if you knew then what you know now. You were a little boy and no boy is ready for such gruesome brutality. You couldn't have changed anything or done anything differently. Your parents knew that and they would never blame you. I couldn't protect my parents either, and I was way older than you, but against a rura, I stood no chance. Just like you stood no chance. I don't feel shame, and you shouldn't either. Think about it, do you *really* think you could've done anything? But you did save a helpless young woman from being a meal, and here we are. I don't blame myself, you truly should not blame yourself either."

He looked at her with a soft expression, tears still in his eyes, before shaking his head slowly. "It feels wrong saying this, but you're right. What could I truly have done? Thank you, Ara."

Tears welled in her eyes, but they weren't tears of sadness. They chuckled and he embraced her in a deep hug that lasted. His slow pulse and warmth made her feel safer than she had in a while, and she treasured the beautiful moment between them.

"I want to take a walk," he said and let go. "By myself. I want to mull this over and think some things I should have thought about a long time ago."

Ara nodded and they rose.

"It's amazing to think Topper and I saved some desolate young woman in a ruined part of a city, and now we're here. I would never have thought this conversation would happen between me and that girl."

"I'm full of surprises," she said with a grin.

"Literally."

It wasn't long before she barely saw him in the dim moonlight, and them he disappeared. She actually felt great. That conversation could have gone a thousand ways, but it had a happy ending. Ara wandered down from the huge wall and towards the pavilions Koradin had set up in the emptied square by the main gate. The soldiers seemed alert, their eyes examining everything and everyone, despite Chronor said they would end tomorrow. For all they knew, he lied.

The soldiers let her through to the pavilions without question, as most of the army knew what she looked like, and she quite enjoyed that. She felt happy seeing Adenar there too, talking with Koradin, Topper, Commander Relen and some other tacticians. Or not 'talking', but rather observing what the others said while scratching his chin.

"If we stretch the army out here," Koradin said, pointing to a battle map, "we'll be vulnerable at the gate."

"That's true," Topper agreed.

"What if we post scouts," Adenar suddenly said. "If they're stationed at equal intervals along the wall, it should be quicker to get reports if Chronor emerges with an actual army somewhere."

Koradin and the others thought about it. "In the light of the moon," Koradin said, "their armour might be possible to spot. Let's do it. Jack, can you set it up?"

"I can," Commander Relen answered and hurried to some of his subordinates.

Ara approached, hoping not to be shooed away.

"The soldiers's morale is low," Topper said.

"I know," Koradin said. "I can see it in their eyes and I don't blame them. The endless supply of shadowwalkers sets fear into me as well."

"Do you think that's his plan?" Adenar asked.

"I don't know," Koradin replied. "And I don't know what I hope for. But we need a plan on what to do if it is. And somehow we need to sneak Ara up next to him with the blade." He looked at her, and she shivered at the thought. They relied on her to kill an ancient voreen god. It felt impossible.

"Where is Khendric?" Topper asked.

"Taking a much-needed walk."

"Find him, we must lay a plan," Koradin said. "His idea worked on getting the voreen blade, so I need his keen mind here."

"I'm here," Khendric said as he pushed through the thick of soldiers. "And I brought company." Of all people, Darlaene emerged.

"Darlaene!" Ara exclaimed. "You're still alive!"

"Of course." She nodded confidently, her long red hair waving smoothly in the weak wind. "I've been through worse."

"How did you get in?" Koradin asked.

"I'm good at hiding and hid until I heard sounds of the battle against the shadowwalkers. Glad I got to sit that one out. During the battle, all of Chronor's minions were in a different state of mind; sluggish and unresponsive. I don't think he can pay attention to what they all see when concentrating on the battle. I simply walked through the massive crowd, and believe me when I say 'it is massive,' inching closer and closer to your wall. It was nerve-wracking, but I got through. I yelled until some of your soldiers threw me a rope and lifted me out of the horde."

"I see," Koradin said. "Guess we get to have some luck."

"Nice to see you again," Topper said, shooting her a glance.

"Good to see you too, Topper, right? That's a better body than that old bag of bones you wore last time."

"I want to keep this one," Topper said.

They returned to staring at the map for a long while, but none offered much substance.

"Any ideas, Khendric?" Koradin finally asked, but he shook his head. "I see," the king said. "For now, Chronor's people are calm, but there have been reports of light attacks on the wall with ladders. We think it's to unnerve us." He turned to Darlaene. "You came from the Passionist District?"

"Yes."

"How is it there?"

Darlaene's eyes fell to the ground and she sighed. "It's . . . worse. It started just like here: an endless horde of people standing outside the wall, but not the district wall. The wall around the headquarters. Elrich didn't do as good a job as you in keeping his district safe."

"They're in a standoff just like us?" Koradin asked.

"No. Chronor's minions stormed the building, slaughtering everyone."

"How did you survive?" Topper asked.

She let out an exasperated sigh. "I don't really know. I acted instinctively and I got out early, but luck played a major part too. I hid until his horde turned unresponsive."

Khendric put his hand on hers. "I really mean it this time: I will lock you up." A charming smile hid the worry behind his eyes, and Ara understood him.

"So, they're all dead?" Koradin asked.

"Or turned," she answered.

Koradin exhaled heavily. "These are grave news. We'll weep for them later. First, we need a plan."

"Got anything so far?" Darlaene asked.

"Not much," Khendric answered.

"We forged a dagger from the doombringer dust you acquired," Koradin said and waved his hand at someone. Forth came an elderly scrawny man with two hairs on his balding head, holding a dagger wrapped in a blanket. An air of eloquence surrounded him still, his blue formal and clearly expensive clothes too clean for this environment. Topper and Adenar gave him a wide berth as he started unwrapping the dagger.

"It was forged that fast?" Topper asked.

"The dust," the old man began, his voice strong. "I've never worked with better material. I could only make a dagger, but I'm honoured to forge it. Thank you, King Koradin." He revealed a weapon seemingly made of pure silver, so white it threatened to blind them. He held it out towards Ara.

"Me? I get it?"

"You got us the dust," Koradin said. "But we also thought it smartest."

"Darlaene was there too, and I already have the blade."

"Blade?" Darlaene asked.

"We got Ara a voreen blade," Khendric said, puffing out his chest. "All my idea."

Topper cleared his throat and glared at him.

"What?" Darlaene exclaimed. "That's amazing! Where is it?"

"Hidden," Koradin said. "Ara brings up a fair point. Do you accept the dagger, Darlaene?"

Khendric pushed the dagger away from her. "It's just going to put her in more danger."

She took a step forward and grabbed the weapon. "I can handle it."

The old smith's eyes opened wide at her sudden movement. "Treat her well," he said. "It's one of a kind."

"Its name?" Koradin asked.

"Godbreaker," the smith said almost with reverence. "Bring truth to the name."

"I will," Darlaene answered, placing a hand on his shoulder. "Thank you for bringing us hope."

"Just kill this vile thing." The elderly smith glanced one last time at his masterpiece and bowed courteously before leaving them.

Darlaene secured Godbreaker to her belt and hid it beneath her cloak. "We should get the sword too," she said.

"I don't know where it is," Ara answered.

"What?"

"It's true, I—"

A messenger on a horse galloped up to them, breaking through the surrounding soldiers. "My king!" the broad man atop the horse yelled, interrupting Ara.

Koradin walked past Ara and Darlaene. Darlaene sniffed the air and wrinkled her nose.

"What?" Koradin asked.

"The book. It has been ruined. Aeba sent me with haste."

"How did this happen?" Koradin demanded with his hard voice.

"We don't know. Several guards were killed and the pages burnt to dust."

"We've been infiltrated," Koradin said with a troubled face.

"Is this really a problem?" Khendric asked. "When we win, we'll drag the real one from Chronor's dead hands."

"I know," Koradin said. "But *how* did he get a hold of our copy?"

"Ponther," Ara suggested. "It has to be him."

"I doubt that," Koradin said. "He may not like me, but he's a Meritocrat to the bone."

"Maybe he struck a deal with the god?" Topper said. "I've seen honourable men turn before."

Adenar and Khendric nodded, and they all dove into theories and accusations, except for Darlaene. Her narrowed eyes stayed locked on the king, seeming lost in thought until Ara nudged her.

"Are you okay?" she asked.

Darlaene shook her head. "Yes, why?"

"My king," the messenger shouted. "My apologies for not saying this before. Whoever burned the copy, left a note." He held out a small piece of paper.

Koradin grabbed it and read aloud. "'You stand no chance, soon you will be mine'."

That sent shivers down Ara's spine, her preconceived notion of their security crumbling.

Commander Relen ran down the stairs of the wall, screaming at the top of his lungs, "Something's happening!"

"What?" Koradin asked and approached him, Khendric, Topper, and Adenar staying close to the king.

Ara stepped forward too, but Darlaene put a hand on her shoulder. "Let's stay in the back. We're the most important individuals here. You need to get that blade."

"They're moving and screaming," Commander Relen shouted through the clatter of moving armoured soldiers. "And soldiers are getting into formation outside the wall!"

"How many?" Khendric asked.

Commander Relen shook his head in disbelief. "I couldn't see the end. It has to be all of Ashbourn's armies except for ours."

"Get into positions, arm the walls," Koradin commanded and captains started bellowing orders. "Flood the square and the wall with soldiers. Place a smaller army where the opposition is regular citizens."

Commander Relen saluted sharply and went to work.

In a split second, the somewhat quiet square had turned into organized chaos. Soldiers flocked together and moved hurriedly to various locations, most of them getting into formations in front of the main gate. Endless screams sounded from beyond the wall; something really was happening.

"Fire!" a captain on the wall ordered, and archers sent a volley of arrows down upon their enemies.

Koradin remained in the middle, Khendric by his side, observing what he could. Ara and Darlaene had moved up to him, and she felt safer.

"What is going on?" the King demanded from a captain descending the stairs.

"They're raising ladders," he reported.

"How many?"

"Two, only."

"Soldiers or citizens?" Koradin asked.

"Citizens."

Koradin shook his head. "It was still the right thing to do. Don't let any ladders settle on our wall."

"No, my King!" he answered back sharply.

"Any reports of Chronor?" Koradin asked as the captain turned.

"No."

Koradin looked displeased. "Where is he? Shouldn't he lead the charge?"

"It feels like we're missing something," Khendric said aloud.

Koradin turned his head and shouted, "Adenar!"

Adenar's head turned away from the strategic map at the pavilions and to Koradin with a puzzled look.

"If Chronor appears," Koradin said to Khendric, Ara, and Darlaene. "Call for me." They nodded, and Koradin went over to Adenar and pulled him into a tent.

"What can be *that* important?" Khendric asked.

"You stay here," Darlaene said to Khendric. "We'll eaves-drop. Come on, Ara." She grabbed Ara's arm and dragged her along through the thick of soldiers. She would object if she wasn't so damn curious as to what the king wanted with Adenar. They neared the tent and leaned closer to listen. The clamour of the soldiers almost drowned his words out.

". . . and we don't have time," Koradin said. "So I will just tell you straight. You will have questions, but there is no time for answers. I am sorry for this. I wish there was more time. Adenar, I am your father."

Ara's heart almost stopped, and she looked at Darlaene, but the woman looked calm as always. *I can't believe it,* Ara thought, putting her hand in front of her mouth so as not to yelp.

"What?" Adenar's careful voice sounded. "I don't under-stand."

"I know. Your mother and I had a relationship, but it ended. We met one night after I had married Lenda and I . . . had an affair. That's why I could never—"

"Ladders!" someone on the wall roared. "Breach!"

"Koradin!" Khendric roared and the king exited the tent faster than Ara and Darlaene anticipated.

"Ladders everywhere!"

He shot them both a glance, and Ara must've looked like the biggest fool in the world. She cringed at her behaviour, but Koradin pressed forward, preparing for battle.

A great commotion erupted on the wall as numerous lad-ders rose. Their soldiers tried pushing them back, but turned citizens lunged up on the wall, attacking with animalistic ferocity. The war had begun. Koradin disappeared into the thick of his soldiers, followed by Khendric and Topper too.

Ara's fingers shivered and her lungs barely let her draw breath. What should she do? She couldn't get her sword, so should she wait? Or join the battle? With her arm she was a dangerous foe, but she shouldn't be wasted.

"We'll hang back," Darlaene said at her side. "They got this. They're both basically immortal. I think we should get the blade."

Darlaene's certain hand on Ara's shoulder provided her with some assurance, and she nodded. "Okay." *They better survive,* she thought, as those three men were the only ones who knew where the voreen blade was hidden.

CHAPTER 10

Pulling the Strings

Rhakta, The Master of Skulls, challenged Chronor to a blood oath, but only if his four best warriors could join the duel. Chronor accepted, longing to show his true might. These four warriors did not enter into a blood oath, and could only hamper Chronor, not truly harm him.

This duel is known throughout voreen history as 'The Battle for Godhood', the skill shown described as "a sight only worthy of gods." The balance between elegance and brutality had us all watching silently and unmoving.

Chronor killed all of Rhakta's terrifying warriors, but it did wind him, and Rhakta took his chance. It ended with them both piercing each other.

From 'The Dark Traitor', chapter sixteen.

Khendric and Topper tried to make their way through the soldiers just like Koradin, but it wasn't easy. Ara hated staying in the back, but Darlaene had some good points.

Adenar exited the tent with an astonished look. His eyes wandered back and forth confused, and Ara completely understood him. How should he react to such little, yet powerful information?

"Where is the blade?" Darlaene asked Ara sharply, tightening the hand on her shoulder.

"I don't know," she answered.

Darlaene grabbed her neck hard.

Ara's eyes shot wide open as pain coursed through her. "Ouch, Darlaene, what—"

"Where. Is. The. Blade?"

"I don't know—"

She tightened her grip around Ara's throat.

She struggled to breathe. *Alright, enough of this.* Ara put her enhanced arm on Darlaene's wrist and pulled it away—except, her arm didn't go away.

Darlaene's hand did not waver from Ara's strength. Panic surged through Ara's body as her lungs ached for air.

"Ara!" Khendric's voice shouted from somewhere.

A dark familiar presence unleashed itself and emanated so strongly from Darlaene that Ara almost fainted—because she recognized its overpowering force. *How?*

A sinister smile grew on Darlaene's face. She plunged Godbreaker deep into Ara's stomach; the pain couldn't be described, but worsened as the blade twisted inside her guts. Darlaene pulled the dagger out and stabbed again, and again, and again. Ara's eyes rolled back and her body wouldn't respond. Her tainted arm lost its grip and fell to her side.

"No!" Khendric, Topper and Koradin yelled. Multiple gunshots rang through the air, and Ara refocused her eyes. The bullets struck Darlaene and dark blood sprayed from her onto Ara's face and stomach, but she just kept staring into Ara's fading vision, releasing the dagger. Confused screams and shouts spread through the army. Blood seeped from the deep wounds, yet Ara summoned her final strength and grabbed the hilt of the weapon and plunged it into Darlaen's side.

While keeping eye contact, she groaned deeply, but that voice couldn't belong to a human. Ara knew who it belonged to. *So this is it, how it ends?* Darlaene let go of her and she slumped to the ground. Her vision blackened, Darlaene's deep laugh the only thing she sensed. The darkness enveloped her. She'd feel fear if she could, but her body was broken and her mind was dying.

"You were brave," Darlaene said, her voice morphing into the voice of Chronor. "Though I'd never give you a weapon that could kill me."

I can't believe he tricked . . .

***

The smoke rose from the barrel of his gun and all bullets had hit the mark, but they did nothing to stop Darlaene from stabbing Ara.

Khendric's mind raced, trying to comprehend the impossibility before him. *It can't be . . .*

"Soldiers!" Khendric heard Koradin bellow. "Form ranks!"

Ara sat slumped against the wall, her eyes open, but she didn't move. *I have to get to her!* But that would prove hard, as Darlaene's body transformed. Thick smoke swirled around her, enveloping her as she grew in size, her skin fading to grey, her clothes tearing and her belt snapping.

Khendric couldn't move. He refused to believe this.

The smoke abated, revealing a tall, dark, menacing figure with spikes on his head holding a massive otherworldly blade. A dark cloak interweaved with green fire formed on his back, akin to the flames in his eyes. Armour blacker than the night protected his muscular body. Chronor stood before them, his back against the wall amid Koradin's forces.

Koradin stepped forward and drew his blade. "You vile creature!" All the soldiers unsheathed their weapons and lined up behind their king, spears pointed at the ancient god.

He looked unconcerned and a self-confident smile slashed across Chronor's face. Green and black smoke emanated from his armour and weapon, setting fear into everyone's hearts.

"Where is Darlaene?" Khendric whispered in horror.

"Your hope lays dead at my feet," Chronor said aloud. He picked up Ara's limp body and threw her far away along the wall. "Though she is not your only hope, right, Koradin?"

"Attack!" Koradin roared as he stormed towards the voreen god.

His soldiers followed, pulling Khendric with them, and his feet moved forward automatically. Rage build within him, and he clenched his jaw so hard his teeth almost broke. His blade found its way into his hand and the army clashed with the god.

Koradin swung his blade towards Chronor, but he spun aside and slashed his blade into the oncoming cascade of soldiers. They flew into the air, thrown back several feet, all dead. Koradin followed and Chronor blocked his sword, barreling into the army and swinging his blade again—Khendric ducked just in time as the god split several soldiers around him at the waist, cutting cleanly through metal, skin, and bone. Koradin pursued Chronor, but the god kept moving and slicing through the army. The soldiers's weapons did nothing, so Khendric fought to get to the wall where Ara had been stabbed.

"You insult me," Chronor said while swatting aside three soldiers with a massive swipe of his blade. He ducked beneath Koradin's massive sword and blocked his next attack. "Show them who you truly are and fight me like it!"

Khendric pushed through the soldiers and fell against the wall. Godbreaker, the dagger laid in a pool of blood. *Ara's blood.* He raised his head to look for her, but a wave of soldiers fell against the wall, while others flew through the air and crashed into it. A jumble of armour and blood fell onto

Khendric, and he pushed it off before realizing it was half a body.

Where's the dagger? Afraid to get trampled by scared men, he got to his knees and saw it between a bunch of feet. He darted forward, got a grip on the hilt and sprang to his feet. Blood stained every piece of armour and clothing, but none of it was his.

With his brain turned off, he pushed through the soldiers again, this time towards the screams. Chronor stood taller than the army, decimating it from within. The battle on the wall still raged, but they had to focus on the god.

He neared Koradin and Chronor as the god planted a foot into Koradin's chest. The king fell to the ground with a loud grunt, and got the tip of a blade at his throat before he could move.

"Come on, "Chronor said. "I want them to *see* you."

The soldiers surged around Chronor, jumping onto him and holding in, forcing him to swing wide. They flew off him as he spun, thrown into the air.

Khendric slid forward, below the deadly blade above his head and plunged Godbreaker through a slit in Chronor's armour. Chronor roared and Koradin rolled to his feet, a literal fire alight in his eyes as he attacked the god viciously with two incredible strikes that dented the god's armour.

Chronor moved backwards, toppling every soldier in his path, as he parried Koradin's mighty blows. "There you are," he said, satisfied.

Khendric followed in Chronor's wake, wanting to flank him again, and saw his chance as multiple soldiers were cut down.

He lunged forward, dagger in hand and—Chronor's massive hand grabbed him lightning quickly by his collar.

"There you are, little insect," he said and flung Khendric over the soldiers and straight into the massive wall. Pain rippled throughout his body as his bones broke. Blood sprayed from his mouth as he slumped to the ground, darkness consuming him.

* * *

Koradin dampened the fire within him as Chronor moved closer to the main gate, but still followed his every step. He slashed and hacked, but Chronor matched his speed easily. It had been ages since Koradin had felt his fire within, and it seemed Chronor knew his true nature. *How? I've never told a soul.* It was supposed to be his secret weapon.

Chronor kept moving towards the gate, and Koradin feared the worst, so he followed. The blood of his soldiers pooled on the cobblestones, and anger fuelled Koradin's strikes. Their swords collided. Chronor didn't care about the soldiers's weapons, only his.

As they reached the gate, Chronor fainted a swing and instead shoved his shoulder into Koradin's chest. Koradin staggered back, and his sword scraped over Chronor's bracer, but caused no damage.

Chronor put his hands on the iron lattice of the main gate. "Time to die." With inhuman strength, he tore it in two. His dark-eyed soldiers poured passed him like a flood, charging into Koradin's armies, throwing themselves at them.

"Fall back," Koradin roared, swinging his sword into Chronor's maniacal minions. "Form a line, block them from breaking down the side streets. We must hold them!" He fought with intensity, slashing through the incoming flood, giving his soldiers enough time to form a wall. As the foes threatened to overpower him, he stepped back and joined his forces.

The disciplined wall of soldiers dealt with the incoming wave effectively, the rabid, undisciplined mix of soldiers and citizens dying on their swords. But Chronor's soldiers kept flowing through, washing over their dead and just kept coming. Even without tactics and formation, the sheer force of bodies cracked Koradin's defences. One enemy became ten became a hundred became a thousand in a matter of seconds.

"Keep formation," Koradin cried, driving his blade through three former soldiers of Ashbourn.

Along their struggling line, sergeants and captains shouted orders, and soldiers established barricades along the streets. But the endless host kept arriving, swarming up the stairs to the wall, decimating the outer defence, slaughtering them all. They stood no chance with enemies in all directions.

Chronor placed himself atop the gate, watching the ongoing battle with glee. His figure, clad in disheartening black armour and a pair of green eyes, made for a terrifying sight. *I have to strike him down and kill him*, Koradin thought while parrying the many strikes made against him. *But there's no path.*

Chronor's armies spewed through the gate, forcing Koradin's contingent back. Most citizens didn't join the battle, instead slipping through and disappearing into side streets or houses, probably looking for victims to turn. The people of the Meritocrat district had not yielded to Chronor, which meant a massive pool of new followers. The largest bulk of Koradin's forces was positioned in the square, but his reserves were stationed throughout the side streets. *Perhaps they can protect the innocent,* but he had his doubt.

Entrenched positions along his long line of defence fractured, and the enemy citizens grabbed and pulled soldiers into their midsts. They didn't kill them to his surprise, just overpowered them and held them in place.

"Koradin!" Commander Relen shouted, yanking him out of his trance. "Chronor's minions are flooding every house, every alley, every crack of the district. They're forcing vials of blood down their throats." Commander Relen had a grim expression. "He's turning them, sir."

Koradin gritted his teeth. "We're out of time." Their foes pushed them further back, more and more soldiers dying or getting snatched.

"I think he's not in his final phase," Commander Relen shouted.

"I agree, he needs more."

"So what do we do?"

"Get me a brazier, right now!"

* * *

Khendric snapped awake, his ears assaulted with thousands of people shouting, dying, or fighting. The battle raged, yet he was unscathed and his wounds and bones healed. Dead bodies lay strewn around him, soldiers from both sides, as well as citizens. Blood stained his armour and clothing. This time some of it had to be his. He pushed his hand to the muddy and crimson ground, feeling Godbreaker against his palm. *That's lucky,* he thought. Except for a headache, he felt normal. He leaned against the wall, surprised nobody had come to kill him in the chaos.

Chronor's minions swarmed every street he looked into, severely diminishing the places he could hide. He looked in all directions in hopes of laying a plan, his eyes suddenly landing on the dark voreen god atop the gate—close to his position. *If I can sneak up on him,* he thought, tightening his grip on Godbreaker.

Chronor turned his head and stared right at him. Khendric froze as the harsh gaze of the god tensed his every muscle. *I'm dead.* He shrunk under the deity's mighty presence. Chronor turned his head away unconcerned, and moments later a shadowwalker landed in front of Khendric, drawing its shadowy short-swords.

Great, Khendric thought, grabbing a nearby sword and flung himself into the fight of his life.

* * *

Adenar carried a heavy brazier with Commander Relen and placed it behind Koradin as he fought the endless horde of oncoming soldiers.

"Good," Commander Relen said. "Koradin! It's ready. Flame's bright."

Adenar marvelled at the king as he pulled back from the defensive line and placed his hand on the brazier. Sweat ran down his face, but he looked fierce.

Through the thick of soldiers surrounding them, Adenar thought maybe Koradin wouldn't see him, but he did and placed a hand on Adenar's shoulder, pulling him close. "You have to promise me something."

Adenar nodded his head, almost falling as a man toppled onto them, but Koradin barely budged.

"Promise me this!"

"I promise!" Adenar shouted through the clamour of battle.

"If I die, take my ashes and kill whatever is born of it."

"What?"

"Go now, my lost warriors," Chronor's voice boomed through the clatter, cutting Koradin off. Three shadowwalkers lunged high into the air, past Koradin's crumbling defensive line, and rained down in the middle of their soldiers, dealing devastating blows, disrupting their order.

Oh no, Adenar thought, watching as the creatures slashed soldiers to pieces. The eyes of the others around him seemed to share the thought. Koradin jerked his head back into focus.

"What?" Adenar asked.

"Did you hear me?" the king shouted.

"Yes!"

"Thank you." Despite being knees deep in the fight for their lives, Koradin looked calmly at him. "I'm sorry we couldn't have more time." Koradin let go of his shoulder and lowered his left hand directly into the burning fire of the brazier, eyes locked on the shadowwalkers.

Adenar's eyes widened as the fire encircled his hand, but Koradin was unscathed by the heat. The Fire violently twirled around his arm like a tornado, absorbed directly into his skin. Adenar couldn't believe his eyes, forgetting to breathe. Koradin's shoulders and long blonde hair caught fire without burning to dust, his eyes turning firey red. The mighty sword in his hand lit up with an intense, almost blinding, orange and yellow flame.

Adenar and the surrounding soldiers stumbled back due to the inferno that was their king. Koradin leapt through his soldiers and into the throng of enemies pummelling his men. He grabbed a vicious shadowwalker by surprise, turned it around, and with the fire live in his hand exploded it into smoke and fire.

"There he is," Chronor's strong voice said from the top of the wall. "The Ashenborn. The true and last king of Ashbourn!"

Before the smoke and fire settled, Koradin dashed through it and across the battlefield, clearing away foes with blistering fire like a tempest, striking down dark-eyed soldiers in bright flashes. He swung his fiery swords without breaking stride, reaching the next shadowwalker with charred corpses in his wake.

It slashed its weapons at him, but he spun to the side and decapitated the mighty foe. It combusted and exploded in fire and smoke. Through the darkness he emerged with blazing flames churning around him, alive like the wind, coalescing around his hand as he plunged it into the earth, sending forth a wave of fire to envelop Chronor's minions. Smoke rose from the dead, and the king's forces advanced for the first time in the vacuum he created. Koradin advanced too with a determined and furious expression. The last shadowwalker landed in front of him and attacked, but movements faster than Adenar had ever seen placed Koradin's hand around the creature's neck. Fire swallowed them both and only Koradin remained as it abated. "Face me!" he shouted. "Chronor! Face me!"

The spirit of their army transformed. Eyes glowed with hope, and the line pushed forward aggressively, winning back lost ground. Adenar fought his way through the thick of soldiers, afraid to be pulled to the front line. He stepped onto the pavilion, for a better view. The endless horde hadn't stopped and poured over the wall as well.

He refocused on Koradin, the raging flame dominating the fight, shining like the sun. Despite his crushing strength, he wasn't enough to turn the tide against Chronor's overwhelming forces. Koradin's troops thinned, the little ground they won had been lost again to their adversaries. More and more soldiers fell into the hands of Chronor's minions, overwhelmed, but kept alive. Adenar felt hope fade, realizing how bleak their future was. Chronor won with sheer numbers, and death would come for them all. He had trouble breathing as his gaze rose to the malevolent god atop the gate, his huge cloak and armour sending shivers down his spine.

The clatter of battle stopped, and Adenar thought he'd gone deaf for a moment. The enemy soldiers had stopped attacking and retreated a few feet back. Koradin's forces looked around confused, keeping their shields up.

"People of Ashbourn!" Chronor's echoing voice reverberated through the square. "You fight with honour. I admire and respect it. You have shown great strength, and for that, I shall offer you one final chance to keep your lives."

Oh no, Adenar thought.

"Swear allegiance to me. Kneel before me, and you will live. Kneel before me, and you will grow richer and more powerful than you can imagine! Kneel before me, and you will lead armies and find immeasurable glory!"

The nearby soldiers exchanged uncertain glances and Adenar understood their doubt. He knew the thoughts in their mind. "We can't give up now," Adenar said, but his words fell on deaf ears. The soldiers didn't even grace him with their eyes, Chronor having their full attention.

"Resist me," Chronor continued. "And you will all die."

Absolute silence rested upon the huge square.

Koradin turned to his soldiers. "Do not listen to him! These are lies!"

"They are not," Chronor answered.

Adenar wouldn't bend to this terrible god. He didn't care for glory or his life enough to serve an oppressive and destructive force.

But all hope died as heads in the crowd dropped. Knees bent.

"No," Adenar said. "No!" But soldiers fell to their knees, all around him. "What are you doing?"

But no one answered, their eyes revealing shame and fear. Like waves, more and more dropped and Koradin's army fell to the mighty words of the voreen god.

"There you see, Ashenborn," Chronor said. "Your own men betray you. They understand the futility of fighting."

"Get up!" Koradin roared, his words reaching Adenar's ears with icy clarity. "You're only making him more powerful! This is exactly what he needs!" Fire exploded from the former king's mouth as he screamed, but none rose to their feet. Releasing a beastly roar, he charged Chronor. None of Chronor's minions reacted, letting Koradin pass.

Chronor bent his head back and spread his arms as molten red fire and smoke whirled around him in a wild inferno. "I am complete!" his thunderous voice bellowed.

Adenar's face paled and his knees trembled as Chronor ascended to his final stage. The molten lava and black smoke abated, and a bright crown burned over his head.

Koradin gazed upon the dreadful god. With flames radiating from his body, he held his huge burning blade towards the dark god on top of the gate. "I challenge you to a blood oath!" Koradin roared.

A rumbling hum filled the air as if Chronor chuckled through the throats of every follower at the same time. His dark and green sword reappeared in his tentacled hand, and a smile crept onto the god's visage.

"I accept," Chronor said.

CHAPTER 11

Oaths of Blood

Rhakta, The Master of Skulls, died and in death became Chronor's ultimate warrior, but landed a mortal blow on Chronor too. As Chronor died he told Rhakta, The Master of Skulls, to enjoy his eternal servitude.
From 'The Dark Traitor', chapter sixteen.

The shadowwalker stopped its vicious attacks when Chronor spoke. Khendric used the moment to catch his breath, while in futility watching the god achieve his ultimate goal. Khendric couldn't do anything while the shadowwalker barred his way.

All of Koradin's armies broke beneath Chronor's will and promises, but the former king remained standing, together with Adenar and Commander Relen too.

Good men.

His breathing calmed, and he thought of dashing past the shadowwalker, but it stayed alert it seemed. Its smokey tendrils churned around its being, and the lack of a face unnerved Khendric.

Chronor descended gracefully from the wall and approached Koradin with heavy steps. His army stayed down like beaten rabdogs, not daring to rise while surrounded by their friends-turned-enemies. The corrupted soldiers looked maniacal, opening and closing their watering mouths while looking at their prey.

If Khendric could get to the king, maybe he could help . . . somehow. He readied his weapons, but the shadowwalker didn't react at all. Perhaps Chronor didn't have the mental power to give it a new command or react to Khendric's actions.—if it worked like that.

The pavilions stood on an elevated area, and given Chronor's walk, that's where he intended to hold the duel. His tall figure ascended the area and he gestured for Koradin to approach. Koradin remained at his station, talking to Commander Relen.

"You let us die," a shadowy figure in his peripherals whispered, but Khendric breathed through it. His hallucinations had gone unnoticed in the heat of the fight, but as it slowed, they reemerged. He pushed away the decades-old shame by remembering Ara's words. *I was a child. I couldn't do anything.* The figure vanished slowly with a final whisper, *"we will never forgive you."*

Begone, Khendric thought, *you're not mother.* Instead, his thoughts went to Ara, and he felt truly sad. After everything they had gone through, she was dead by the god's trickery. His muscles vibrated with fury and his eyes refocused on the foul being that had spread his corruption through the city. *You killed her, you monster.* And what about Darlaene? Had he killed her too? He gritted his teeth as dread coursed through his veins. *I have to kill him.*

As he stepped to the side the shadowwalker followed suit, and Khendric halted. "So you are paying attention?" He tightened his grip on his weapons and stared the creature down. "Let me pass."

It didn't react, so Khendric made it react. The two near-immortals spun back into a vicious fight, and Khendric used every fibre of his body to try and break the foe in front of him.

***

Koradin walked through his cowardly kneeling army. The shame in their eyes befitted them. They had ascended Chronor to his final phase, forcing Koradin's hand.

This duel set fear into his very heart, and his fingers shook. Losing meant becoming Chronor's eternal servant in his afterlife, an unstoppable force of destruction. He didn't know what to expect from Chronor either. But fear was also good. It would push him to fight with his soul, and give everything to beat him.

"Matt?" Koradin whispered into the wind as he passed by his shameful soldiers, his voice shaking more than he anticipated.

"Yes, we can," Matt replied in his mind. *"We will beat him. I will aid you."*

Koradin let out a strained breath and felt some tension melt away as he entered the duelling ground. "What's dying like?" He swallowed, uncertain if he should ask that question.

"I . . . don't know. I don't remember pain."

"That's good," Koradin whispered. Nervousness felt strange to him, as he hadn't been nervous in almost a decade. By the pavilion, Adenar stood tall, chin high and shoulders back. There hadn't been enough time to show him how immensely proud he was of his son, and not enough time to deal with the guilt either. He'd abandoned the boy, and the shame had to be clear in his eyes. Their gazes locked, and Koradin wished to say so much, but couldn't. He couldn't believe his son had been the one to *almost* save Ashbourn. Koradin nodded to him, and Adenar returned it with vigilance. His wife and daughters entered his mind next, loading his nerves with more tension. *I have to beat him.* The thought of them turning into mindless followers or killed, ate him up. Despite being locked inside the safe room of the Meritocrat Headquarters with a small army, they wouldn't stand a chance. *Perhaps they will make it out of the city,* he thought.

Chronor's heavy footsteps came to a stop and Koradin lifted his gaze. They stood at each end, and the muscular monstrosity held a satisfied smile. Koradin sighed and for some moments wished he'd never been put in this situation. But if not him, who else could rival the god?

To his pleasant surprise, Adenar and Jack joined his side, alleviating his feeling of loneliness to some extent.

"When you win," Jack said with a rye smile, "rip his heart out and make him eat it."

Koradin chuckled slightly. "Adenar," he said, facing the young man. "There are so many things I want to say, but most of all: I'm sorry."

"You can tell me afterwards," he answered.

"It is an honour to fight an Ashenborn," Chronor said, his deep voice reverberating across the square, bringing Koradin back to the deadly matter at hand.

Deep anger manifested in his gut. "You talk of honour," Koradin said. "Yet you sacrifice the young to reach your end."

Chronor narrowed his eyes. "It almost escaped me; you being more than human, but I got close enough to smell you."

"You're a coward! You killed Ara in cold blood with your dirty tricks and—"

"Oh, come now," the ancient god interrupted harshly. "It's war. You made your own secret plans. Mine worked better. I have killed many, though few as special as her. Truly magnificent. But she was dangerous, and I didn't want to end her life, but it had to be done."

"She was just a girl."

"You know that is not true, Ashenborn. I was pleased to learn your true nature. Not even *you* would dare challenge me as a simple human, but an Ashenborn would, and I *need* a willing soul. You are worthy of becoming rosh'gar, for many reasons. I've met few with your courage and those I have met, are now my eternal servants."

"I will never serve you," Koradin roared with a hard tone, but his fear didn't yield.

"You will." Chronor's huge armour started bleeding thick black smoke, and it slowly vanished from his huge dark body. "It would serve you well to remove your armour too, Ashenborn. My blade will carve through it easily, and you'll be quicker without it."

"Why are you removing yours?" Koradin asked.

"It's what's fair. Your sword is special and can kill me, but it would have a hard time getting through."

"How dare he?" Matt said.

Koradin hated that Chronor gave him advice. The god's confidence unnerved him even more. Though Koradin fought better than any human, in truth he doubted he would win. He let out a deep breath before turning to his loyal commander.

"Help me remove my armour."

Jack walked up to Koradin. "Don't listen to him," Jack said as he loosened the breastplate. "He's trying to scare you."

"It's working," Koradin said.

"I've never seen anything like you in this war. You were an inferno, a tempest. Don't doubt yourself."

"I'll certainly do my best," Koradin replied, nodding curtly. He unsheathed his mighty blade, but felt naked with only a sleeveless shirt and his trousers. Jack grabbed his hand and the two butted heads. "It's been an honour, Commander," said Koradin.

"Truly," Jack replied. "Don't let it end here."

He then grabbed Adenar's head and did the same, but didn't know what to say.

"For Ashbourn," said Adenar.

"For Ashbourn," replied Koradin.

Chronor summoned his massive dark-green blade amidst a whirl of smoke, and Koradin shivered. It looked to be alive, its deadly surface slowly morphing. Chronor gripped it with both hands and pointed it at Koradin. Perhaps it had been a mistake to remove the armour?

"Will you hold against that?" Koradin asked.

"Nothing can break me," Matt answered.

"I thank you for your confidence. I need it."

"A good choice to remove it." Chronor moved his other-worldly sword through the air, flexing the black tentacled muscles of his body. Koradin tried not to waver at the threatening display. "Let our blood unite," Chronor said, cutting a small wound in his hand. He offered it to Koradin, waiting for him in the middle of the grounds. Koradin's heart raced as he neared the god. Chronor towered over him, and from within a mass of writhing tentacles, five fingers emerged.

Koradin ran his palm up along his sword's edge. Red blood flowed from the wound, red blood to bind him in a dangerous oath. He inhaled and grasped Chronor's hand. The dark god's disgusting tentacles crept around Koradin's wrist, but he stared defiantly into those burning eyes. He felt a burning sensation within him as their blood mixed; the oath had been sealed. *There's no going back now.*

Chronor let go and walked back to his side of the duelling ground. A bead of sweat ran down Koradin's temple, but hopefully the fear would sharpen his senses even more than being an Ashenborn already did.

"Any rules?" Koradin asked.

"An honourable duel," Chronor said as he turned. "No tricks. No explosions. I will not use any of my tricks either."

"I accept." He didn't know any of the god's tricks anyway.

"Then are you ready?" Chronor asked, a daunting, sinister smile spreading across his lips. Koradin inhaled slowly and his sword caught fire.

I am ready, Matt said.

"I am," Koradin said, letting the sword fall into place.

***

Sweat dripped down Adenar's forehead, and he gripped the pommel of his sword to keep it from shaking. This fight was their only hope, and Adenar could do nothing but stand and watch, though that seemed to be a lot more than what most did. Only Koradin, Commander Relen, Khendric, and Adenar visibly opposed Chronor, and Khendric was still trapped in combat. The beast hunter had impressive stamina, but if the fight dragged on, the shadowwalker would win. Adenar could do nothing to help either, as an army of Chronor's minions blocked their path.

Chronor entered an alien battle stance, and Koradin fell into his own. Slowly, the two warriors approached the middle.

They clashed together, Chronor with a blow which Koradin blocked with apparent ease—the sound of the clashing swords loud enough to deafen Adenar. Koradin stepped forward and retaliated with an unnaturally quick swing for such a large weapon, but Chronor's blade slashed it away. The god punched at Koradin's head, but he dodged and parried the quick swing coming for his guts.

It became clear why anyone fighting Chronor needed to be a god in their own right. These opponents fought with supernatural speed and strength. Yet, the most terrifying aspect was the clash of the swords—sounding like a hundred swords striking simultaneously.

Chronor struck downwards, but Koradin sidestepped and swung. Chronor leaned backwards and came at Koradin with a jab he easily parried.

"You are skilled," Chronor said, stepping away from Koradin. Neither duellist showed signs of exhaustion. "The pharlanax you killed must have been strong. Had we time, I would like to know how you did it."

Koradin didn't hesitate; he didn't respond and reengaged with a violent flurry of slashes, but Chronor dodged or parried them all. To Adenar's surprise, Koradin landed a solid hit with the hilt of his sword into Chronor's jaw. Seemingly unphased, Chronor swung his blade at Koradin, who tipped his sword downwards to parry the blow, delivering another devastating punch into Chronor's stomach—the blow lifted the god from the ground, but he landed and raised his sword before Koradin could capitalize any further.

Perhaps Koradin could actually win, and Adenar felt a glimmer of hope.

They reengaged, and Chronor headbutted Koradin, stumbling the king back. He parried Chronor's quick jabs at his chest—barely. Chronor darted forward, and Koradin swung his blade wildly, missing every strike, but it kept Chronor away until he regained his footing. They came to a standstill.

Koradin wiped blood from his brow. "They aren't your soldiers! They kneel in fear."

"They will find it to be more rewarding than what you could ever give them."

"Your words are poison."

Chronor battered his sword at Koradin with a fury unlike anything Adenar had ever seen. The king parried the lightning strikes, but Chronor latched onto his arm and flung him into the air. He crashed into the ground, but masterfully used the throw's momentum to roll back onto his feet with sword in hand, as Chronor lunged after him and swung his blade. Koradin blocked it, but the god kicked him in the knee, making Koradin kneel. He groaned in pain, yet still managed to grab Chronor's hand to stop the deadly edge coming down on him—but didn't see Chronor's knee coming for his forehead. From the sound it made, Adenar knew it would kill a regular man. Surprisingly, Koradin rolled backwards, ended up back on his feet and swung the blade in an arc Chronor barely dodged, giving himself time to shrug off the crushing blow. He fell into stance, matching Chronor a few feet away.

"Together," Chronor said with a sickening smile, "we will conquer the world."

"I will not be your warrior," Koradin answered and spat blood.

"No, you will be *so* much more."

***

Khendric did his best to fend off the shadowwalker's continuous blows and stabs, but he *was* starting to feel the wounds and exhaustion taking their toll, for they would have killed an ordinary man hours ago.

The creature bled smoke from multiple gashes, indicating it was hurt, but Khendric probably had even less time—so he had to take a different approach

He fought his way towards Koradin and Chronor's duel, trying to keep the shadowwalker's shadowy blades away from his skin. The god and king's blows echoed through the air, their speed frightful. None of the turned soldiers reacted to Khendric or the shadowwalker, not even when their blades cut them accidentally. It had to be because Chronor was busy in the duel.

He neared the duelling grounds, and shouted at the top of his lungs, "I challenge you to a blood oath!" The shadowwalker's attacks broke off immediately, and Khendric turned to watch Chronor disengage from Koradin.

"Halt," he commanded the previous king of Ashbourn.

Koradin did so and took some deep breaths.

"You challenge me?" Chronor asked, striding menacingly towards him. "You have no weapon."

"I have this," Khendric said, showing him Godbreaker, the dagger.

"That cannot kill me, healer."

"I don't care. It can hurt you. I only agree to the duel if you let me fight alongside Koradin. You're going to have to take us both on."

Chronor seemed puzzled, twisting his head. "You know you are no match for me?"

"So what have you got to lose?" Khendric asked, anger boiling at the sight of Ara's killer. "You can have two moltens before the night is done, instead of one. I'll die either way, but this way you'll get more out of it."

"Khendric," Koradin said aloud. "Don't do this."

"I accept," Chronor declared. "Obviously." He stretched out a hand to Khendric, the same one Koradin had shaken. "The blood is fresh enough. Your cut will have to be deep, healer."

"Don't do this, Khendric," Koradin said. "You're a skilled fighter, but humans have no business here."

"Just keep him off me," Khendric answered and entered the grounds. All eyes were on him, even the turned soldiers and citizens followed his movements. He cut deep into his palm, watching as blood gushed from the wound. They shook hands, and Khendric felt a burning sensation in his body.

"It is done," Chronor said, walking to the centre of the stage. "I've rarely seen bravery like this in my lifetimes. Perhaps others among you are as brave as this." Chronor faced Koradin's remaining army. "If anyone of you are brave enough to challenge me, I will reward you with the great honour of becoming my rosh'gar. I accept all blood oaths from brave souls! Once I am done with the Ashenborn, you can use his weapon to fight me!"

Only the rustling of the wind and the burning in the braziers sounded through the night. Not a single person stepped forward.

Chronor waited patiently, but no brave words rang through the square. The god suddenly turned his head rapidly in all directions, as if an annoying insect flew around his face.

"No one is stepping forward," Khendric said. "Are you done?"

Chronor looked quizzically at the ground with his eyebrows narrowed. "Yes, few possess the bravery you displayed tonight."

Or rather the insanity, Khendric thought to himself, but the oath had been sealed.

"Now, find your positions," Chronor said as he lifted his blade into position.

Khendric placed himself on the far side of Chronor from Koradin. *Keep him off me, Koradin,* Khendric thought, hoping the god's focus would be on the king so Khendric could create some opportunities for him.

"You disappoint me," his mother's voice bled into his ears. A false apparition of her stood in the crowd of soldiers, all ragged and bloody. *"Just like you did when you killed me."*

Khendric forcefully shook his head and she disappeared. It felt like being this near Chronor made the hallucinations stronger, yet they didn't bite as hard as before, so another thought surfaced in his mind. "Where is she?" he roared to Chronor and a disgusting smile emerged on his dark lips.

"She is dead. Drained of blood."

"You're lying!" Khendric shouted, feeling his air completely leave him.

"She was strong. One of the strongest I've met, but she is gone."

Khendric's lower lip quivered, his control slipping. "You're just trying to make me lose it," he said as his fingers, toes, and chest vibrated with anger, despair, and fear.

"Darlaene is dead, healer."

"Don't you speak her name!" Khendric bellowed.

"Fine. Since you will become my rosh'gar, I grant you such respect."

"Stop!" Khendric shouted, his eyes wet with water. He hated that Chronor talked of respect, wanting him to display anger or regret. But he stayed ever calm and confident. "I will kill you," Khendric said through gritted teeth.

"So let's fight," Chronor said. "Whenever you are ready."

"I am ready," Koradin said.

"Then we begin." Chronor swung his sword in a wide arc, reaching as far as his tip could, heading straight for Khendric's gut. By sheer ingrained reflex, Khendric leapt backwards out of the way. The blade grazed his stomach, leaving a shallow gash. It healed immediately, but burned more than usual. Khendric drew a sharp breath. *I'm alive. I'm alive. Good.* The booming sound of Koradin and Chronor's blades clashing brought him back to the matter at hand. Chronor focused on Koradin, who assaulted him heavily.

Chronor blocked Koradin's mighty blows and countered with a horizontal swing. Khendric darted forward, but Chronor's sword passed by Koradin and came around in a full circle, almost splitting Khendric at the waist a second time had he not thrown himself to the ground. He slid forward and used the momentum to lunge and plunge his dagger into Chronor's lower back.

Chronor groaned and arched his back before his large hand swung around lightning quick and knocked Khendric away. He flew aside crashing to the ground, but kept his wits well enough to see Koradin capitalize on the opportunity: his burning blade cutting into Chronor's thigh. The god roared and elbowed Koradin away, and attacked with newfound ferocity.

Khendric shook his head and ran back into the fight, dagger held high. The dark god spun, kicking Koradin's feet out from under him, and slashed downwards at Khendric. Khendric threw himself to the side as the deadly edge buried itself into the ground, but Chronor pulled it free and stabbed at Khedric too fast for him to possibly react. The blade headed for him and suddenly jerked upwards, flying over his head.

Khendric couldn't believe it. While on his back, Koradin had planted his heel into Chronor's calf, saving Khendric's life.

With a roar, Chronor faced Koradin and attacked him relentlessly. Koradin and Chronor slashed, parried, and dodged one another with godly speed. Khendric approached and tried slashing the god, but he spun in a full circle, parrying Khendric's dagger and continued fighting Koradin. Khendric slashed again, but Chronor blocked it too and punched, but Khendric sidestepped it. He tried again and again, but Chronor either repositioned himself, dodged or parried the attacks—until he slipped slightly on his own blood.

Koradin struck at him, but the unbalanced god grabbed his arm—Khendric stabbed the dagger into Chronor's hamstring and Koradin punched him straight in the jaw. Chronor didn't release Koradin's arm even after the second punch, so the king locked eyes with Khendric. "Take it!" Koradin dropped his huge sword and Khendric lobbed him the dagger.

The blade fell into Khendric's hands.

With the dagger, Koradin slashed at Chronor's sword hand and he dropped the weapon, finally releasing Koradin's now empty hand.

Khendric drove the burning sword through Chronor's calf, and he roared in pain.

Koradin plunged Godbreaker into Chronor's chest.

Khendric retracted the sword. *Time to finish this.* He swung at Chronor's side.

Chronor grabbed Koradin's hand, twisted the dagger free, pulled it out of his chest, turned, grabbed Khendric's wrist and crushed it with overwhelming force. Koradin's sword flew from his hands as he screamed in agony, while Chronor's blade reappeared in his hand.

Khendric stumbled back, clutching his shattered wrist. The pain was unbearable, but it tapered off as he healed. With no focus on the duel, he hoped no sword gutted him until his pain subsided and his eyes dried up from the tears.

Aching seconds passed, and no sword cut his head off. Once the wrist healed, his vision cleared, and regained his focus. Koradin fought with both the sword and the dagger, though Chronor's two-handed strikes were hard to parry with only the strength of one hand on either blade

As Khendric re-engaged in the fight, Koradin tossed the dagger to him with acute precision. The dagger landed perfectly in Khendric's hand, and he ran past Chronor, adding a slice to his thigh.

Koradin delivered a punch to Chronor's cheek, but the god quickly elbowed him in the head. Koradin shrugged it off and sliced his blade at Chronor, who ducked and swung his deadly edge back. Koradin blocked and barreled his shoulder into Chronor, who rebuffed the force, roaring and pushing Koradin away, swinging his blade right over Khendric's ducked head.

Khendric darted forward and plunged the dagger into Chronor's back. The god's body arched, but kept parrying Koradin's blows. Koradin turned up the speed, hacking viciously at him, but Chronor held his blade up, blocking the attacks while trying to shove Khendric away. Koradin made it near impossible for Chronor to deal with Khendric, who stabbed the dagger into Chronor's back again.

Too close to Chronor to use his blade, Koradin shouted, "Khendric," and lobbed his sword over the god, creating the perfect opportunity to end this evil ancient being.

Khendric's hands wrapped around the hilt of the blade—Chronor's clenched fist punched into the weapon with unmatched strength. Khendric couldn't hold on, and it flew out of his hands.

"No!" Khendric screamed.

Chronor headbutted Koradin in the chest with all his might, creating the dangerous distance he needed. Before Koradin could recover, Chronor grabbed his throat and held him fast—aligning his otherworldly blade at Koradin's chest. Khendric stabbed and stabbed the dagger into Chronor's back, but he didn't falter. Koradin's eyes opened wide as the tip of the blade touched his chest. He clasped both hands on each side of the sword to keep it from entering his body.

"Welcome to servitude," Chronor said, driving the blade into Koradin's chest. He screamed in pain as the blade kept going through his body. He fell to his knees in front of the towering dark figure.

Khendric stumbled back in horror, losing all hope, dropping to his knees in futility.

"No!" Adenar roared. Commander Relen held him back, but even he looked devastated.

It happened so quickly, as if Chronor planned it. Khendric felt fear manifest as he stared at Koradin, knowing he was next. He felt his insides churn and threaten to spill out on the ground.

On his knees, Koradin coughed blood and gazed up at Chronor. Anger filled his face.

Chronor let go of the blade and kneeled, putting a hand on Koradin's shoulder. "You are incredibly skilled. I'm honoured to have you serve me."

"I will . . . never . . . serve."

"Yes. You will."

A violent fire emanated from Chronor's weapon, scorching Koradin's flesh. He roared in agony as the dark molten flame consumed his entire body. A whirling tornado of black smoke engulfed him, hiding him in an inferno. Chronor's eyes hungered, while Khendric crawled away as the heat wave struck him.

The brutal transformation abated, leaving behind a truly horrifying sight that shook Khendric to the very core. For he wasn't just about to die—he would experience the same fate.

From the dying fire, Koradin rose with molten fiery skin split by dark cracks emanating tendrils of smoke. His dark eyes held none of the former hate for Chronor.

"My rosh'gar," Chronor said proudly. "Summon your weapon."

A glowing orange blade coalesced in Koradin's hand as if from mist, lava dripping off the burning edge. Chronor's voreen blade paled in comparison to this terrible weapon of mass destruction.

Khendric realized what he had done. He'd given Chronor two unstoppable warriors, and the world would burn for it. He couldn't beat Chronor alone. As soon as the duel resumed, he would fall alongside the former king.

Khendric didn't fear death, but this was far worse—eternal servitude under the reign of a malevolent god. Even if someone killed Chronor, he'd become a shadowwalker.

He couldn't breathe, reality dawning upon him. His fingers trembled and barely functioned. He desperately wanted to flee, but Chronor would catch him easily. *I'm trapped. What am I supposed to do?* He found Koradin's sword, but his fingers would barely lend him the strength to grasp it. Chronor turned his attention to him as he lifted the shaking weapon.

"You have given me more than you can ever imagine, healer."

The sword felt so heavy in Khendric's hand, as if it didn't belong to him.

"I feel your fear," Chronor said. "You will do great things."

Khendric said nothing.

"Do not worry. It will be over quickly."

"I doubt that," Khendric answered, looking at Koradin, who stared ahead without emotion. Fire danced over his molten skin; a being of pure destruction. Khendric couldn't see a glimmer of the former man beyond the shadowy veil surrounding his new molten form.

"It is time," Chronor said, and Khendric savoured his last breaths. His insides churned as Chronor's blade reappeared in his hand. He steeled himself and levelled the fallen king's sword towards the monstrous god.

"Stop!" yelled a voice cutting through the air. A huge, broad man wearing a ridiculous amount of armour strode through Koradin's broken army with red-hot anger on his face. All the soldiers had understandably risen during the duel, and shuffled back and forth. Khendric recognized the man immediately: Topper. *I thought he'd been killed for sure,* Khendric thought, a faint smile finding its way to his lips.

A wide black cloak hung around his neck, reaching to the ground. The metal pieces clanked together as he walked forward, passing by the shameful soldiers.

"You murdered her!" Topper roared. Khendric had seen him angry many times, but this anger came from deep within. "She was just a sweet, little girl and you stabbed her like a coward! You truly are evil incarnate, you plague upon this world!"

Chronor frowned. "Be silent, or your death will—"

"I challenge you to a blood oath, you monster!" Topper shouted, stopping as he neared the end of the army.

Khendric wanted to scream at him to shut his mouth, but kept silent against his better judgement.

Topper clenched his jaw, eyes locked on Chronor.

Dead silence lay over the large square, but for the rustling of the wind. Not one soldier opened their mouth. Chronor's turned soldiers and citizens remained still too, maniacal looks cladding their faces.

Chronor examined Topper's figure, taking a step closer. "What are you?"

"I am Commander Royce," Topper said sternly, shaking with anger.

"*What* are you?"

"I am a man."

"No, you are not. You are *something* else."

"You said you accepted any blood oaths," Topper said and put his hand forward. "But only if you let us both fight you."

Chronor remained, eyes drilling into Topper, seeming to want to figure out Topper's game as much as Khendric wanted to know. "You are foolish."

"You are a coward," Topper bellowed back harshly. "You murdered Ara in cold—"

"Enough," Chronor said, waving a hand Topper's way. "I tire of your accusations."

Topper barred his teeth, something Khendric had never seen him do before. *Has he simply snapped? Has he gone mad?*

"How dare you?" Topper asked the god, and Khendric admired the audacious bravery, though Chronor seemed like he wanted to just kill him.

The god looked at him angrily, his nostrils flared like a beast, but then the animosity seemed to melt away and that sinister smile slashed across his face. "You *are* brave, I will give you that." Chronor's gaze wandered to Koradin's burning figure. "And such bravery should be rewarded." The god walked with heavy steps towards Topper, but stopped a few feet away. "You feel . . . familiar."

"What are you talking about?" Topper asked.

The god hesitated.

"Let me have my revenge, you monster." Topper drew his sword and cut into the palm of his hand. Blood flowed from the wound and dripped to the ground.

Chronor's mouth opened slightly, his eyes growing hungry as Topper's blood stained the ground.

"I will need a weapon," Topper said. "The dagger will be enough, trust me."

That must have struck a chord with Chronor, as he licked his lips and grinned. "Fine." The dagger lay at Chronor's feet, and he kicked it towards Topper.

Topper remained standing, hand outstretched.

Chronor closed the distance, staring Topper down, but he held firm.

Khendric had no idea what was happening. Should he try to stop Topper?

"I accept," Chronor said and cut open the wound in his palm once more. "Your armour will not help."

"Yes, it will," Topper said.

Chronor offered his hand and Topper clasped it hard.

Khendric let out a strained breath, knowing they had doomed the world. Dread filled his stomach and—

A huge dark blade shot out through Topper's chest with lightning speed, his arms and head thrown backwards. The tip pushed forward, digging into Chronor's chest. His mouth opened with a terrible growl, but the blade kept going until the tip protruded out of his back. His scream died. The menacing sword in his hand fell to the ground and vanished into a pool of smoke. He fell to his knees together with Topper's limp body, revealing a young woman holding a massive voreen blade.

Khendric didn't move an inch, no sound leaving his lips.

"H-how?" Chronor asked, his entire being leaking smoke. Ara stared the dark voreen god down. The clothing over her stomach had been torn to pieces from Chronor's stabbing, yet Khendric saw no wounds.

Ara pulled the sword out and Chronor groaned deeply as his flaming crown crumbled. His fingers withered into dark flakes that blew away in the wind.

"There was . . . no oath?" Chronor asked confused, clutching his chest with his diminishing hand.

Ara said nothing, clenching her jaw, holding pure courage in her eyes.

Chronor bent forward as his skin turned to dust. "Carry my gift . . . with you," he said with a faltering, yet deep and rumbling voice. His head vanished, followed by his shoulders, and in the end, only a pile of black dust remained.

Khendric couldn't believe his eyes. Chronor was dead? Just like that? And Ara still lived? He ran over to her and grabbed her tightly.

She threw her arms around him and cried heavily.

"Well done," he said. "You did great." She clutched him even tighter. "You were amazing, Ara."

In the embrace, he laid his eyes upon Koradin. His body faded out of existence, but Khendric swore he spotted a hint of a smile on his blazing lips.

Khendric had tremendous respect for the King of Ashbourn, who gave *everything*—more than his life—to save them all. Tears of joy and tragedy ran down Khendric's cheeks, for they had defeated the god, but Koradin remained an eternal servant forever. He hugged Ara tighter, still having trouble believing that she was in his arms again. And he hoped Koradin knew his people were safe.

* * *

As her tears stopped flowing, Ara let go of Khendric, and they looked upon all the people surrounding them. Koradin's army seemed astounded, despite having seen Ara behind Topper's back the whole time. They still looked like they didn't dare to move, but if that was shame or shock in their eyes, Ara didn't know.

The dark eyes of the turned soldiers and citizens faded, and they gazed around in confusion. Many began crying, some hugged each other, but mostly, pain surrounded them. Too many had died, and mind-controlled people had to live with the gruesome acts they had performed. The huge mass of people—every last citizen and soldier of Ashbourn—began dispersing, slowly clearing the square. No cheers rung through the air. Too many dead laid in the gutter in the streets. Ara felt the same feelings; thrilled Chronor had been defeated, but mournful for the loss.

Adenar pushed through the crowd with a pouch around his shoulder. Ara's lips split into a smile, but he barely looked at her, focused on something else. He kneeled at the pile of white ash left by Koradin upon his death. Ara had barely witnessed it, as she'd been busy putting all the armour on Topper.

No corpse remained after the king, but Adenar gathered the ash into his pouch.

Ara and Khendric walked up behind him. "He really was a great man," she said, hoping it was the right thing to say.

"He was my father," Adenar said, his lower lip shaking, holding some ash in his hand before he poured it into the pouch.

"Do you know how?" Ara wondered, knowing the 'secret' already.

"Something about a relationship and then an affair, but there wasn't enough time. My mother will know."

"So Koradin wasn't strictly human," Khendric said. "Does that mean you aren't either?"

"Khendric," Ara said, furrowing her brows. "You can't ask that."

"It's fine," Adenar said. He stared at the ash in his hand. "I don't know. Perhaps, but I've never felt any different."

"Are you alright?" Ara asked him.

He let out a breath and rose. "Yeah. I mean, I didn't really know him, so it doesn't feel like I've lost my father." No matter what he said, Ara saw some sorrow behind his eyes.

"But," he continued, "he truly was a great man and I'm honoured to have his blood coursing through my veins." With red eyes, he stared at her. His frown turned into a half-smile and he hugged her deeply. "We did it, Ara. We saved Ashbourn."

She embraced him, shivers running down her spine as he tightened his arms. "We did. We did the impossible."

"You're amazing," he said and she felt herself blushing.

Thank the stonepudders he can't see my face, she thought.

He let go of her and cleared his throat when he saw her red cheeks. "Sorry for crying," he said and wiped away some tears.

"No-no, it's fine."

"I have to go and find my mother. I need to know that she is alright."

"Of course."

He turned and jogged away, and she hoped Olenna was alright.

"So, how did you kill him?" Khendric asked, stealing her attention.

"You were there, weren't you?" she taunted, trying to lighten the mood.

"You know what I mean."

"When you shot him after he stabbed me, his blood sprayed onto my stomach and our blood mixed. I don't remember much more of what happened after, as I was dying of blood loss. Next, I woke up in an alley with Topper."

"How did you survive?"

"The bags of blood you gave me. Topper forced it down my throat."

A smile dawned on his face, and he chuckled. "I can't believe it."

"You saved my life again, with some help. I've been wearing them on my belt ever since I got them. Luckily, Topper and I were in a secluded area where none of Chronor's minions searched. We snuck inside those buildings." Ara pointed to the buildings behind the pavilions. "Then we tried to concoct some sort of plan while sneaking glimpses at the duel. I saw you challenge him. Do you remember when he said something along the lines of 'I accept all challenges to blood oaths from anyone'?"

Khendric nodded.

"Well, without really thinking, I just whispered that I accepted and felt a burning sensation within me. I then realized what I had done, which I'm sure you can relate to."

"Very much so," he said.

"After the initial panic, I realized two things: I can now kill him, and I had a voreen blade . . . somewhere. Topper and I snuck to where he had hidden my blade, and almost got caught several times, but we made it. Then we actually had to make a plan, but, looking at the duel we quickly realized we were running out of time. I couldn't fight him, that was obvious, so we had to trick him. Under heavy pressure, we came up with the most ridiculous plan, and started cladding Topper in as much armour as his body could carry."

"So he wore that big, bulky, ridiculous armour on purpose to conceal you?" Khendric asked.

"And the cloak, but yes, essentially that was our plan. I just had to ram the sword through them both, or become a molten. We prayed none in Koradin's army would squeal. I had to hold the blade pointed at Topper's back all the time, which got heavy, but I heard Topper clasp hands with Chronor and I pushed through with all my force."

"What a stupid plan," Khendric said and laughed.

She nodded with a smile. "I'm just glad you shot him when he transformed from Darlaene and his blood sprayed on me."

Khendric's features darkened immediately, his smile vanishing.

"Darlaene!" she exclaimed, but Khendric had already taken off running. She would follow, but he ran faster than lightning and was gone around a corner before she could even think.

An older man in white robes walked up beside her, standing next to the large blade. Ara hadn't thought to see Ponther again. He'd fled like a coward when laying eyes upon Chronor's army, but apparently, he hadn't gotten far.

Ponther sighed, and walked to where Koradin had been killed with a grim expression on his face, staring at the ground. "I am a coward, that's apparent to anyone. I'll live with that, and let the fate of the city in such events be handled by better people. My deepest thanks to you." He looked sincerely into her eyes. "Koradin truly was a *great* king, and I have my regrets. I fear his death is Ashbourn's biggest loss." He looked back at the ash that remained in Koradin's stead. "I'm sorry, old friend, for not listening to you." He put his fist to his chest in a sign of respect. "Do you know if Koradin revealed Adenar's heritage to him?" Ponther asked, surprising her.

"Uhm," Ara stuttered. "You knew?"

"Yes. Our families have always been close. I swore to secrecy, but I think he might be what Ashbourn needs now, at least for some time."

"What do you mean?" Ara asked.

"We need someone to rule, at least for the time being."

"And you want Adenar?"

"I do. The people know Koradin fought to his last breath for them. I think they'll be comfortable with his son as the new king until we hold a new coronation."

Ara didn't know what to say, simply blinking her eyes multiple times.

"We will be by his side," Ponther said, clearly seeing her expression. "We will aid him."

Ara chuckled and shook her head. The lowly assistant at the Meritocrat Headquarters, Adenar, was the son of the king, and would become king himself. *This is too bizarre to be true,* she thought.

"Thank you," Ponther said, offering his hand. "For saving us all."

She laid the sword down and grasped his hand with her dark arm. He shook it and bowed graciously. "I will go find the new king and break the news."

Ara remained alone on the duelling grounds, but a large number of soldiers had assembled around it, waiting. Her eyes ran along the growing crowd, uncertain as what to do. She swallowed dryly and felt her heart beat harder.

One soldier stepped forward and turned to the others, raising a hand into the air. "All hail the Hero of Ashbourn!"

"ALL HAIL THE HERO OF ASHBOURN!" roared the army loudly.

Ara lost her ability to speak at the humbling display of gratitude and tears welled in her eyes. The energy of the thousands of voices still vibrated deep in her chest, and her heart kept beating harder.

One by one, the soldiers kneeled.

The girl once beaten by her parents, the girl grown from nothing, the girl who'd never known more of the world than the Rundowns of Kalastra—that girl had saved an entire city, and thousands of soldiers saluted her. With cheeks redder than ever she had trouble believing this, but . . . it was real. As real as could be.

She raised her voreen blade and the soldiers rose and cheered wildly. A triumphant smile grew on her face as they ran towards her with happy faces and bolstering screams. They encapsulated her and patted her on the shoulders and head, staying clear of her blade. Hands grabbed at her thighs and before she knew it, they lifted her above their head, cheering at the top of their lungs. They also lifted Topper's body, screaming "martyr," and carried them both,

No deathwalker had sprouted from Topper's corpse, which she guessed was a good thing, and hoped he'd get back to Ashbourn quickly to see the result of their plan.

Tears of joy ran down her cheeks as they carried her off. They had done it, they had saved Ashbourn.

CHAPTER 12

The Hero, the King, and the Martyr of Ashbourn

"Are you alright?" Ara asked.

"No," Khendric answered. His head hung low, his eyes distant. Sunlight barely made its way through the small opening of the tent, dimly lighting his grim features. Normally, she'd be nervous about going on a large stage in front of a city, but the sadness drifting in the air dampened the emotion. The occasional cheers from the massive crowd outside reacting to Adenar's speech rekindled her nerves, but they settled quickly. Ara and Khendric sat inside their empty tent on the large stage, waiting to be called out by Adenar, the new temporary King of Ashbourn by Ponther's hand.

"I'm so sorry, Khendric."

"I know you are." He didn't look angry, just sad. "He had drained her completely of blood. Only her hair still had any colour." He twirled a lock of Darlaene's red hair around his finger. "I hoped he lied, but I knew he didn't."

Ara felt little dark thoughts sprout from his head. It seemed grief clouded his mind, and not a manifestation of anger or hatred. Despite the terrible circumstances, Khendric had learned *something*.

Two days had passed since Chronor's defeat, and the city slowly returned to a sense of normality. Adenar stepped competently into his new role, effectively establishing new caravan deals to feed a starving population. Or, starving until he uncovered the hidden Warborn food chambers, housing enough to keep the city alive for a week at least.

"I didn't put her in a coffin," Khendric said. "I burned her." He raised his hand to stop her from voicing her concern. "I know it's dangerous regarding kindlers, but it rained, and I had a moment of clarity after hours of holding her in my hands. If I didn't burn her body, I'd go my whole life trying to bring her back."

Lost for words, she put her dark hand on his shoulder.

"This is almost impossible to say without feeling like a terrible human being," he continued, "but if I'm being completely honest, strangely, I've been prepared for this. I mean, she was a *beast hunter*. I would have died numerous times without my abilities, so I knew someday she'd get in too deep and . . . that would be it. For being just a fantastic, ordinary woman, she's the best beast hunter I've ever known." Tears stained his beautiful light tunic and black tabard with white rims, until he wiped them away. "But then suddenly it hurts so much. The thought that I'll never hear her voice again or hold her close is unbearable." He lifted his red eyes from the ground and met hers. "But I know that I'll get through it, thanks to you." Khendric embraced her in a hug. "Thank you for showing me that all scars can heal."

Incredible appreciation washed over her and she tightened her grip, feeling tears force their way out of her eyes. "Thank you for saving me too," she said.

He let go and grabbed her shoulders, smiling. "This is a day of celebration. Let's celebrate."

They both heard Adenar's muffled voice through the tent. "*These* are the heroes of Ashbourn!"

She felt her heart almost skip a beat in a mix of nerves and excitement, and followed Khendric's lead. The rays of the sun momentarily blinded her, and the roar from the people threatened to deafen her too. At the end of the stage stood Adenar with his hands out towards them, wearing his father's crown, looking strikingly handsome in his blue royal attire. They stopped in front of him, and the cheering died down. She made sure to show her tainted arm, as that's what Adenar had wanted. Displaying it to the world like this made her feel proud. What had once caused her shame had led to their salvation and Chronor's downfall. Adenar had purposely set the celebration up in the marketplace where she killed the voreen god.

"Thank you, both of you," Adenar said loudly. "We owe you everything for saving our great city!" To her surprise, Adenar kneeled, his entire ensemble on stage following suit. Thousands of knees touched the ground next, and she felt all of their gratitude. Even Khendric looked like he struggled to keep his awe in check. Ara didn't bother, and her red eyes let free the tears wanting to cascade down her cheeks.

"Ara and Khendric," Adenar spoke loudly as he rose, the people rising in turn, "as a token of our gratitude, you will always have housing in Ashbourn should you wish to stay here." Adenar leaned closer and whispered, "this is where you kneel." Both she and Khendric did so. "Ara, to you, I, King of Ashbourn, bestow the estates that belonged to Eranna Carner."

She couldn't believe her ears, rising to protest the massive gift.

"Stay down," Khendric said, laying a hand on her shoulder.

"To you Khendric," Adenar continued. "I, King of Ashbourn, bestow upon you the estates of Ronoch Steelbane. We hope the two of you will keep an eye on the Warborn District in the future, though it is not your responsibility. I also grant you the military rank of Commander, giving you legal authority to inspect any Warborn-owned building or equipment without question." Adenar unsheathed a beautiful sword. "I lift you to nobility, meaning you will have to pick a family name for yourselves. Ara, what do you choose?"

Her mind froze. *Why didn't he tell me beforehand?* She remained on her knee and didn't say a word. Sweat formed on her forehead as thousands of people remained silent.

Khendric leaned closer, whispering, "What about 'Godkiller'?"

"What? That's ridiculous." His contaminating mischievous smile made her chuckle. Ara's eyes met Adenar's. "I choose my family name to be Godkiller," she said proudly.

"What?" he asked, blinking his eyes repeatedly.

"You heard me." His eyes darted to Khendric before a yielding smile grew on his lips.

"I hereby name you Ara Godkiller, The Hero of Ashbourn!" He touched the blade to both of her shoulders. "You may rise. Khendric, what will be the name of your family?"

He remained kneeling, and said with a mournful tone, "Dawnsun, in memory of Darlaene."

"I hereby name you Khendric Dawnsun, The Challenger of Gods!" Adenar touched the sword to Khendric's shoulders too, and the beast hunter rose. "To you, Khendric, I give Godbreaker—a dagger forged from the dust of a doombringer!" Commander Relen approached and offered the dagger to Khendric on a beautiful purple pillow.

"Thank you," he said, lifting the dagger proudly.

"To you, Ara," Adenar continued. "Not that we have a choice, but under my authority, I grant you leave to wield the voreen blade, given that you use it responsibly. For obvious reasons, we cannot formally hand you the blade, but it is yours nonetheless."

Chuckles and a soft murmur spread through the crowd, and Ara smiled deeply.

Adenar resumed his position at his panel, and Ara and Khendric took some steps back. He fit the role so well and she hoped he'd win the coming coronation and become a lasting king. "There are of course some heroes who did not live to see the end of this battle, "Adenar said. "Darlaene gave her life in the investigation of Chronor, and was captured and killed by Chronor himself. Without her, we would have lost. I am erecting a statue of this beautiful woman, who gave her life so that we could have our freedom, in the Passionist District, named 'The Martyr of Ashbourn!'"

Khendric bore a sombre expression. The public didn't know about their love, which was probably what he wanted.

"Koradin Banner, King of Ashbourn and my father, also gave his life for all of us in the fight against Chronor. His bravery is unmatched, challenging the god alone. I am proud to be his son and you should all be proud that he was your king. For King Koradin Banner!"

"KING KORADIN BANNER!" the citizens of Ashbourn bellowed, giving Ara goosebumps. Despite having known him briefly, she would miss the former king. He was a true man of honour.

"There is also one more who both did and didn't give his life," Adenar said when the crowd quieted. "Without Topper, Ara wouldn't have stood a chance!"

The truth about the morgal had been revealed, serving two purposes: he would be known for his heroic deeds, and no criminal charges could be leveraged against Ara for the murder of Topper. The latter would probably never happen anyway.

"He has not returned to us yet, but when he does, he will also be elevated to nobility, and given a family name and property. In his and Ara Godkiller's names, another stature will be forged and placed at the exact spot where Chronor was killed, depicting the epic moment when Ara drove her blade through Topper and into the dark god!"

Ara gawked, wanting to see it right away.

"Give our heroes one last round of applause!" Adenar bellowed.

Ara, Khendric, Commander Relen and Adenar all bowed one last time to the cheers of the deafening crowd.

"As you all know," Adenar continued. "In three months there will be a new coronation. The Warborn party is not allowed to enter a candidate, and the party will undergo serious investigations at all times for a long time. The council has been disbanded and all surviving members questioned about their involvement in Chronor's rise to power. For the time being, the city's armies will be handled by the king directly, together with one representative from each of the three remaining parties, hereby named 'The War Council.' Once the Warborn party can be trusted again, they will regain their former duties. I am the Chosen of the Meritocrat Party, and I hope to win your support during my brief time as king. I have formed new trade deals with villages and cities, and new shipments of food and other essentials are on their way." Adenar waited for the applause to die. "There is a book called 'The Dark Traitor' that holds all the information needed to defeat Chronor should he ever return. Without it, we would have stood no chance. Hence, it is being copied and distributed to all libraries, schools, and public buildings as well as all cities in the Sangerian Grasslands. We are even sending it to other kingdoms, hoping to make Chronor the most infamous god in the world! Thank you for all your support."

Adenar ended his long speech and transported them all in carriages to the huge castle in the middle of the city. Citizens cheered them the whole way there, hoping they would catch a glance at the new heroes. Ara waved all the way to the castle with her enhanced arm, relishing the heroic feeling. Khendric mostly stared out the window, giving a half-wave at best.

Once the carriage stopped, he put a hand on her shoulder. "Imagine if we hadn't walked past your house that night. This city would have been doomed, and maybe even the world. Perhaps it was fate."

"Or just luck."

With a mused expression, he said, "Probably just luck."

The carriages entered through the castle gate and stopped. Together with other numerous people, Adenar walked in front with Commander Relen and Ponther. Ara didn't despise Ponther anymore. She didn't like him either, but she saw he regretted not trusting Koradin, doing whatever he could to help Adenar.

An officer approached Adenar as they climbed the stairs leading inside. The two shared a few words before Adenar turned and waved both Ara and Khendric over. "It seems Topper is back. Or someone claiming to be him."

Ara felt a burst of relief. A growing worry had been that Topper had for some reason not survived the voreen blade.

"We'll be the judges of that," Khendric said. "Bring him forth."

Two guards escorted a dark-haired man with a slim build towards them. A huge grin dawned on the rather handsome face, and he stopped a few feet away from Ara and Khendric.

"Well?" Khendric asked.

"Hmm," the stranger said. "What terrible quote shall I resurrect back to life this time?" He rubbed his hands together. "I'll go with a classic one: the secrets of the past are always hidden in—"

Ara burst forth and embraced him.

His arms wrapped around her. "I can't believe it worked. That blade hurt more than any previous death, but the worst part was not knowing if it worked or not."

Ara let go of him and Adenar leaned closer, reaching out his hand. "I must also thank you."

Topper grabbed it and pulled Adenar close. "I hear you're doing pretty well as king. Don't screw it up."

Adenar grinned. "If I do, you know I'm possessed by some monster."

"Okay-okay," Khendric said. "Stop ignoring me. It's good seeing you again. You're not looking terrible. In fact, you're quite handsome." He examined Topper's new body. "Perhaps a bit *too* handsome. I feel threatened. Maybe I have to kill you."

"I'll kill you first." They shared boyish smiles and clasped hands.

"I would like to talk to you about some rewards," Adenar said. "But if it is alright with you, can it wait? I would like to talk to Ara in private if that's okay?" Both Khendric and Topper gave the young king daunting stares and whistled at him.

"Stop, or I'll throw you in the dungeons," Adenar said, blushing profusely.

Khendric and Topper walked away with mocking expressions, leaving Ara alone with Adenar after all of his other advisors and commanders left too. Her stomach churned with a mixture of both anticipation and worry as she looked into his starry eyes. For some moments they just lingered there, looking at each other as everything finally stilled around them, alerting her of how hard her heart beat.

"So," Adenar said, losing all sense of authority. In a moment he became the same earnest and nervous young man from when they met. "I would like to, uhm . . ." His lips trembled, and Ara's spread into a grin, hoping she knew where this was going. "I would like to ask you, that perhaps maybe you . . . Ara, would want to . . . Uhm . . ."

"Is the King of Ashbourn nervous?" Ara said, taunting him. "I think I'll add this as my biggest achievement: made the King of Ashbourn speechless."

Adenar forced a smile and composed himself. "Ara," he said with a determined voice. "I would like to court you."

"Let's start with dinner," she said and, without thinking, leaned forward and kissed him. *What am I doing? Did I just . . .?*

She felt his lips return the kiss and placed her hands on his chest. An inferno of emotions welled up within her. *My first kiss. And to a king.*

"My first kiss," Adenar said as they departed, cheeks red. "And to a god killer."

Ara laughed sharply and awkwardly.

"I'll . . . see you tonight then?" he asked.

"I can't wait."

EPILOGUE

The Dinner of Fates

Night covered Ashbourn, but the moon cast its light over the city as a reminder that hope had survived and won. Peace rested over Ashbourn once more, and Adenar felt he could breathe again for the first time in a long time. They'd defeated Chronor, and the rebuilding had begun. Despite being demanding work, his current job as a temporary king left him less exhausted than his time as an assistant, which he found amusing and chuckled to himself.

"What's so funny?" Olenna asked, still tidying up his new massive royal quarters within the castle, where Koradin had lived for twelve years.

It seemed even kings needed mothers. "I found it more stressful being an assistant than being king," he answered and turned away from his grand terrace.

"Just you wait until the coronation begins," she warned.

He smirked. "Mother, how did it all happen? With you and Koradin? How did you come to court a king?"

"He wasn't king back then," she said, fluffing up his pillows. "Just an idealist with a fire in his eyes unlike anything I'd ever seen."

"Did you know about him being ashenborn?" Adenar sat down on a nearby chair.

"No. He never told me. We met while we studied and had a pretty good relationship."

"Why did it end?"

"Foolish youthful things, like jealousy." She seemed pleased with how his bed looked and sat down next to him. "It's so long ago it's hard to remember."

"And how did I come to be?" Adenar asked.

"You were a terrible mistake," she said.

Adenar sighed, rolling his eyes.

"You know me too well, but it was a detrimental mistake at the time. We met once, at a gala many years later. His wife didn't attend and we began talking, reminiscing about the olden days, while getting drunker. The night pressed on and I kissed him . . . or was it he who kissed me? I don't rightly remember. The kiss prolonged and . . . we made you."

"I get why you said 'mistake,'" Adenar joked.

"Your father was scared to death when I told him. I knew how much becoming king meant to him and how much good he could *actually* do in the position, so we agreed: he would help support me as best he could and I kept the secret. He kept his word, always looking after you, sending letters asking how you were doing. He cared for you, a lot."

"Wow," Adenar said, feeling a tear forming in his eye.

His mother hugged him. "I should go to my 'new home' right down the hallway. Don't freak out too much over this date with Ara. She's gorgeous. If you misbehave and she slaps you, I think your whole face would disappear."

"I agree." At the thought of the date, his nervousness reappeared. *What if she hates it?*

Olenna disappeared out the door. He always felt better after talking to her, and they weren't done talking about the past. He wanted to know so much more, but hopefully, he could bring the two families together first.

He had met Koradin's three daughters—his new sisters—for the first time today as well. They had all done their best to be nice around him, but sorrow had a mighty grip on their hearts. Adenar understood them well, and appreciated the effort. Lenda, their mother, struggled more with hiding her grief and bitterness, but he couldn't blame her. He would give her as much time as she needed, understanding that seeing him was a living reminder of her husband's unfaithfulness. It helped tremendously that his new sisters wanted to form relationships, and he enjoyed their company, looking forward to meeting them tomorrow. But for now, he should focus on the upcoming dinner.

He walked in front of the mirror, inspecting his hand-picked clothes for the evening. A simple deep blue shirt made out of silk with a black vest over it. His advisors had told him over and over again how this didn't befit a king, but he didn't care much. A pair of black trousers accompanied the shirt and vest. He'd sworn to wear his crown—the only way to make his advisors shut up. It looked ridiculous in these clothes, but he had given them his word.

A crack sounded through the room and Adenar turned quickly. Several more followed, originating from the urn holding his father's ashes. The urn had been placed on a pedestal with painted-on flames. It shook slightly and almost toppled to the ground. Adenar grabbed a nearby dagger, his father's words repeating in his ears.

Take my ashes and kill whatever is born of it.

The urn suffered a push from the inside, crashing towards the ground. It broke, and the ashes of his father spilt all over the floor. Adenar got down on his knees next to it.

A small head rose from the ash—a bird's head. It revealed more of its small, featherless body, taking some clumsy steps before staring at Adenar. How had this come from his father's remains?

Slowly, the bird's skin caught fire until its whole body burned bright. A glance at a window revealed its wish to flee.

Is this what you meant, father? You want me to kill this small, beautiful bird? It felt so petty, but this clearly wasn't some normal beast. It tried to flap its wings, but it couldn't fly just yet.

Adenar sucked in a deep breath and grasped the knife in his hands. Koradin had not been a fool, and there was probably a good reason why Adenar *should* kill it. His father *knew* what this was, and Adenar didn't. *That's really the only reason I need, and I won't disobey his final wish.*

It felt wrong, but he drove the dagger easily into the small chest of the flaming bird. It exploded into a violent inferno, consuming Adenar with it. He screamed in pain—his skin roasting. The flames ate him up, burning him alive.

* * *

Adenar gasped for air as he shot up from the white ash surrounding him. When he breathed, it felt like his lungs expanded for the first time. He opened his eyes, but his blurry vision only allowed him to understand he laid in his royal room at the Ashbourn castle.

What happened? He remembered an all-consuming fire, and . . . a flaming bird?

"That was cruel," a voice spoke from within his mind.

Adenar tried to locate the origin of the voice, but it proved difficult with his swimming vision. He opened his mouth to speak, but his dry throat put a stop to that. When his vision finally cleared, he found himself to be alone, sitting in a pile of crystal-white ash.

"But Koradin did tell you to do it."

"W-what?" he finally managed to croak.

"You killed me, and now I am yours."

"Am I an Ashenborn now?" Adenar asked after a couple of coughs.

"Clever for an assistant."

"Actually, I am a king."

"We shall see."

He rose on wobbly legs and found a mirror, finding himself to have put on some pounds of pure muscle. *Now I understand why Koradin looked so regal.* He ran his fingers through his now blonde hair. "Koradin's hair wasn't always blonde either?"

"No. It was like yours used to be. You are now a part of a long line of kings and heroes. You now have powers that—"

"My clothes!" Adenar exclaimed. They had been burned to dust, and he had nothing to wear for the date. "What do I do now?" He stormed out of the room in what remained of the handpicked clothes to find something new to wear in a hurry, tearing through his royal closet of royal clothes.

"As I was saying—"

"Not now, bird," Adenar said while running almost naked through the corridor after finding nothing befitting in his wardrobes.

"Did you just call me 'bird'?"

"Sorry about that," Adenar said as he rounded a corner with great speed and inhuman balance. "I have an important dinner to—"

He turned sharply around a second corner and crashed into a large man wearing a great robe. Adenar fell towards the ground, but his reflexes helped him roll back to his feet with ease. "Wow," he said in awe. *This is amazing.*

The man he had collided with remained standing despite the collision. His monocle gave him a distinct look, especially with seeming a little too young to wear it. Adenar would place him at the same age as his father. The cane in his hand probably helped his balance too. Something glimmered in the air around the man, and a golden coin landed on the ground. Adenar had knocked it out of the stranger's hand.

"Must be an important dinner," the man said, keeping his air of eloquence.

"I'm so sorry," Adenar apologized. "Are you alright?"

"It's not every day you're run down by a king," he said.

Adenar chuckled—though nervously.

"Could you help out an old man and pick up that coin?"

Adenar frowned. Looking at his face he shouldn't be *that* old, but the cane and monocle said otherwise. The coin laid right by Adenar's foot. He bent down and picked it up.

"Careful," the man said sharply. "Don't turn it."

Adenar made sure not to, holding it flat in his hand. It depicted an arm ending with a hand holding a skull. A rope passed through the skull's eyes and coiled around the arm. He had never seen such a coin before. The man leaned closer to examine it too.

"Who are you?" Adenar asked. "I haven't seen you before."

"Most interesting," the man said, his eyes on the coin, murmuring, "so you did kill the bird."

"What?" Adenar asked, wondering if he'd heard correctly.

"It's a huge castle. Surely you haven't seen everyone in it in your short time here."

"What did you say about the bird?" Adenar pressed, closing his hand around the coin.

"You killed it, yes? It seems you have tethered yourself to fate again, young King. Tell me, is it a right or left hand on the coin?"

"What?" Adenar asked. "Shouldn't you know?"

"Look at the thumb," the man asked.

Adenar opened his hand again. "Left."

The stranger paused, his mouth staying open. "I see."

"Why? What does that mean?"

"We shouldn't talk. Don't you have an important dinner to get to?"

Adenar frowned, but the man grabbed the coin with a quick hand and resumed walking around the corner. A pack of gnurgles followed closely beneath his robe.

"Hey, wait," Adenar said.

"I can't. I have places to be," the stranger said. "And so do you."

He wanted to ask more, but the stranger had a point. Adenar *did* have an important dinner to attend.

* * *

Ara had never worn such a beautiful blue gown before, and spun in front of the mirror repeatedly, loving how it swirled around her. She felt so pretty, even liking how well her dark veins fit with the colour.

"Maybe," Khendric said, lounging on her bed, eating grapes, "you should spin two more times for good measure."

Ara snorted and rolled her eyes back.

"You do look beautiful," he added.

Khendric and Topper hadn't been able to keep their mouths shut about the dinner, making a fool out of her as often as they could, sprinkling in some nice words here and there to keep their conscience clean.

Despite having gotten separate houses, they all spent time together in a cramped room within the castle. It fit perfectly with her, being closer to Adenar. Topper gazed out the window, seeming contempt.

It felt so good to be with them without having a case. They could just make fun of each other, laugh, and talk about the craziness they had survived. Naturally, Khendric's mind often spiralled, but he really tried his best to keep himself in check for her big night.

Ara finally dragged herself away from the mirror. "I think I'm done," she said, making Topper turn away from the window. "What do you think?"

"If he doesn't like it," Topper said. "I'll beat him bloody."

"I don't think beating up a king is very wise," she said.

"What's he going to do, kill me?" he said and chuckled.

"Good point," Ara answered with a laugh.

"You look beautiful," Khendric said as he examined her. "He's one lucky guy."

Ara blushed. "Thank you. Now I've got to go."

"Remember," Topper said. "Wise is the woman who dresses as the night, but appears as the day."

Ara stopped halfway out the door, furrowing her brows and looking at him. "What?"

Topper looked to Khendric for approval, but found a similar expression on his face. "You'll get it when you're older."

Khendric slid off the bed and onto his feet. "No-no, I think you should explain it here and now."

Topper opened his mouth to protest, but no words came.

"I think it's vital for me to understand these . . . *profound* words," Ara said mockingly. "Else I might not be safe on this date."

"Well," Topper began. "You see, the night is dark, and so is your gown, but you have the demeanour of . . . the day, and so, therefore . . ." He waved his hands in small circles, probably hoping one of them would save him, but both Ara and Khendric waited patiently.

"Therefore?" Khendric pressed.

"Alright, fine!" Topper roared. "I just thought it sounded smart. I have no idea what it means!"

"Thank you," Ara said and closed the door, and stormed into the hallway. After walking up several staircases and through numerous hallways, passing countless guards, she found herself in front of where Adenar had planned their dinner. She breathed heavily, hoping her sweat didn't show too well. *This has to be the very top of the castle*, she thought.

"You may come in," Adenar's voice rang through the heavy doors. She pushed them open and discovered she was, in fact, at the very top. The wind caught her hair immediately as she stepped outside on a tiny balcony with a table and two chairs. The balcony offered a view over Ashbourn, with certainty being the highest point of the city. It was breathtaking, so breathtaking that she almost missed Adenar leaning against the railing.

"It's beautiful, isn't it?"

Ara placed her hands on the railing too. "Yeah. I've never been this high up before, ever. Everything seems so small."

"Dinner is being prepared and will be brought up to us soon."

"Oh, brought to us? Being a king has its advantages. What are we having?"

He nodded with large eyes. "Yeah, it really does. We're having steak together with some . . . other things, I don't really remember. It's going to be good, I hope."

"I believe you," she said with a smile, getting lost in his eyes. It felt like eels crawled inside her guts, and her fingers tingled. He was so handsome, but he looked different. "What happened to your hair? It's . . . blonde?"

His hands went to his head right away. "Oh, right. Thought you'd like it, and—"

"It reminds me of Koradin. You look like him." Knowing their relation made it impossible *not* to see their similarities. "Did you do it to salute your father?"

"Uhm, yes."

"I like it."

He looked into her eyes and then down at her gown as his face turned red. "Oh," he said, shaking his head. "I forgot; you look beautiful."

She did a spin for him, and he seemed to gawk. "Thank you, I was hoping you would notice."

"I'm sorry," he said, chuckling nervously.

The quirkiness he displayed now was such a huge contrast to the kingly demeanour he held to his people, and Ara liked it. She got to see the secret side to him that the citizens wouldn't, his true nature.

"Don't worry about it," she said and put a hand on his shoulder. "Let's sit."

Shortly after, two people entered the terrace and placed food before them. It didn't look like the beef Adenar talked of, and one of the servers explained it was octinara meat.

It tasted decent enough, but it was way too salty for Ara.

"It's supposed to be a delicacy," Adenar said, drinking the rest of his water and pouring more from the canteen.

"I believe you," she said, trying not to grimace. "Because you'd have to be nobility to have enough water to eat this."

Adenar laughed and they begged a guard waiting on the inside to bring more water.

The beef finally arrived and she dug in, experiencing the most succulent meat she had ever tasted. It melted on her tongue and she couldn't stop herself from taking the next bite. Neither of them spoke, but they shared awkward giggles and before long the main course had been gulped down.

"That was . . . tasty," Adenar said and leaned back on his chair.

Ara stared into his eyes with admiration. Adenar had never tried to be anyone but himself, and luckily she really liked him for him. As her eyes examined him, she thought he seemed more muscular.

"I have to ask you about something," Adenar said. "And if you don't want to talk about it, just let me know." She nodded at him to continue. "When do you think Chronor captured Darlaene?"

"It must have been when we infiltrated their headquarters when she passed for an arranger," she answered, having pondered the same thing.

"I thought so too."

"That's when we got separated and Topper was killed," Ara continued. "Hence, she was alone. She must have been captured then and he used her blood to gain her appearance, just like he did with Ronoch Steelbane."

Adenar let out a sigh. "It must have been terrible."

"Yeah. It's eating Khendric up, I can feel it. I hope he gets better with time. I've been thinking back to every time I met her after the infiltration and there were small things I should have picked up on. When I told her Khendric and Topper had left Ashbourn for good, I felt no dark thoughts emanate from her mind. Considering that she almost murdered me because I attended a political party with him, she should definitely have felt something."

"But why help you get the dagger?"

"I'm not sure. He knew it couldn't kill him, so I've been thinking it was to give us enough hope to come out and face him. He needed us to be brave, I think, so that breaking our spirit would hurt as much as possible, increasing the chance we'd give in to him. But I'm not sure."

"That might be. It certainly worked. He snuffed out our greatest hope right in front of us. Every one of our soldiers knew you were the one that could beat him." His gaze fell to the table. "It tore me apart seeing what he did to you."

"It tore me apart too," she answered. "Literally." They looked at each other with blank stares, before bursting out laughing.

"I have a question for you," Ara said.

"As king, I allow it, but just one."

She chuckled. "You said you didn't know how you got the job as an assistant?"

"That's right. It didn't even seem like anyone at the Headquarters knew."

"I think Koradin got you the job. I think he pulled some strings."

"I think so too, at least according to my mother. It's nice to know he was watching over me."

"Are you angry with him?" she wondered. "For not being there."

"Yes," he answered. "But I understand him too. I want to be angry, but it won't do any good."

They sat down on a bench together, and Ara instinctively leaned her head on his shoulder, realizing afterwards what she had done. A moment of anxiety hit her, but he seemed calm, so she stayed. It calmed her heart down somewhat, but she still felt the excitement hanging in the air.

"Thank you, Ara," he said. "Just for, everything."

Ara almost kissed him again as their eyes locked, but she restrained herself. *This time it's his turn.* Adenar did nothing though, and the moment turned awkward.

She sighed. "You should get some of your father's courage."

He leaned close and pressed his lips to hers. Sparks shot through her body and to her fingertips. She put her hand behind his head, and he clasped his hands around her, but someone opened the door. She shoved him away by reflex, way too hard with her tainted arm, but he placed his feet strategically into the ground and grabbed the railing, negating her push almost instantly. *Wow,* she thought.

"Uhm," the advisor in the doorway said, seeming to know exactly what he had interrupted. "Terribly sorry, my King. I just want to remind you of how much you have to do tomorrow."

With a sad expression, Adenar said, "He's right. But, uhm . . . I want to see you again—"

"Tomorrow?" she asked eagerly.

"That would be lovely."

Ara and Adenar walked through the endless staircases, followed closely by the advisor who didn't want to let them out of his sight. They stopped before a great hall, where apparently they would part ways.

Adenar gave her an awkward shake of the hand. "I will see you then, Miss Godkiller."

She chuckled and dramatically kneeled before him. "Yes, my lord and liege. We will."

Adenar's weird demeanour broke into his regular smile, and even the advisor let a grin sprout on his face. Adenar left her, but he winked at her with one eye, making her stomach feel all tingly again.

Despite staying in another part of the castle, she had a little journey ahead of her and started walking, feeling something she had never felt before. A certain happiness coursed through her whole body, and she couldn't help smiling on her way back to her quarters. Khendric and Topper could say what they wished, nothing could hurt her now.

She entered one of the castle's many gardens on her way back, relishing in the starry night. Guards stood posted at all entrances, but didn't inquire about her intentions or anything, making her feel quite important. She skipped along the small brick road as she passed the many plants and flowers in the garden.

She rounded a corner and found a man sitting on a bench, wearing large dark robes with a hood covering his head. Several gnurgles ran around his feet, eating small pieces of bread he tossed to them. "Miss Godkiller," he said as she walked by.

Ara turned sharply, alert. "Who are you?"

"Don't worry. I am not here to hurt you. I am here simply to observe and . . . predict."

She frowned and stayed ready for an attack nonetheless.

"You did very well," he said, "in saving Ashbourn, I mean. The first time we crossed paths, I felt only a slight disturbance in fate."

"What are you talking about? I've never seen you before."

"It was long ago. You were . . . not as you are today." She wanted him to lift his head, so she could see his face. A cane rested against the edge of the bench. "You've changed significantly. Even fate calls your name."

A part of Ara told her to run, but she wanted to know what he talked about. "Fate calls my name?" she asked. "What does that mean? Who are you? Show your face or I'll tear your hood away."

The stranger flicked a coin her way, revealing a younger face than she anticipated. The coin spun through the air, and instinctively, she caught it. Opening the palm she laid eyes upon the strangest of symbols.

"What's the outcome?" he asked, staring back at the ground, only his mouth visible.

"What are you?" she countered.

"Tell me the outcome and I'll tell you."

"It's a hand holding a seed," she said. Vines grew forth from the seed, tangling themselves around the arm.

"Is it a left or right hand, according to the thumb?"

"Tell me who you are."

"I will if you answer my question. You are in no danger, I swear it."

She examined the symbol on the coin. "Right hand."

The man's lips spread into a thin smile. "I am the right hand of fate. And when fate calls, you must do as it says."

"What do you mean?"

"I don't know yet. Something is coming, and if my predictions are right; something old. You are lucky."

"How so?"

"You may not need a twist of fate to survive."

"A twist of fate? What do you mean?"

"A twist of fate is to change a prophecy as it's coming true."

"Prophecy?"

The stranger locked eyes with her. "You must know: nothing is certain until it happens. The prophecies regarding yours, Khendric's, Topper's, and Adenar's futures are not written in stone."

"You better start making sense," Ara pressed, getting annoyed.

"What's on the other side of the coin?"

Ara flipped it, seeing a similar symbol, but with a skull and a rope instead, still held with a right hand.

The wind rustled and when she looked up, the man and his gnurgles had disappeared. She closed her hand around the coin, but felt nothing in her hand. It had vanished too. She looked around the garden, but saw no sign of the mysterious stranger.

She felt troubled, rushing to an entrance to find two guards. "Did you see a man with gnurgles?"

They looked confused. "No. Is everything alright?"

"Are you certain?"

"No one has entered or exited the garden through this entrance," the other guard said.

It left her feeling dissatisfied, and she pondered upon the meeting the whole time back to her rooms.

As she opened the door, Khendric and Topper greeted her with smiles and laughter, teaching her a new game they apparently had been playing since she left. It helped her push the strange meeting to the back of her mind, which she needed for now. *I'll tell them another time,* she decided and simply enjoyed their company; the company of her new family.

She joked, discussed, talked, and laughed heartily with them, even shedding some tears at her happiness, feeling beyond blessed to have been saved by them so long ago.

After *everything* she had been through with these two weird men, they had given her exactly what she had yearned for all her life: family.

BEASTIARY

Deathwood

Known location: throughout Dimbar forest and some distance outside as well, depending on the wind. If the seeds are caught in a whirlwind it could be a disaster if they land in other regions.

Type: seed

Weakness: cold temperatures

Rarity: common

If you ever find yourself in Dimbar forest and feel like you start seeing shadows resembling people in the corner of your eyes; run. The deathwood is a type of forest spreading within Dimbar forest, praying on living creatures, especially humans, characterized by looking like trees and plants growing out from corpses—because that's exactly what it is.

What happens is this: a deathwood tree releases its seeds in the wind, and it lands on the skin of a creature or human. If it is not removed before burrowing through the skin, all hope is lost. It will move through the body, slowly growing.

Victims of a deathwood seed will take a slow turn for the worse, and depending on where the seed settles, vegetative growths will occur. The seed grows and will protrude from the body, and its location determines how long the victim will live. On the arm it will be slow, while close to the heart or the brain, death comes fast. Vines or branches may grow forth from anywhere, for example: on the arm, from the mouth, through the chest, from the armpit, or anywhere else on the body. Once the victim is dead, the growths continue until it becomes a large tree, sprouting through skin and bone, releasing its own seeds in spring.

The roots and vines growing forth from the person's body will try to attach themselves to the ground or objects. That's why many victims within the Dimbar forest are standing up, desperately trying not to fall asleep, but the seed always wins. At some point, the afflicted must rest, and in later stages, the roots are active, quickly growing into the ground. Some people also become near-immobile or immobile quickly due to the seed's location and are doomed to grow into their environment in early stages. Some truly unfortunate souls have multiple seeds burrow into their skin and growths emerge from multiple places. It's a painful death, and those affected are exiled to the Dimbar forest to keep the contagion under control. If you see trees grown out from human or beastly bodies, run.

The important thing to take away is this: don't go into the Dimbar forest in spring. You might never come out.

Alec

Rembar

Known location: Kolridge and Varanos

Type: humanoid

Weakness: general weapons

Rarity: common

*Rembars are tall and lanky creatures of peaceful na-
ture and are prone to fleeing from any conflict. They have
short brown fur, and long snouts and ears. The teeth in
their mouth are not sharp, used for eating grass, bark
and such. They may unhinge their jaws to make their
maw circular to gather rainwater efficiently. While this
looks disturbing, it has no sinister purpose. For being
thin creatures, their stomachs are strikingly spherical, as
if they had all swallowed a huge canon ball. They live
either near the ocean or up in the mountain ranges where
it rains a lot, needing a substantial amount of water for
their remarkable stomach abilities.*

*Rembars naturally brew ale in their stomachs, and
rembar-ale is renowned around the world for its incredible
taste. They sustain themselves on their brewed ale, needing little other nourishment, as long as they have access to
water. During autumn, rembars store their ale for the
coming winter, their bellies growing large, making movement harder.*

*It is believed that the rembars near the ocean and
those in the mountain ranges are different tribes. The
ocean rembars have evolved to brew ale with saltwater,
something the mountain rembars can't, giving the ale a
salty taste.*

*Rembars are unfortunately hunted for their ale, and
since they don't fight back, they are easy prey. There are*

few rembars left, and if they go extinct, the ale is lost forever. This human fear is currently what keeps them alive, and Brindenborg, Hirren, and Mountainmorg have stationed designated soldiers to kill poachers, trying to save the species. Poachers are especially active during autumn when the rembars are getting ready for winter. The hope is that we can find a way to extract the ale without killing the rembars. These creatures are peaceful and friendly, and I've walked amongst them many times. Please help protect them from black market poachers.

Alec

Children of the Snow

Known locations: Norda, Ponteria, Paradrax, and further north

Type: humanoid, parasitic, ghoul

Weakness: fire and a warm environment

Rarity: Rare

The origin of the children of the snow is unknown, but they have some ghoulish features. They resemble children around six to eleven years old, but with blue and frozen skin. Their eyes and hair are crystal white, and their nails are long. These children are truly frightful, and none know exactly how they come to be, but they have one clear omen foretelling of their arrival.

If you live in a village, and as winter ends, the snow doesn't melt, be aware. If the snow in the surrounding area does melt, but not the snow in the village, you have two options: flee or fight. It's a peculiar phenomenon seeing a clear line between spring and winter, where over a village it might snow, whilst outside the sun shines brightly. This means that during winter, the children of the snow have arrived.

The villagers who won't flee have to light torches immediately, as the children hate heat. The best way to combat their infestation is to burn pyres and as much wood as possible to heat the area. The more snow that melts, the better. My advice is to burn all the lumber you have saved up and send as many people as you can out of the village to chop down more. I actually think this is vital, especially since many have burned up almost all their timber during winter. Another tip is to burn down the houses of any who are taken by the children, as long as that won't set fire to other houses of course. If you heat the village for long enough to a sufficient temperature, the children of the snow will disappear. If you cannot heat the village, the snow will continue to fall until moving outside becomes almost impossible. If this happens, there isn't much hope, especially if everyone is isolated.

The children of the snow will kill everyone in a village, most often at night. They start with the coldest houses, often belonging to the poorer residents who can't afford or acquire wood to burn. The children knock on the door first, but you must not open up. Light any light source you can. If you have a weapon, find it. When you don't open the door, they will move to the windows and knock there, but you won't see them. Children's voices will ask for help, saying you have to save them from the cold. It's a trick, do NOT listen to them, no matter how much they beg. Board the windows if you can. The snowfall will increase, reaching higher up the wall of your house, but it's too late to deal with that. Focus on heating as much as you can. Your door will begin to creak as something pushes against it. This is the weight of the snow and the children pushing on it, trying to break through. Use what you can to reinforce it. The same goes for the windows. If they break a window, repair it as fast as you can, or else the cold will quell your warmth. Snow may fall down your chimney too. If so, remove it so your fire doesn't die and the smoke won't choke you. If you survive this until the next day, you have another chance, but their attacks will intensify.

Most people won't survive this, as either a window breaks, the door bursts off its hinges, or their roof collapses due to the weight of the snow. After your door breaks open, nothing will happen at first. Your warmth will be swallowed by the cold as snow enters your home. You'll start to freeze, your breath turning to fog, as you stare fearfully into the white nothingness outside your door. Children start to sing. Gusts of wind throw more snow into the house as the song intensifies. Children as white as the snow and blue as the ocean reveal themselves as shadows in the distance, creeping ever closer, growing larger in numbers. They enter your home with sapphire eyes and barred teeth, singing their song as they come to claim you. Fight with all you have, though they will most likely overpower you and drag you out into the snow, ensuring your cold death.

The victims are left in the snow to freeze to death until the prolonged winter finally abates. I have found a village full of corpses splayed out on the ground, with seemingly no explanation for their deaths as the children of the snow have disappeared, taking their winter with them.

We don't know where they come from or who they are. They can't be defeated it seems, only stopped for the time being. If you find yourself in a village with unending snow in the spring, get out quickly, or it will be your tomb.

Alec

Emeron

Known location: bound to no Location

Type: beast

Weakness: none

Rarity: legendary

The emeron is a large beast with thick, green skin, walking on four short legs with a large bulky body. Their long head ends with a snout sporting two dangerous horns.

The emeron is only mentioned in legends, but they are real. According to legends, emerons find people brought to the brink of death by evil acts. The beast licks the dying person, bestowing lasting regenerative effects upon the victim.

This sounds divine, but it is not. Though your body heals, your mind doesn't. Nightmares, visions, and horrible memories stick with you forever. These creatures are not saviours. You're brought back from something you should have died from, and you'll never be whole again. Emerons are hateful beasts that leave you with a plagued mind.

Khendric

This entry was written in anger, sadness, and despair towards the emeron. I had issues to deal with and instead took it out on the beast that saved me. These creatures are saviours, and because of them I've done so much good in my life, and saved so many people. One of them saved me as well.

*Khendric, after talking to Ara on the wall of Ash-
bourn.*

The Draug

Known location: the sea

Type: ghostly, ghoul, humanoid

Weakness: unknown. Sailing on shallower waters seems to help

Rarity: horror (meaning there is only one of this specimen)

The Draug is a horrible monster bound to the ocean, attacking boats and ships, dragging them into the depths of the sea. Weirdly, the monster has a humanoid shape with oceanic features; two arms and legs, but gills along the neck and webbed skin between the toes and fingers. Endless short tentacles clad its legs and back, while shells and seaweed riddle its arms and chest. Its head is large and round, with tall rectangular haunting eyes. Its mouth reaches almost around its head, allowing it to open so wide that the top of the head rests against its back. Doing so reveals a circular set of serrated teeth with the oesophagus in the middle. When the Draug is barely beneath the surface of the water and with its head split like this, it creates a powerful whirlpool almost impossible to escape for sailors falling overboard. The teeth shred unlucky souls apart before they are swallowed.

The Draug attacks very few ships, but there are telling signs if it's haunting you. As far as I know, legends won't say much of its origin, other than it used to be a beautiful woman cursed to the ocean for eternity, searching for the man that betrayed her. Apparently, she fell in love with a sailor and joined him on his ship, where he locked her in a cage to sell her across the sea. How she became the Draug is beyond my knowledge. Some sources claim it's a curse, while others some rare affliction, but I do not know.

It's speculated, and to some extent proven, that the Draug seeks out ships with men who have wronged women, be it unjust or just, and it may have slowed down human trafficking by a lot. If the stories are true, the Draug has attacked ships with men who claim to have caused slight offences to women or even left them for good reasons, to men who are cruel, violent, or even murderers. It's hard to know who's telling the truth, but the Draug doesn't seem to separate. It should be said that most voyages across the sea go unimpeded by this gruesome monster, despite horrible souls being aboard, but when it strikes, it strikes hard and with reason.

As mentioned, there are signs that your ship has been targeted by the Draug. One sign seems to be the sudden absence of wind, which is a natural phenomenon as well, happening from time to time. But if it starts happening frequently, be aware. We cannot know if this actually is an omen of the Draug or not, but it's been reported too many times to leave out.

On moonful nights, sailors have reported seeing two rectangular light sources in the far distance, shaped like two doors, though it's apparently hard to make out. This can be many things, but the peculiar aspect is that no matter how fast the ship is sailing, the lights keep the same distance. It has been speculated that this is the top half of the eyes of the Draug reflecting the moonlight, following the ship through the night. I believe this is accurate, as these sightings have been confirmed multiple times.

As the days go by, these light sources appear to come closer and a terrible smell has been reported to loom over the deck from time to time. At this point, the crew usually starts pointing fingers, trying to reveal the culprit. Many men are thrown overboard as sacrificial bodies, hoping they are the sinister soul wanted by the Draug. None of those sacrificed ever return, and only if the signs stop, will they know if they have made the right choice.

One of the final signs is infrequent female screams of agony stemming from the ocean. This is a sure sign that the Draug is close. If the water turns bioluminescent at night, it's too late; the Draug will attack.

It shakes the ship, climbing aboard if it can. If not, it tries to tilt it, sucking in as many sailors falling into the sea as it can until the correct one ends up down its maw. If successful in boarding the vessel, it does its best to sink it, but sailors have repelled this attack before. These facts are gathered from survivors who lived because the heinous man was eaten before them.

The Draug is the reason it's considered bad luck to bring men across the sea who have recently left their wives. And many captains are sceptical of anyone with rumours hanging over their heads of misdeeds towards women.

Alec

Oxin

Known location: The Sangerian Grasslands

Type: beast

Weakness: general weapons

Rarity: common

Oxin are majestic creatures from a safe distance, and incredibly dangerous should you be unfortunate enough to walk through their area at the wrong time. Theories suggest oxen are a related breed to oxin, though whether this is true is hard to confirm, as there are bodily similarities, but also striking differences. Though sharing a similar build, an oxin's skin resembles nature, giving them natural camouflage and making them harder to deal with. Their grey skin is riddled with stone and grass. Their green mane, eyes and teeth also set them apart from oxen. The green mane of the oxin is long, almost reaching down to the ground. While an ox has its eyes on both sides of the head, an oxin has both eyes looking forward like a predator, which is what they are. Their teeth are sharp, meant to rip flesh from bone.

Oxin always wander in large packs and can be devastating to villages and other wildlife, but if these creatures are this common, why mention them?

Oxin have a long hibernation circle, sleeping for almost an entire year, but they wake in the summer. While hibernating, they sleep on the ground and their natural camouflage makes them next to impossible to spot. With their hard skin interlaced with rocks, moss, and grass, it's hard to differentiate if you're standing on actual stone or an oxin. Standing on a hibernating oxin isn't dangerous, unless you happen to be within their pack as they all wake from their deep slumber. Suddenly, all the lumps around you come alive, and large majestic oxin rise, and they are hungry. If you find yourself in this situation, the best thing to do is to spot the largest one, jump on its back while they are still coming to, and hang on for dear life. The oxin won't be able to tell you are on their back and fight off any other oxin coming for you, thinking they are trying to dominate it. Once they start sprinting across the fields of the Sangerian Grasslands, let go when you feel you won't die and hope you won't get trampled. Don't wait for nightfall with hopes of sneaking off, because the oxin won't sleep for two months, before going back to hibernation.

Alec

Claylin

Known location: Bodera, the Mud Lands

Type: replicator

Weakness: heat and general weaponry

Rarity: common

Watch yourself while wandering through the marshes in Bodera, and tread not into the deep mud or water unless you have to. There is a certain type of pinkish clay floating in the water, or hiding in the mud, and your skin must not touch it. If some part of you comes into contact with this clay, it will begin to transform and attract more mud until it fully forms a person looking exactly like you. This is a claylin, now turned into a replica of you, seeming to hold all your memories up until the point in time you made contact.

A claylin will emerge from the marshes with one goal: to take over the life of their real self. Having all their memories, it usually finds 'home,' and are often successful at killing their maker. After doing so, they assume their normal life, donning their victim's clothes. With all the memories of the true them, they can act fairly normally, not often causing suspicion to family or friends, but there are clear tells.

Claylins don't age, and their hair doesn't grow. They don't breathe, instead mimicking breathing, but they can forget to do so if stressed. Once a claylin feels safe, secure, and trusted, they turn dangerous again, most often going after 'their real' family. They kidnap their husband or wife, and throw them into the marshes, drowning them after making sure their skin touched the clay. Then the duo do the same to their kids or friends until the whole village is turned. Claylins seem to hate humans, wanting to eradicate and replace as many as possible. It should be noted that claylin can look like any other organic creature too, if they were unlucky enough to touch the clay, like rabdogs for example.

To kill claylins you have to shatter them. General weaponry will hurt them, but don't expect them to stop coming for you without a head. Once you smash them into enough pieces they stop moving. I cannot stress this enough: do not touch this clay, as it holds the same property as that in the marshes. Scoop it up and burn it, or put it in a deep hole in the ground. You can also melt claylins with torches and other heat sources, and they don't seem to like that. Pistols work wonder against them, so stock up on ammunition if you find an infested village.

The best thing to do if you step deep or fall into the marsh water is to set up camp nearby. It usually takes up to four or five days to form a claylin, depending on your size. Kill it as it emerges. You can damage it while it's growing, but it usually heals and keeps growing anyway. With a weapon in hand, you can slash and hack at it easily until it stops coming after you.

Alec

The Woman of the web

Known location: Bodera, the Mud Lands

Type: humanoid, arachnid

Weakness: fire and general weaponry

Rarity: horror

The woman of the web is an old legend with so many different origin stories it's impossible to know what's real or not. Some scripture claim she's the mother of spiderlings and needlers, while others say she's been afflicted by them. Some folktales mix in the magic of a darkora, and it's just impossible to know what actually happened.

The only thing I know for certain is that she's been around for a long time since legends date back centuries. Or perhaps we're fighting descendants of the original web woman, and they're somehow breeding, but who knows?

There have been no reports of her presence outside of Bodera, which could mean she has some connection to spiderlings.

The woman of the web looks like a regular woman wearing a cloak, but she is a monster. Multiple survivors say she hides an arachnid body under her black robes. Tucked and hidden below her robe, along her rib cage, are eight spider legs. Countless black ball-like eyes occupy her throat and two powerful fangs are attached to her clavicles. A slim mouth full of sharp teeth is ready on her chest to devour her prey. It's been questioned whether her human head has a function or is just there for appearances, but survivors claimed she used her eyes and spoke with her mouth. It seems she makes use of both her bodies. Where her belly button should be, she instead produces thick web to wrap around her victims. Despite looking like normal skin, her torso feels like a carapace and can take a lot of stabbing.

The woman of the web either attacks people out travelling, which seems to sate her hunger for some time, or if she's starved, enters a village to find sustenance. When finding prey out in the marshes she crawls with terrifying speed on her spider legs, and all the person sees is a woman's body seemingly hurdling towards them until she strikes.

In villages and cities, she's more subtle and scary. She'll climb silently through open windows and sit outside the bedroom, tapping her spider legs on the floor to toy with her victims. She also likes to wrap and stick people to walls and ceilings, saving them for later consumption. If she feels safe after having eaten a family, she might move to another house and wrap her new victims in web. I've heard stories from other beast hunters where they've come upon a dead village with a bunch of thick spider's webs in all houses and corners, with only body parts left. This behaviour is unlike that of needlers and spiderlings, so I assume it's her.

I do believe she can be killed, though it would take a lot of soldiers. She's fast and dangerous, especially on her spider legs. If you're going up against her, be aware and bring a lot of fire. She seems to hate it.

Alec

Yenferd

Known location: can spring into existence anywhere, but bound to that location

Type: spectral

Weakness: burning sulfur

Rarity: rare

A yenferd is a ghostly entity bound to a location born out of immensely strong emotions stemming from heartbreak, betrayal, anger, or jealousy. Once a person experiences something so horrible it threatens to break them apart, they may create a yenferd while on the brink of destruction, in a way saving themselves. The yenferd will embody the emotion, and remove it from the person's mind, making them feel better instantly. They won't realise what they've done, just feel strangely puzzled together . . . almost. They'll be confused, but no longer threatened to have their mind broken.

The yenferd won't be visible or act out at first, but some records state that people who have created yenferds thought it suddenly smelled like raw eggs.

From this point on, the person seems free from the emotions that should rightly follow whatever they just experienced. They'll go back to living their life, seemingly unaffected. This might puzzle family and friends.

The symptoms from having created a yenferd seem different from person to person. Some are almost normal, usually having increasingly disturbing nightmares, while others seek to cause others the same kind of pain they should have felt. It's as if they are unable to feel that emotion anymore, whether it be jealousy or heartbreak. This makes them seem colder than normal, which is a sign you should look out for. One thing no one escapes is the increasing nightmares haunting their dreams, always of the location where they spawned the yenferd.

In the beginning, it isn't that bad, but it will make them fear going to sleep. Most people revisit the place of their dreams at some point in their life, hoping it will bring an end to the nightmares, but it won't.

While all of this is going on, the yenferd manifests itself at the location of their birth, holding in these terrible emotions, unleashing itself upon anyone unfortunate enough to enter their space. They'll get increasingly aggressive, starting by moving items around, putting out lights, and showing unnatural shadows. As time passes by, they'll show themselves, resembling a twisted and bent version of their creator, with horrific elements, such as unnaturally wide or long mouths, broken necks, sharp teeth, or broken limbs. They'll scream and claw at the victims, trying to bar any escape if possible. The longer people stay, the more it will manifest and attack. To purge the location of the yenferd, the creator must be brought back to face it.

As a beast hunter, what you want to do is: stay at the location until you get a good glimpse of the creator, get out and find them, and bring them back. Make sure you have sulfuric compounds you can burn. This will weaken the yenferd.

Without it, it will assault the creator's mind, inflicting them with tenfold the original emotions and breaking their minds completely. This will also make the yenferd go away, but the creator may die, or be as good as dead. Their mind will be destroyed. Some will go into an endless maniacal rage, or simply never utter a word or function again. Though this solves the problem, it's not a good outcome, so bring sulfur.

When the yenferd manifests its physical form, burn the sulfur and attack it. Make sure the creator stabs it too, who is the only one who can kill it. The yenferd will disappear and unleash a final attack of the mind of their creator, but with way less force. The creator should be able to not have their mind broken, but some of the original emotion will return. This will make them fully human again, and they'll have to overcome the traumatic experience, but at least now it's possible.

The worst outcome is if the creator dies somewhere else in the world, and the yenferd's captured emotions remain unresolved. Then it will haunt the location until the end of time. The location stays uninhabitable.

On a quick side note, don't go to these places: the black lonely house near the Green Gate, the old manor in Carahadrim, the hut on Stake Island, or the Salty Dog Inn in Brinne. The creators of those yenferds have died and with the knowledge we have so far, cannot purge these locations.

Alec

The Right Hand of Fate

Known location: bound to no location

Type: unknown

Weakness: unknown

Rarity: unknown

I know very little of the Right Hand of Fate, but he seems to have something to do with the future. I met him after the battle against Chronor, and he seemed to predict something with a coin. He had a lot of gnurgles around him and stated that we had met before. I think this was in Kalastra, on the day the rura killed my parents, but I am not sure. Those memories are fuzzy.

He said that fate would call me again and that I must answer. I don't know what this means, but I am just noting it so that I won't forget.

Ara

AUTHOR'S NOTE

If I'm being honest, this is my favourite book in the series (so far, haven't written book 4 or 5 yet). It's the culmination and finale of all that book one began. My heart pounded so hard when writing this book: the Darlaene twist, Koradin's death, the final duel, the voreen battle. I shed a tear when Khendric and Topper left Ara, despite knowing I would bring them back. To me, it felt so real. Ara really believed they left. It took so long to plan the ending, and I am really satisfied with it. It's bittersweet, which I feel brings some reality to it. I never wanted it to be only a happy ending. It had to come with some sacrifices because it makes it all the more real emotion-wise. I hated killing Koradin and Darlaene, and really tried saving her life, but I couldn't do it in a way that didn't seem cheap. I strive to not give my characters any plot armour, and it's hard, but letting her survive wouldn't be believable.

A dear friend of mine said he was emotionally exhausted after finishing this book, just laying in his bed staring at the ceiling. I felt like that while writing all those emotional scenes and had to step away and watch a movie or walk my dogs to disconnect. My girlfriend couldn't understand why I came out of the office with tears in my eyes, and when I told her it was because of the book she gave me a deep hug. Even though it's all in my head, it feels real while I write it. I feel like as I write those pivotal moments, *that's* when it's happening. I really experience their emotions to some extent, but I believe that is what makes any book great. You have to be able to feel the love between the pages.

If anyone will ever read this, I cannot thank you enough for finishing my first trilogy. I hope it has been an amazing journey, and that you love the characters as much as me. I wish I could meet you in person, whoever you are, to talk about the world, the characters, and the story. I'd have countless questions about what you thought about this and that, and you'd grow tired of me within minutes. Anyhow, thank you for reading my book about Ara, Khendric and Topper.

I've been asked who my favourite character is, and many people guess it's Khendric or Ara. To have it in ink: my favourite character is Koradin Banner. I think he's everything I wish to become, and have projected my own best self onto him, or at least what I wish my own best self can be. I wouldn't have the courage he had in defending his city, but I dream of being so brave.

Ara holds a special place in my heart. I put her in such a bad place in the beginning: beaten down and battered. But now she's saved the whole of Ashbourn (with help) and become a new person. She has an uncanny drive, maybe because she's fictional, but that's what I love about her. In book one, she forgot her insecurities because she was so interested in the beasts of the world, and that drive is clear in this book too when she refuses to go with Khendric and Topper to leave the city. I am proud of this world, and hope to write more about it.

I wish you a good day, and remember: watch out for monsters.

STAY IN TOUCH

Thank you so much for reading **The Beast Hunters Blood Oath**, the third book in **The Beast Hunter of Ashbourn** series. If you have read my books, but haven't read my **free short stories,** then please go ahead and sign up for my newsletter to get them if you wish.

The Dollmaker of Kalastra is about Khendric and Topper's last case before saving Ara in Kalastra.

Bleeding Ink is about tattoo magic fuelled by blood ink and a mystery at a blood ink factory.

https://www.authorcalende.com/newsletter-signup

Facebook: www.facebook.com/christer-Lende-108798154062930

Twitter: twitter.com/ChribsterL

Author website: www.authorcalende.com/

Instagram: www.instagram.com/christerlende

ABOUT THE AUTHOR

Christer Lende is an award winning author whobegan writing in a library, which sounds fitting, only he was supposed to be there working on his engineering degree. He is a professional screenwriter, working with the Norwegian movie producer behind 'One Love,' 'Who Killed Birgitte?' and 'All About my Father', Bjørn Eivind Aarskog. Together, they are developing the manuscript for a Norwegian thriller. Bjørn hired Christer after reading *The Beast Hunters*, trusting he could bring his vision to life.

Christer lives in what Norwegians call a city, but people from actual cities would call a town. Of proud Viking blood, he honours his ancestors by heroically sitting in front of a computer writing Fantasy and Science Fiction books. He believes in writing a little every day, through weekends, Christmas, New Year's Eve, even his own birthday. When he's not writing, he takes care of his two dogs and tries to broker peace with his girlfriend. He's often found at the gym, trying to compensate for his height issues, or lazily playing video games.

Christer did get that Master's degree in Electrical Engineering, despite procrastinating by writing fiction in the library, and works for a large IT firm, but writing and storytelling are his passions.

For more information, you can visit:
https://www.authorcalende.com/about.